CHANTAL ROOME

Book Cover by Chantal Roome

2nd edition 2023

Print ISBN 9781777707668

ebook ISBN 9781777707675

For my kids, who sometimes let me get some writing done. I love you more than anything.
Now, don't read any further in this book until you're older.
Like maybe 85.

I Call Dibs

Johnny

THE CROWD IS INSANE tonight, rushing the stage as soon as the lights come up, screaming so loud that the floor rumbles beneath me. We've played a lot of shows in a lot of really cool places, but it's always good to be home. And not just because the hometown crowd always screams the loudest.

Being in one spot for a longer period gives me the chance to find her. You know, 'the one'. Someone to date for longer than a few days or weeks at a time. The guys like to give me shit for ghosting women after a few weeks, but when I know, I know. Why would I waste my time on a person once I've figured out they aren't the one? Plus, it's not like I disappear without telling them first. I always break up with them before I block them.

It's not like I'm a complete asshole. I'd probably call myself a romantic, actually. I'm looking for that 'love at first sight', 'sparks and fireworks' kind of love.

That's why I pay extra attention to the faces in the crowd during a home show. I'm aware it's probably not a good idea to look for my future wife in the crowd at one of my shows, but who knows when and where fate will bring me my other half? There is always the risk of the woman I meet using me for my fame and money, but no risk means no reward. And it's not like that hasn't happened before. Besides, she wasn't even a fan, just a model who was using me to boost her career.

We're halfway through our set list when the lightning strikes. When I see her, my heart stops and tingles run down my spine. She's not in the crowd, not really. She's in front of the fence, standing near security, and pointing a huge camera toward the stage. Toward me.

And she's scorching hot.

She's dressed casually, in jeans and a tight t-shirt, her curves making them look painted on. Her chin length, dark hair is just asking for me to run my hands through it. She has tattoos up and down both of her arms, and it looks like she has a chest piece as well.

I'll need to get a closer look at those, for sure.

Fuck, I hope this is the photographer Denise was talking about. The one who is shooting the meet and greet after the show. Either way, I'm meeting her.

Tonight.

I'll make sure of that.

Somehow.

I give her a subtle wink and a little smile. She lowers her camera and looks me up and down, her eyebrows raised, a little smirk on her dark red lips.

Oh yeah, I need to meet this woman. She clearly doesn't care who I am. She's giving me shit with merely a look and fuck if it isn't making me hard.

We play a few more songs and I can't tear my eyes away from her the entire time. I'm probably creeping her out, but thankfully she's working and not paying much attention to me. I know I'm coming on a little strong, but I have limited time to make this happen. I don't want to rely on the off-chance that I'd be able to find her if she disappeared right after the show.

Suddenly, Connor announces we're playing an acoustic song that wasn't on the set list at all. My guitar tech runs out and swaps guitars with me. I point out the photographer and tell him to get Devon, our head of security, to invite her backstage.

Denise said no sluts backstage tonight, but this is my future wife we're talking about here, not some run of the mill groupie.

By the time I look back at her, she's gone.

Fuck.

There's nothing I can do about it now, though. I have to finish the show.

We play a few more songs, and an encore, and finally the show is over. If that photographer isn't in the dressing room when we get there, my plan is to ask Denise to track her down. If anyone can find someone, she can. She has her hands in everything involving our shows, going way beyond standard practice for a manager. She probably already knows everything there is to know about this photographer.

Once I step into the dressing room, I realize I won't need to get Denise's help. The sexy photographer is already here.

"Who is *that*?" I ask somewhat less than casually when my eyes catch on the two women near the entrance to the dressing room. I hope my interest isn't too obvious. The last thing I need is someone giving me a hard time about my love life. Again.

We're scheduled for some meet and greets after the show we just played, but usually, they give us a few minutes before letting people in. We all like a few minutes to contain some of the adrenaline coursing through our veins after performing before having to be on our best behavior. I think I'll let it slide this time, though, since it means the sexy photographer is here.

The woman with the camera is without a doubt the hottest woman I've ever seen. I *need* to get to know her. The other woman is also attractive, but the photographer is way more my type. Black hair, dark eyes, ass and tits to die for, and she's covered every inch of visible skin in beautifully done tattoos. I couldn't see them well from the stage but I can see now that the artwork is amazing.

As is the canvas.

I need to know where else on her body she has tattoos. Where do they stop? If I trace the flower on her right arm, does it go to her shoulder? Her back? All the way down to that sweet ass?

I tear my eyes away from her when Devon answers me and I almost feel a physical loss. Some force is pulling me to this woman and I don't even know her name.

Devon looks over at the other side of the dressing room. "The photographer? Her name's Becca. The other one is *Alex*." He raises his eyebrows at me and Ryder, putting emphasis on the name 'Alex'.

"Holy shit. Are you serious? Like '*Alex*', Alex? '*All I Ever Want*' Alex? '*Better off Dead*' Alex? Connor's long-lost songwriting muse and true love, Alex?"

Ryder lists off song titles from our first album, all of which Connor wrote for Alex, his first love and first heartbreak.

"Yes, Ryder. All of those things." Devon says. "He doesn't know she's here, so this could be interesting."

Ryder cracks open a bottled water and passes it to me before grabbing another for himself. "Okay, well, dibs on the other one, then."

Anger bubbles up inside me as I think of Ryder with Becca. She can't be with someone like him. He's a cool guy, but he's a man whore. Different chick almost every night. He would never treat her the way she deserves to be treated.

I know I'll treat her right, but how can I know if we're compatible without us spending at least a little time together? I always start out with the intention that a woman could be the one. Because that's what I'm looking for. I want to find my other half. Does that make me blind to a woman's true nature? Sometimes. But I'd kiss a million frogs if it meant I'd find my princess.

"Fuck off, Ryder," I growl at him. "Stay away from her."

He raises his hands in surrender and backs away. "OK man, no problem. You got dibs."

"Shit. Sorry, Ryder. I didn't mean that. I just… I don't know, man." I run a hand through my hair and look at the floor in front of me. What the fuck is wrong with me? "I want to get to know her, that's all."

He slaps me on the back and shoots me a wide grin. "No worries, man. I get it. You're in love again." He laughs. "Now that I look closer, you seem like you'd be more her type, anyway." He leaves me and walks over to talk to Denise and Travis.

How will I get to know Becca better? I need a plan to get her alone. From the way she's talking to Alex, it looks like they came together. If Connor doesn't invite them to the after party, then I will. I just need to make sure none of the fans hear me when I tell her. The last thing I want is to be surrounded by fans when I'm trying to talk to her. Maybe I should ask them right now, before this all gets started? I take one step in their direction when Connor comes storming in, head down, bee-lining to the bar on the opposite side of the room.

"What the fuck? Where's the fucking whiskey?" Connor yells.

I sneak another look at Becca and Alex. Looks like the real show is about to start. It's too late to ask them now.

"You guys don't even drink whiskey, and it's not like I've had enough for you to hide the bottles on me now. Don't tell me this meet and greet is some kind of bullshit intervention." Connor looks accusingly at me and the rest of the band just as Alex shoves the whiskey bottle into his hand.

"Oh, shit. I'm so sorry. I was nervous, and I needed to fortify myself with many drinks. Um, here you go."

From where I'm standing, I can see Connor's eyes widen and his jaw drop. I see his entire life change before he even turns around to see that it's Alex. My gaze drifts to Becca, and my heart pounds hard in my chest.

I want that.. I want a love that lasts more than three weeks.

Maybe Becca's not that person for me, but maybe she is. All I know is I'm desperate to talk to her and find out.

We get busy going through the motions of the meet and greet, but I sneak looks at the sexy photographer every chance I get. When she's not taking my picture, I get to watch her work, and I love it. Seeing the way she lines up each shot is mesmerizing. I've never been that into photography, but Becca makes it look so good that I might need to add it to my list of interests.

After the meet and greet, we all go over to Rough Mix, the bar where we played our first proper show, and I snag the seat next to Becca. She's sitting on my right and we're close enough that I can feel her thigh pressing against my leg, close enough that I could easily rest my hand on her knee without stretching. And I want to touch her so badly. I'm able to restrain myself, but barely. She looked hot in the dressing room, but now that I'm right next to her, I can see how beautiful she really is. That, and she smells amazing. Every time she turns her head I get a whiff of some spicy scented shampoo or perfume. Whatever it is, I'm sure I look ridiculous when I breathe deep every time she moves.

Not creepy at all.

"Ha! I can tell you about that." Becca jumps up off the seat and into the space next to the table where she acts out the story of Alex catching her boyfriend cheating.

I can't tear my eyes off of her as she describes, in detail, Alex getting home and thinking there is a burglar, only to realize it's her boyfriend fucking some other chick in their bed. Becca acts out Alex's umbrella-destroying home run hit on the dude's ass, the other woman's embarrassment, and the dude's crying and whining about being sorry. A hilarious story, especially with Becca's reenactments of erratic humping, swinging umbrellas, and cheering crowds.

We're all laughing, Becca back in the seat beside me, when Connor turns to Alex and says, "So, Alex, you seem pretty okay for finding out about this today. Are you? Okay, that is."

"Oh, she's totally used to this. It's happened to her before." Becca says, wiping her eyes and letting out a small chuckle.

Alex's face drops. "Okay, Becca. I think that's enough story time for now. These guys don't need to hear this."

"Wait," I say, my eyebrows bunching in confusion. "This isn't the first time?" Alex is a very attractive woman, and she seems pretty fun too. How does someone like her get cheated on repeatedly? She must have terrible taste in guys. Except Connor. He's a good dude.

"Not at all," Becca says, looking directly at me, not noticing the venomous look Alex is giving her. "She's nearly into the double digits with cheating boyfriends."

Suddenly Alex shoves Aiden out of the booth and slides out after him. "Okay, cool, yeah. Thanks for the drink, Connor. It was really nice seeing you again. Nice to meet all of you," she says to the rest of us. "I need to get going, though. I need to work early tomorrow. Maybe we can do this again sometime?"

Alex turns and sprints to the exit, with Connor not far behind.

"Oh, fuck," Becca says, running her hand down her face. "I really need to learn when to shut up." She grabs her bags from under the table and stands up. "Nice to meet you guys," she says, and then she disappears into the crowd.

"Wait," I call out after her. "Becca."

Shit. I didn't even get her number. Now, how will I find her again? Because I'm sure this time, it's real.

She's definitely the one.

2

Please, No Pictures

Becca

I PULL INTO THE venue with minutes to spare and park in a spot far from the building, leaving the close spots for wedding guests. Helping Alex with her hangover issue this morning has put me a little behind schedule, so I slam the car into park while undoing my seat belt before jumping out and grabbing my equipment from the back seat. I bolt to the entrance weighed down by several bags, already sweating under the many layers of my suit.

Please don't let me be late.

This client's wedding is a massive opportunity for me. They're connected with all of Westborough's high society and if I impress them, I could find myself booked solid for the next year. And I need all the help I can get for my business. I'm barely scraping by as it is. If I don't book at least four more weddings this year, I'm going to have to get a regular job. Considering it's already almost September, the odds aren't good that I'll reach that goal. But this wedding could be what I need to get my name out there in a meaningful way.

If I had my way, I'd be back at the apartment nursing my own hangover. I would have much rather stayed out last night and investigated whatever was happening with Johnny. When he winked at me from the stage, it was easy enough to brush it off as typical rock star stage flirting. You know, the shit they do to make the audience feel special. But once we got to Rough Mix, he seemed like he might have some genuine interest in me.

At least for a night, which is all I would have wanted, anyway. It gets too hard to hide myself from guys if they get more than one shot at me.

Too bad I'm here to document the most romantic day of someone else's life instead of home recovering from what could have been the most sexually adventurous day of mine.

After huffing my way across what feels like ten miles of parking lot, I finally make it to the entrance. I struggle with my bags but eventually get the door open, and standing inside is Mrs. Carmichael, the mother of the bride.

So nice of you to open the door for me, I say to her in my head.

"Good afternoon, Mrs. Carmichael. Lovely day for a wedding. If you'd kindly direct me to your daughter's dressing room, I can get started on the getting ready pictures." I was hoping I'd have the chance to wipe my sweaty face before seeing anyone, but this is good, too. The sooner we get started, the faster this day will go by.

Mrs. Carmichael rolls her eyes slightly and somehow manages to look down her nose at me, even though I'm several inches taller than she is. "That won't be necessary, Ms. Morris. We have made alternate arrangements, and we will no longer require your services."

My mouth drops open.

"I'm sorry. What was that? I don't think I heard you right." The mother of the bride couldn't possibly have said what I think she did, could she?

"I think you heard me. A check to return the deposit will be fine."

Yup. She said it alright. It's the day of the wedding and they've hired a different photographer. And they waited until I got here to tell me.

"You do realize that when you booked me months ago, you paid me a non-refundable deposit?"

"Well, that's ridiculous. If we will not be using your services, I don't see why we should have to pay anything."

"I'm afraid that's not possible, ma'am. The *non-refundable* deposit is to ensure my availability on the date you chose. I turned away several other opportunities to be here for you today. So I'm definitely keeping the money."

The mother of the bride huffs and stomps her foot. "Well, I never."

"Have a nice day, ma'am," I say, picking up my equipment and walking out of the church. I'm not interested in arguing with her any further. This is the reason I have all of my clients sign contracts. Someone always wants to get the deposit back. I get photographers can be expensive, but they can't expect me to block off my day for them and get nothing if they change their mind at the last minute. Some people have such overblown senses of entitlement, it's disgusting.

So much for this wedding opening doors for me. I can almost hear them slamming in my face as I get further from the building.

I trudge back to the far end of the parking lot, the heat of the early afternoon sun turning my tailored suit into a sauna. Once I reach my car and put my equipment bags in the back seat, I take off my suit jacket and loosen the buttons on my blouse. I never let the clients see my tattoos if I can help it. And I damn sure never let them see what the tattoos are covering, ever. As a photographer, I'm there to capture the beauty of the day, not introduce my monstrousness. I can deal with the odd passerby noticing the ugliness, but when I'm trapped in a room full of strangers, I refuse to give them the opportunity to ask questions.

My ass buzzes, distracting me from my thoughts and letting me know I have a call coming in. I pull out my phone in time to see my mom's face before the call disconnects. Great, looks like this day is about to go from bad to worse.

Now I really wish I'd taken advantage of what Johnny was offering last night. I probably could have banged him in the bathroom before rushing home to apologize to Alex. She would have understood eventually.

Not that I would actually do that.

I'm strictly a 'lights off' kind of girl.

I get in the car and crank up the air conditioning, waiting for the inevitable call back from dear old mom. She doesn't leave messages, and she doesn't text. She hangs up and calls back repeatedly until I answer. I think the record for most phone calls in a row is seventeen. Thank god I had my phone turned off for that series of calls.

As predicted, my phone buzzes again, mom's face lighting up the screen once more.

"Hi Mom," I say, forcing as much fake cheer into my voice as I can stand. "How are you?" She never calls unless she wants something, even though it's usually just to complain about life not going her way. For some reason, she thinks the world is out to get her.

"Oh, Rebecca. I'm so glad I caught you. You'll never believe what happened to me at the grocery store today. I saw Mrs. Johnson, and she said hello. Can you believe it?"

I rub my temples with one hand. I have enough to worry about today without dealing with my mother and her persistent feelings that someone has wronged her.

"Should she not have said hello?" *Fuck.* I pound the side of my fist against my forehead. I should not have asked that. Now I'm going to get sucked into more interaction with my mother than I want to deal with today.

"Of course she should have. But she didn't even thank me again for all that help I gave her when her husband was sick a few weeks ago. I brought them dinner every day for a week, you know."

I hold the phone away and let out a quiet sigh. "She did thank you, I thought. Didn't she bring you that angel food cake and a beautiful thank-you card?"

"Yes, but she still should have said thank you again. A whole week, Rebecca. That's a lot of meals to make for someone. And it's not like I'm made of money. Lord knows you haven't helped me since you moved out on your own."

"That was fifteen years ago, Mom."

"Hmph. Well, I still don't see why you couldn't have stayed with me. After everything I did for you after your accident. Remember how I took care of you? Remember how everyone looked at me like I was the worst mother in the world? I did everything for you. And you don't even care."

Shit, not this again. I hate talking about the accident, and I hate trying to make her feel better about it. She's not the one living with the lifelong consequences. I am.

Time to try distraction.

"You know what? How about I grab dinner and come over for a visit? My client canceled on me at the last minute, so I have an unexpected day off. I'd love nothing more than to spend it with you." Not true. I can think of many things I'd rather do, including going back to my apartment and checking on how Pukey Mcbucketface is doing with her hangover. But if I don't appease my mother right now, she'll subject me to weeks of guilt-inducing phone calls, and I don't want to deal with that.

"Oh. Are you sure, dear? I don't want to put you out. I know you probably have much better things to do than spend time with your mother. I wouldn't want you to feel obligated just because I'm still suffering from your accident."

I roll my eyes so hard it wouldn't surprise me if Mom heard it through the phone. "I'm sure, Mom. I insist. I'll see you in about an hour, OK? I'm going to run to my place and change out of my suit first, but then I'll come over with that sushi you like. Sound good?"

"That sounds fabulous, Rebecca. You always know what to do to cheer me up. See you soon."

She doesn't even wait for me to say goodbye before hanging up on me, which is typical. She got her way, so no need to be polite. I know I should stop letting her run all over me like this, but I can't just leave her to fend for herself. She is still my mother, after all. I need to remember I owe her everything.

Not that she'd ever let me forget it.

3

I Want More

Johnny

"You should give her some time to get used to being here before you demand information," Travis says. "It's only been a few hours since she found out she's working for Connor. I'm sure she has enough on her mind without you trying to hook up with her best friend."

Fucking Travis. Why does he have to make so much sense? As soon as I saw Alex, I wanted to ask her for Becca's number, but Travis is right. I guess I should let Alex get settled before I ask questions. But I won't be happy about it. Becca has been on my mind all week, and nothing has distracted me. I was almost ready to launch a stalking strategy like Connor had, but having that entire neighborhood thinking two of us are sketchy fucks wasn't all that appealing.

"Fine, I'll wait to ask. But I'm not waiting long. Becca is special. I can feel it."

"Yeah, just like Amber. And Tasha. Oh, and we can't forget Sherry," Travis chuckles while ticking the names off on his fingers. "You fall in love all the time, Johnny. Maybe you should forget about this one altogether. Getting involved with Alex's best friend probably isn't a great idea. Look at the way Connor looks at Alex." He gestures to where Connor is currently pulling Alex into a hug. "He's not letting her go anytime soon. Breaking up with Becca could cause problems for all of us. Set your sights elsewhere."

I nod, not because I agree with his assessment, but because looking like I agree is the only way to get Travis to shut up. I know he has a point, but Becca is different.

I've always been more romantic than most guys. I wouldn't say I have my wedding planned out, but I definitely have some ideas about how I would like it to go. (Nothing stuffy. Short and sweet. Lots of laughs.) The only thing I haven't been able to find is my bride. Travis is almost right. I have had many girlfriends. I always go into a relationship with the intent that it will last. I just prefer not to stick around long after I know she's not the one.

I'm expecting fireworks and explosions and that classic 'love at first sight' feeling that I read about. Yes, I read romance novels. I've learned a lot about how to treat a woman from the books that I've read. Not all of them, of course. Dark romance is one thing to read, but in reality, most women don't like to be treated the way the dudes in those books treat female main characters. At least not outside of the bedroom. My mom tells me I'd probably fall into the cinnamon roll category if I were a romance novel hero; I'm a sweetheart, and I'm okay with that.

"You guys coming?" I catch the end of whatever Connor was saying. Looks like we're heading to the studio.

"I'm not afraid of helping you, Alex, but I really need to keep an eye on Connor in the studio. I have a feeling he's bursting with the desire to write love songs tonight." Travis laughs and runs off down the hall to the studio.

"Something's going to be bursting with desire tonight," I joke, waggling my eyebrows and winking at Alex before I follow Travis. I hear her chuckle as I walk away.

I think I'm going to enjoy having Alex around, and not only because she gets me one step closer to Becca. Connor already seems happier than he has in years. Not sure what that's going to mean for his songwriting, or for the band, but he's my friend first, and the lead singer of Sleeping Dogs second. His happiness is more important than that other stuff.

See? Sweetheart, and not just when there are ladies involved.

When I get into the studio, Connor is already pacing, talking about how he can't lose Alex. The guy's got it bad. Good for him. I walk over and pick up an acoustic guitar and start messing around.

We're kidding ourselves if we think we're going to get any work done tonight. Connor is too worked up about Alex to settle down and get some writing in. I missed most of the conversation in the kitchen, but I think we're in here to give Alex a little time to herself. Well, to herself, with Devon and Ryder. They seem to have befriended her more quickly than the rest of us.

"It can't bother her that much, can it?" Connor asks. He's referring to the story Becca told last week at Rough Mix, about how Alex has been cheated on by every boyfriend she's ever had, besides Connor when she dated him in high school.

"Oh gee, I don't know, dude. If you'd been cheated on a bunch of times, would you be interested in starting a relationship with someone? Let alone someone you could google to see evidence of the countless other people they've been with?" My voice is dripping with sarcasm.

Connor dated a lot when we first got popular with the band. There are pictures of him online with hundreds of different women. I don't know for sure what Alex would think of that, but it certainly doesn't paint a pleasant picture. It makes him look like a whore. Which makes sense, because he was kind of a whore. I think we all were. I was a misguided whore looking for love, while the rest of them were just getting their dicks wet.

The conversation continues this way for a while, with us talking about Connor and Alex, until Devon and Ryder come back from the kitchen.

"Hey guys," Connor greets them. "Dinner done already? That was fast."

"Nah," Ryder says. "Lasagnas just went in the oven. She made her own noodles, man. I've never had lasagna made with fresh noodles. If you fuck this up, I'm going to be so pissed."

"So before Connor asks, did Alex say anything about him?" I ask, knowing that's the only Connor can think about right now.

"Not much. She's calling Becca to talk right now, though." My ears perk up at Ryder's mention of Becca, but I drift off into my thoughts again when it's clear the conversation won't be about her.

I continue to pick out a melody on the guitar while my mind wanders. Thoughts of Becca take over and I lose track of what the guys are talking about.

I wonder how her pictures from the show turned out? She must be an amazing photographer. Is that her full-time job or if she does something else too? Maybe she models? She has almost a pin-up quality to her look, with her short Bettie Page bangs and that dark red lipstick she was wearing last week.

Would that lipstick end up all over my face if we kissed? Maybe she has some extra long-lasting lipstick that won't come off on my face. I'm not sure which I would prefer. I can't say I'd be mad if we both wound up with red lipstick smeared over our faces. Everyone would know I was hers and she was mine that way.

Connor's voice intrudes on my thoughts. "I can't help it. I'm fucking in love with her guys. Tell me what to do."

"In love? You just met her. Is that even possible?" I look over at Connor, disbelief and hope both plain in my voice.

"I didn't *just* meet her. I've been in love with her all these years but I never thought I'd get another chance. I didn't think I'd ever see her again."

"Okay, yeah. That makes sense." Plus, if he can fall in love this quickly, then there's nothing saying I can't.

Sure, it's a little different because I did just meet Becca, but at least this shows it's a possibility. Travis has already guessed what's going through my brain, and he's subtly shaking his head at me. He always knows what I'm thinking. I wonder if something about us being the only two boys in a family with seven kids gives us special powers, like twins. At least he somehow uses our strange brain connection in his favor. Most of the time, I end up thinking he's hungry, even when he's not. Either he's great at reading my thoughts, or I'm *that* predictable.

I widen my eyes at him, hoping he gets the message. I know what we agreed, and I will give Alex some time before I beg her for information about Becca. But not too much. This is my destiny we're talking about, after all. If I leave it all up to fate, it might not happen.

The guys go back to talking and I take up the melody I was working on again. My fingers find the strings while my mind dreams up thoughts of Becca. Maybe she'd want to come out on our next tour. Not for the whole time, of course. She has a life of her own, after all. But for a few weeks or a month? I'm sure we could work something out. And with Alex in Connor's life now, she wouldn't be alone during shows. I'm sure Alex will come on tour as well. They haven't officially gotten back together, but that's only a matter of time. Connor is like a lovesick puppy.

"Let's head back to the kitchen. Alex just texted to say that Becca is coming to dinner too, and she should be here soon," Connor says, already halfway to the door. "I'm going to see if Alex needs any help."

I scramble to my feet, dropping the guitar in my haste. The guys all turn to look at me because of the sound it makes when it crashes to the floor.

"Calm down," Ryder says. "You can answer the door when she gets here."

The other guys make noises of understanding, with some 'ah, young love' and 'Johnny's in love again' thrown in for good measure.

Fuck these guys.

I push past them and join Alex and Connor in the kitchen.

"Tell me what you need, oh kitchen mistress. I am here to serve." I bow to Alex, and Connor rolls his eyes at me. Alex points out things that need to go to the dining room and I begin taking things over. With all of us bringing items, it only takes a few minutes to get the table ready and soon we're sitting around waiting on the lasagnas to finish cooking.

When the doorbell rings, I jump up and run to answer it before anyone else gets a chance. I know it's Becca because the only other person yet to arrive is Denise, and she has her own key. With my hand on the doorknob, I stop and take a deep breath before swinging it open.

"Becca," I say, grinning like an idiot. I can't force the smile from my face. All I can hope is that I don't look too crazy. "Come in. I thought I would never see you again." *Good one, dumbass. Nothing like being over dramatic to make yourself not look crazy.*

She steps in and I close and lock the door behind her. I sneak a look back at her when we stop in the entryway. She's dressed casually again, in jeans and a long-sleeved henley shirt. I can't see the tattoos on her arms at all, but I glimpse her chest piece. There's something about it that looks a little familiar, but I can't place it. And it's not like I can get a good look at it without coming across like a creep who's starting at her boobs.

"Hey Johnny, hi. Umm, hi," Becca tucks her hair behind her ear and looks down at the floor. *She's nervous. She likes me. Yes!* "Should I take off my shoes?" *Or she's polite and worried about getting the floors dirty. Shit.*

"Oh, leave them on. It's fine. Let me show you to the kitchen." I lift my hand to take hers and she jerks her arm away from me. "Oh, I'm sorry. I just... that was... Sorry." Well shit. There goes my thought that Becca is my fate. She's so not interested that she jumps away when I get too close.

"Oh, no. It's okay. It's just, um..." She takes a deep breath and blows it out. "I'm just not a big fan of having my arms touched.

It's not you." She reaches out and pats my hand, but doesn't linger. "I was hoping I'd see you tonight, actually."

I look back at her, and she smiles at me, making my heart pound. "Yeah?" I pull my phone out of my pocket. "Well, then first, let me get your number so we don't have to rely on our friends making plans in order to see each other." I hand her my phone so she can put her information in.

She passes it back. "What's the second thing?" She looks at me and her eyes flicker to my lips, making my dick stand at attention. How is it possible that anyone this beautiful exists?

My hands reach up toward her face, and I take a tentative step, desperate to get close to her. "Can I touch your face? Your hair?" If I don't want her to feel uncomfortable and after the way she jerked away from me, I know that I definitely need to ask before I touch her anywhere again. I whisper, "Your lips?"

She nods, surprising me by reaching out and grabbing my shirt, pulling me forward, forcing me against her. I angle my head, skimming my mouth across her cheek, my fingers threading into her hair and tilting her head up. Brushing my lips against hers, not quite kissing her, I taste her breath as she gasps. Her arms circle around my waist, pulling me closer, as she chases my lips with her own. Grinding against her, letting her feel what she does to me, I press my lips to hers, teasing her with a soft swipe of my tongue, barely holding myself back. My body is on fire with the desire to touch her, with not being able to do more than kiss. She opens her mouth for me and I slide my tongue along her lower lip before plunging into her kiss. Her tongue dances with mine as she pulls me ever closer, little whimpers escaping her mouth all the while. I want to slide my hands down and lift her up by the backs of her thighs, but the only safe space I know my hands can be right now is in her hair. So I hold her face to mine and kiss the hell out of her while I grind my rock hard dick into her hip. I meet her whimpers with moans of my own.

The sound of keys jingling on the other side of the door drags me back to reality. A disappointed groan escapes my throat and I pull back. I place a gentle kiss on Becca's lips once more before letting her go and stepping away.

"That was so much better than I imagined it would be," I whisper, and sneak in one more kiss just as the door opens.

"Oh, hey guys," Denise says as she walks in. "Am I late?"

"Nope," I say. "You're right on time. Have you met Becca? Becca, this is Denise, the band's manager. Becca is Alex's best friend, and she was also the photographer after the show last week."

Denise and Becca make small talk as we all walk to the kitchen. While their backs are turned, I take a moment to adjust myself, willing my dick to go down before anyone notices. I'm sure my stupid smile and Becca's just-kissed lips and slightly messy hair will speak volumes when we get there, but I can't bring myself to care.

That was the best kiss I've ever experienced in my life.

And I want more.

4

I Do the Touching

Becca

I PULLED INTO THE drive at Alex's new place, not quite half an hour after we got off the phone. After the week I've had, it didn't take much for me to agree to Alex's invite to dinner. Especially after she mentioned Johnny would be here. I've been reminding myself not to act desperate the entire drive over here. To Connor's house.

I still can't believe Alex's mystery client wound up being her long-lost first love. If that isn't some sort of cosmic sign they should be together, then I don't know what is.

I'm keeping the moving boxes in my car in case, though. Alex has bad luck with her boyfriends cheating and forcing her to move in a hurry, so I've been keeping an emergency box stash in my car for a while. Well, boxes and the bat I started keeping in there for revenge on said cheating boyfriends. I hope Connor doesn't turn out to be one of them, but it never hurts to be ready.

I've prepared myself for this dinner by wearing long sleeves. I don't know if these guys will ask questions, but it's usually easier on everyone if I keep covered up. I learned that, at least, from my mom. She hates looking at my arms, and she doesn't hesitate to tell me if I ever make the mistake of wearing short sleeves in her presence. Which I did last weekend after that disaster of a wedding that I didn't end up shooting.

I was so hot when I changed out of my suit that I threw on shorts and a tank before I picked up lunch and went over to her place. It was like she couldn't even look at me, the disgust on her face clear. She thinks the accident was her fault, and she has issues with looking at the results of her actions. And it's not even that obvious anymore, not since I've had my tattoos done. They do a great job disguising things, unless I'm in a certain light. But with mom, every light is that light. No wonder I try to hide my hideousness from everyone. My own mother won't look at me.

She hasn't let me forget that mistake for the past week, either. Calling me every day, asking if I did it on purpose to make her feel bad for the accident. Blaming me for people thinking she's a terrible parent. Saying the accident is the reason my dad left us all those years ago. Telling me again how lucky I was that she stayed and took care of me. That other parents would have put me into foster care rather than deal with the issues the accident caused.

That woman is terrible for my self-esteem. The therapists that I've seen off and on over the years assure me that none of it is my fault, but my mother's voice in my head is too loud. One day I will set proper boundaries with her, but I'm not ready yet.

I don't know if I ever will be.

Pushing thoughts of mom and therapists and scars aside, I take a deep breath and get out of my car. These guys won't even see my arms, so I don't need to worry about that tonight. I repeat that to myself as I walk to the door and ring the bell, only stopping my internal monologue when the door flies open to reveal none other than Johnny.

I jump a little, surprised to see him at the door. I was hoping to see him tonight, but I wasn't expecting him to be the first person I would see.

The moments pass in a blur, with Johnny attempting to grab my hand and me pulling away from him abruptly. I can't let him feel my scars, or he'll never look at me the same again. I'll get that combination of pity and disgust that I've seen more times than I care to remember, and I can't bear to have that happen tonight.

"Oh, I'm sorry. I just... that was... Sorry," Johnny apologizes, the hurt shining from his eyes.

"Oh, no. It's okay. It's just, um..." I take a calming breath. "I'm just not a big fan of having my arms touched. It's not you. I was hoping I'd see you tonight, actually." His eyes light up immediately, my words having their intended effect.

Johnny says something about phone numbers and he passes his phone over, I think for me to put my number in. I wish I knew for certain, but I was too busy watching his lips as he spoke, wondering how soft they were. They look soft. He smiles, waiting for me to add my phone number, and the little heart he has tattooed high on his left cheekbone crinkles with the smile lines. His smile reaches his light brown eyes, doing funny things to my insides.

"Can I touch your face? Your hair? Your lips?" he breathes.

My chest erupts in tingles as I nod frantically and grab his shirt to pull him against me. So much for not acting desperate. The only way I could seem more desperate would be if I'd jumped him as soon as he opened the door.

At least I said hello first.

He teases me, brushing his lips against mine, and my body chases the kiss, pushing my lips closer even as I pull him against me. I keep my fists wrapped in his shirt, not trusting my hands to behave themselves if they get the chance to feel his chest. As it is, the backs of my hands are burning with the feel of his muscles pressing against them.

Fuck it.

I wrap my arms around his waist and pull him to me, forcing our bodies closer. Johnny grinds his body against me, pushing his erection against my hip. I crush him closer, deepening the kiss, kneading the muscles in his back as I furiously attempt to touch every inch within my reach. Johnny's hands stay in my hair, tilting my head this way and that, his lips and tongue exploring my own with a reverence I've never experienced. He hasn't even tried to move his hands lower, and that alone fills me with ravenous desire. I can feel the liquid heat pooling in my panties, making me ready, inviting him in.

Just as I'm about to suggest that we leave and continue this elsewhere, Johnny pulls back and a disappointed groan escapes him. He kisses me softly and lets me go.

"That was so much more than I imagined it would be," he says, tilting forward and kissing me again just as the door opens.

"Oh, hey, guys. Am I late?"

"Nope," Johnny answers. "You're right on time. Have you met Becca? Becca, this is Denise, the band's manager. Becca is Alex's best friend, and she was also the photographer after the show last week."

"Yes, hi." I compose myself enough to make conversation. "We spoke last week, I think."

"Yes, we did. I saw some of your pictures on the radio station's social media pages. You made the guys look so good. Wholesome, even. I was shocked." Denise laughs. "You have a gift. No wonder the station called you for this assignment. Have you ever thought of working in image management? You could really help some of the more deplorable celebrities get back into the public's good graces."

It's my turn to laugh. "I hadn't ever thought of that, honestly. I'm not sure I'd be comfortable taking part in that level of deception. Some of those celebs deserve the shit they get."

"Ha! You've got that right."

We enter the kitchen together, and Alex greets us right away. She talks to Denise a little, since it's the first time they've had a real chance to talk since the interview for the position. From what Alex said, Denise had to run off and take care of something this morning before they could really say much.

"So what are you doing after this?" Johnny slides beside me and whispers in my ear.

"Umm, I had no plans," I say. "Alex is out of my apartment now, so I was probably just going to sit around and watch Netflix. You?"

"I was hoping I could take you out?"

Shit. He wants to take me out? Like on a date? I like the guy well enough, but I wasn't really looking to start anything serious with him. I'm comfortable with my usual routine of hook up and move on.

I wonder if that would be too difficult to pull off with him, considering our friends are dating now? Maybe we should go ahead, consequences be damned? The aftermath of that kiss is still coursing through my body, making me reckless.

"Why don't you come to my place?"

"Oh? You don't want to go out?"

"I've had a long week, and I just want to relax. Besides, we're already eating dinner here. We don't really need to go out any-where."

Johnny backs me into the hallway, away from everyone. "Are you sure?"

This time I'm the one grabbing his face and pulling him to me. I slam my mouth to his and kiss him deeply, thrusting my tongue in his mouth, leaving no doubt what's on my mind.

"I'm sure," I say after breaking the kiss. "I'll send you the address after I leave and then you can meet me there."

Johnny's eyes are dark, his intentions clear. "You're going to need to give me very specific instructions for touching, then. Because, god, Becca. I'm dying to touch you." He sneaks anoth-er kiss before turning back to the kitchen, leaving me to follow behind him.

He's going to be surprised when he finds out what the rules entail. Because when I fuck someone, I do the touching.

5

Short and Stout

Johnny

I STAY BEHIND AT Connor's place after everyone else leaves to help clean up and to give Becca some extra time to get home. I'm not entirely sure why she wanted to wait until she left to give me her address, but if I had to guess, I'd say it's because she didn't want Alex and Connor to know about us yet.

Not that I've been acting very cool about it. I know for a fact that the guys suspect something. You'd think they'd all be more worried about their own love lives, but that's not really how it works with us. We're a family, and we're always getting up in each other's business.

My phone buzzes in my pocket and I take that as my cue to leave, guessing that it's Becca's address coming through in a text.

"Alright guys, I'm going to head out. I've got a date after this and I don't want to be late."

"Oh? In love again?" Connor asks, following me to the door.

"I'm taking it a little slower this time. But I'm pretty sure she's the one."

He laughs. "You know you say that every time, right? I think maybe you want it too bad to think properly when you meet someone new."

He's not wrong. I do want it badly. I want what my parents have. They've been together for almost forty years and they seem more in love every day. They got married at nineteen years old, so I'm already way behind. Regardless of when I get my family started, I already know that it's probably too late to have as many kids as my parents. I'm not sure I'd want that many, anyway.

Seven kids are a lot.

Especially when five of them are girls.

"Yeah, I know," I tell Connor when we reach the door. "But I can't help it. I'm a romantic at heart. My true love is out there somewhere." *And I'm almost positive she's who I'm going to see tonight,* I add in my head. "But you need to stop worrying about me and start worrying about Alex. Get in there and make sure she knows you're serious. Don't let her slip away again." I grab Connor's shoulder, letting him know I'm rooting for him. "I'll see you later, man. Have fun. Be safe."

"Later, Johnny," Connor says, closing the door behind me. I hear the lock click before I walk out to my car.

Another buzz in my pocket reminds me I haven't looked at Becca's address yet. I get in my car and start it up, pulling my phone out to check my messages. One is the address from Becca, like I thought, but the other is from Hunter.

> **Hunter-** Got a client needing to book in with you. When are you available?

Hunter owns Ink Revival Tattoo. We apprenticed together under the same artist when we were young. He runs the business with his other artists, and when I'm home, I donate my time to help. He's also Ryder's brother, but I didn't find that out until years after the band got big. Ryder was pretty surprised to see me there one day, consulting with an older woman, when he visited with Hunter.

> **Johnny-** Anytime other than tonight works for me. I already have plans.

Hunter- I'll book you in and
let you know.

Johnny- *thumbs up emoji*

Becca's address is near downtown, which I was expecting since I know she lives near the gym Connor goes to. The gym that we all recently found out Alex's grandfather owns. How Connor and Alex haven't ever run into each other before now is a mystery for the ages. They've been in close proximity so many times over the years that they really should have. And if they had, maybe I would have met Becca sooner. I can't worry about lost time, though. All I can do is move forward and make sure Becca becomes mine.

After a quick stop to pick up some of my favorite craft beer, a delicious, locally brewed coffee stout, I'm on my way to Becca's place. Mom always taught me a guest should never arrive empty-handed, and despite what I led Becca to believe, I'm only going to be a regular guest this evening. Not an overnight guest with special benefits.

I mean, do I want to get my hands all over her eventually? Obviously, the answer is yes. My hands are dying to squeeze her ass. But if she really is the one for me, then I need to take my time and get to know her better first. Plus, the situation with Connor and Alex complicates things further, and I need to be sure of what I'm doing before I mess anything up. I hate to say that Travis is right, but... Travis is right. I need to tread carefully, no matter what my heart is telling me.

I find a spot on the street near Becca's building and I send her a text letting her know I'm here. My hand shakes a little as I run it through my hair, but other than that, I don't think I'm too nervous for a man walking to his destiny.

Becca is waiting for me at the entrance to the building. She's changed into comfortable-looking shorts with a matching shirt and an unzipped, well-worn, hoodie over top. Tattoos cover her right leg all the way to the tips of her purple-painted toenails, with a large Freddy Krueger dominating nearly all the space on her thigh. Surprisingly, her left leg only has one large piece on her thigh.

My mind races with thoughts of what I could put there. The thought of my art marking her leg makes my heart race. I'm tattooing something on her as soon as possible. All I need is to decide what.

The tattoos on both of her legs extend into the bottom of her shorts, so I'm no closer to figuring out where they end than I was before. Do they continue down from the ones on her arms? Or do they end somewhere under her shirt and start up again, lower down?

"Hey," she says, pushing the door open for me. "Come on up. I kicked the rock out of the door when I got home and the buzzer has been on the fritz lately. So you get a door-to-door escort."

I follow her up the stairs, her ass swinging in front of my face, and I'm barely able to stop myself from grabbing it. Her legs are the perfect mix of shapely and strong, her muscles flexing under the softest looking skin. I wonder what it would feel like to run my hands up the backs of them and bury my face in her pussy from behind?

Plenty of time for that later. I'm here to get to know her better. Not get into her pants. Not yet, anyway.

"Here we are," Becca says, opening a door at the end of the hallway. "I'm sure it's less than you're used to, but it's treated me well for a long time."

She leads the way into the apartment, stepping out of the way to close the door behind me. It's a decent sized space, with the kitchen on my right, a dining area on my left, and a living room area directly ahead. A couple of lamps light the space, giving it a relaxed vibe. It looks comfortable.

"Drink?" she asks, pointing to the kitchen. "I've got beer, wine, whiskey, and soda."

I hold up the six-pack that I brought with me. "Actually, I stopped and grabbed my favorite on the way." Her nose scrunches, but I continue before she can say anything. "I'm particular about beer and I'd love to share this one with you. If you even like beer, that is?"

She smirks at me in response, and motions for me to follow her to the fridge. She opens up the door and stands back so I can get a better look.

"What do you think? Do I like beer?" She chuckles a little.

Her fridge has five different brews in it, from a light ale all the way to an imported dark stout.

"Uh, I think maybe you like beer?" I laugh. "I guess I made a good choice, then."

She pulls out two of the bottles I brought and opens them with a bottle opener she has mounted on the wall. Holding one bottle out to me, she takes a long drink from the other. She closes her eyes and opens her mouth a couple of times, tasting the flavors as they dance along her tongue. It's unintentionally hot and I can't look away. I'm really invested in her opinion of this beer, like I don't know what I'll do if she doesn't like it. How stupid is that?

"This is nice," she says, finally opening her eyes and taking another small sip. "I don't normally like a coffee stout, but the coffee flavor is subtle in this. Good find."

"Phew," I say, pretending to wipe the sweat off my brow. "Nailed it."

She huffs a small laugh, taking her beer to the couch, where she sits smack in the middle. *Yes! I won't have to decide if I should sit close to her or not. She's decided for me.* When I sit beside her, she turns to face me, tucking her legs up underneath her and leaning one arm on the back of the couch. The front of her sweater opens wider, one side slipping off her shoulder, leaving her upper chest more exposed. I can see her nipples through what I now know is a tank top, not a t-shirt, and my dick twitches in response. She looks amazing like this. The front of the tank dips low and I can see so much of her chest piece tattoo I suspect it flows down between her breasts and connects to a sternum tattoo as well.

She has more tattoos than some of the people I know that work in the industry, and I'm dying to ask her why. It's too soon for that, though. It will have to wait until we know each other better.

"So," she says, tipping her bottle toward me. "Question time. Can I trust Connor with Alex? I won't need my bat with him, will I?"

I splutter a laugh through a mouthful of beer, narrowly avoiding spitting it into her face. "Yeah, you can trust him. He's so in love with her, I'm betting he'll propose before the end of the year. They'll be married before any of the rest of us."

She flashes a grin at me, her shoulders dropping. "That's good to hear. He seems like a good guy, but I'd be remiss if I didn't do my best friend duty and check him out. And, of course, threaten him in some way."

"Your dedication to your friends is admirable. Everyone needs someone who's ready to go to bat for them," I say, tilting my face and looking up at her through raised eyebrows, silently questioning whether she understood my lame joke.

"Oh, I see what you did there," she teases me and smiles. "'Go to bat' with my bat. Good one."

I chuckle. "Thanks, I couldn't resist."

"You want?" Becca asks as she gets up to grab another beer. I nod and watch as she walks away.

God, this girl is gorgeous. She can't be more than around five foot six, but her shorts are so impossibly short that her legs look endless. What was my reason again for not sleeping with her tonight? I can't quite remember, not when my dick is hard enough to cut glass and suffocating in my jeans. And not while Becca walks around like some previously undiscovered goddess, unknowingly inciting lust in all who see her. And right now, I see her.

Boy, do I ever see her.

I lean forward and place my empty bottle on the coffee table, taking the new one she offers when she gets back.

"Thanks," I say, taking a drink.

I'm feeling nervous suddenly, and the hard-on I'm sporting isn't helping matters much. Becca sits beside me again, much closer than the last time, and looks at me with heat in her eyes. She reaches forward with the arm she's placed on the back of the couch, her fingers curling into my hair, her nails scratching softly on my scalp. I can't control the guttural moan that escapes my throat.

Becca places her beer on the coffee table before taking mine and putting it next to hers. We still haven't discussed the rules for touching and I'm seconds away from sitting on my hands, so I don't grab her and pull her against me. The need to feel her, to touch her, to consume her, is growing faster than I can control. She let me touch her hair earlier this evening, so I assume that is still safe, and thrust my hands through her dark waves, pulling her lips to mine. She scrambles into my lap, straddling me, returning my kiss, her tongue tangling with mine frantically, like she'll never get to kiss me again.

Fat chance of that happening. She's mine. She can kiss me anytime she wants to, from now until forever.

Fuck getting to know her better. I know enough. She's the one I've been looking for and I refuse to wait any longer to make love to her.

"What are the rules, Becca?" I ask, my lips against her mouth, unable to break away from her kiss completely. "How can I touch you? Tell me what I can do. I need to feel you."

Becca thrusts her tongue in my mouth before leaning away, dropping her sweater, and ripping her tank over her head, leaving her in her tiny shorts and nothing else. My mouth waters at the sight, imagining how it will feel when I finally get to kiss, lick, and touch her all over her beautiful body.

She puts a hand against my chest as I lean forward, intent on tasting her tight little nipples, and stops me in my place.

"I do the touching," she says with a smirk. "You can put your hands on my waist, and my head and hair as I said before, but that's it. And you can use your mouth on me. But no other touching is allowed." I must look as stunned as I feel when she adds, "Oh, and this is just for tonight. You only get one night with me."

6

Dream Girl

Becca

"Oh, and this is just for tonight. You only get one night with me." I tell him about my long-standing rule. Usually the guys I sleep with are all for this one, but Johnny looks upset.

He drops his hands from my hair, folding them in his lap. At least he's being respectful of the no-touching rule. I did say he could put his hands on my waist, but that was something new I was trying with him. Usually, I tell guys not to touch me at all, just to lie there and let me do everything, and they're more than happy to oblige. Poor Johnny looks like he was looking forward to touching me, like he'd been waiting for this night his whole life.

Which is stupid, considering we only met a week ago.

"What do you mean 'one night'?"

"I mean, one night, and then we don't do this again." I shift and move off of his lap. I have a feeling this night won't go as I planned when Johnny first kissed me at Alex's place. My face heats in shame as I snatch my tank from the floor and tug it over my head, immediately covering it up again with my hoodie. Johnny grabs his beer from the table and takes a big drink. Yeah, this isn't going as planned at all.

Fuck.

"Becca," Johnny begins, before taking another drink of his beer. He's looking down at his lap instead of looking at me and I'm reminded of all those times when I was a kid and people would avoid looking at me because of my scars. Calming myself takes more effort than it should, especially considering it's been thirty years since the accident and I've had so much therapy I should know how to deal with it. But the panic always threatens to take me when people look too closely, or, like now, when they don't look at all.

"I don't want that," Johnny says, finally looking up into my eyes. There's a pain there that I didn't notice before. "One night isn't enough for me. You mean more to me than that. I want all of your nights."

"Okay," I drawl. I don't even know what to think about that, really. "But one night is all I'm offering. I don't do more than that." I'm not telling him why I don't do more, because that isn't any of his business. "But we can be friends if you want? I'm sure we'll see each other often because of Alex and Connor."

"I mean, yeah, friends is good. Great, even. I was coming here to get to know you better, anyway. I may have come on a little strong at Connor's place, but I really wasn't looking to bang you and then fuck off. Not that I minded what we were doing a moment ago. You're incredible. And so fucking hot," he growls, almost making me believe he means it. "But I can't have sex with you tonight, no matter how turned on I am, knowing that it will never happen again." Johnny stands up, hands me his beer, and takes a step toward the door before turning to face me. "I need to get going now. I need a little time to get used to the idea that we're going to be friends and nothing more." He gestures to his groin, and adds, "And this guy needs some time to calm down. You are the sexiest woman both of us have ever seen, not to mention you're one hell of a kisser, and, well, he's having a hard time adjusting to this new plan." He turns back and walks to the door and I follow.

"I'm sorry, Johnny," I say, not sure why I'm apologizing, but it seems like the right thing to do. He seems genuinely sad, as though he really has feelings for me, which baffles me. I mean, he's hot, and his kisses are like an electric jolt right through me, making me tingle ev-er-y-where, and he's fun to hang out with, but that doesn't mean I'm in love with him. Does it?

Nah. Not possible.

"Don't be sorry. We'll be friends. It will be great." He leans forward and kisses me on the corner of my mouth, not quite a friend kiss and not quite a romantic kiss, but tingle-inducing nonetheless. The butterflies in my stomach need to calm the hell down. "I'll call you soon so we can do something, yeah? Actually, let's do something tomorrow. We're working on the album for a bit, but why don't you come over after that? I'll text you the address."

I nod my head, words escaping me at the moment. Johnny raps his knuckles on the door frame, releases a breath, and walks away, leaving me standing in the doorway. I watch until he makes it to the stairs before closing and locking the door behind him.

What the fuck just happened?

Did I just throw myself at a man only to be turned down? Again?

I know he said it's because he wants more, but old wounds are hard to heal and in my head, I hear the voice of the boy who broke me the first time.

Dropping onto the couch, I grab what's left of my beer and down it. I lean back with a huff, forcefully shoving my back against the couch and crossing my arms. A tight burning works its way through my stomach, scorching all the butterflies, and leaving me fidgety and anxious.

I hate remembering that day. It's the main reason I avoid having a love life.

Milo.

I hate that fucking name.

I hate lots of other names too, but Milo Matthews is the boy who betrayed my trust, and Milo Matthews is the boy who owns most of my ire.

Groaning to myself, I get up, grab another beer, and pick up my phone before sitting back down on the couch. I try to distract myself by scrolling mindlessly through TikTok, but no amount of thirst traps and silly dances can distract me from ruminating. My mind is already taking an ill-advised, and unwanted, trip down memory lane, and I'm merely along for the ride.

Oh joy.

I had just turned fourteen when Milo first started talking to me. He was a popular kid at school, a fantastic baseball player, and was well-liked by everyone. I was the weird girl who always wore turtleneck sweaters and long pants, no matter the weather. When he sat next to me in the library that first day, I was sure he'd made a mistake. Milo Matthews was not someone who would sit by me voluntarily, and since there were many other seats available, I thought he'd mistaken me for someone else. It was only when he said my name that I actually believed he'd meant to sit with me.

Milo soon became my friend; my only friend. I was always too shy to make friends with anyone before, and no one else had ever reached out to me. I never expected anyone would, anyway. Mom had explained clearly that my scarring would probably scare all the other kids away, like they had my dad. But I was happy enough alone, I guess. I did a lot of reading, and I took a lot of pictures with the camera my dad had left behind. None of the other kids had paid me much attention, so I was naïve to the ways they could be so cruel to each other.

Turns out my naivety is exactly what Milo was counting on when he befriended me. Because he wasn't doing it to be nice. We spent some time together, but he still hung out with his baseball friends and the other popular kids. When he was with them, he treated me the same as they did, which is to say, he ignored me. But when we were one on one, he made me feel so special. He told me I was the girl of his dreams. How could I help but to swoon?

If it hadn't ended the way it did, I probably would say that Milo was my first boyfriend. He was my first date, my first time holding hands, my first kiss. He probably would have been my *first* too, but he wasn't willing to go that far for the trick he was playing on me.

See, he had never actually liked me. He'd told his friends he was going to figure out why I was always fully clothed, head to toe, and figured the best way to do that would be to pretend to be my boyfriend.

And, of course, I was dumb enough to fall for it.

One night we were at his place, making out in his room instead of studying like we were supposed to be, and he convinced me, finally, to take my shirt off. Even with how dim the lights were, I knew he'd be able to see the scars on my arms, chest, and neck, but I stupidly thought that he actually cared about me, and that it wouldn't matter to him. Too bad that wasn't true. As soon as my shirt was off, he grabbed a camera from his nightstand, took a picture of me in my bra, and said something I'll never forget.

"As if *you* could be the girl of my dreams. More like the girl of my nightmares, Freddy Krueger." Then he burst out into laughter. It took me a minute to figure out what he said before I burst into tears and scrambled to get my shirt back on.

Worst day of my life, not including the day that I got the scars.

There's only one good thing that came from that entire ordeal with Milo. When I was running out of his house that day, I ran face-first into his Uncle Silas. Literally ran him off the sidewalk. We crashed into a heap on the lawn and I was crying so hard I couldn't even apologize. He hadn't even expected me to. I ran him over and he apologized to me. That's how nice he was.

I remember he asked, "What's wrong, pretty girl? A lovely young lady such as yourself shouldn't be crying so hard." I was still so angry and upset that I pulled my right arm, the one with the most scarring, right out of my shirt, and said, "This is why I'm crying. Because I'm a freak. I'm a girl of nightmares."

Then this man, a virtual stranger to me, gave me the first genuine hug I'd had since my accident. He sat on the lawn with me for an hour that day, consoling me all the while. He's the only person I ever told of how strained my relationship with my mother had become since I'd been scarred. The only person who knew my dad left because of me.

And he's the only person who offered to help me.

That night I got the first of many tattoos. I got a full-color tattoo of Freddy Krueger on my right thigh as a fuck you to Milo. Uncle Silas tattooed me secretly, and for free, for a long time after that night. He perfected techniques for tattooing on scarred skin that he could then use in his tattoo business, and I gained a way to keep my scars covered up without always wearing turtlenecks.

The kids at school all started calling me Freddy thanks to Milo and his stupid picture, but once I started wearing regular clothes and showing my tattoos, they all left me alone for the most part. Then, when Alex moved to town a little over a year later and we became friends, none of what the other kids said ever bothered me. Alex is the best friend I could ever have, and she made every day better for me just by being in my life. She didn't know me before the tattoos, but I know she wouldn't have cared. She's not like that.

Of course, the first time my mom saw the tattoos, she was understandably upset. I was underage, after all. But Uncle Silas helped me sort all that out as well. She still hates the tattoos, but not as much as she hated the sight of my scarred flesh.

She still doesn't hug me, though.

Throwing my head back against the couch, I release a harsh breath. I wish Uncle Silas hadn't moved away. Ever since the accident, he and his husband Patrick have been the only people who actually felt like family. They were like a mom and dad, the ones that I should have had. Uncle Silas is an enormous bear of a man, in more ways than one. Uncle Patrick is a big man, but not as big as Uncle Silas. They always made time for me and always made me feel welcome in their home in a way my mother never did in ours.

They showed me what caring parents should look like.

Blowing out a breath, I quit swiping through TikTok, and take myself to bed. I've had enough of feeling sorry for myself for one day. A good night's sleep will get me back on track.

Too bad I know I'm going to dream about kissing Johnny.

Fuck, that man kiss.

7

Dream Guy

Johnny

WELL, SHIT. THAT WAS not how I expected this evening to go.

What does Becca mean, she doesn't do more than one night? Hasn't she ever wanted to fall in love? To have someone know her, inside and out, and love her beyond all reason?

I've always wanted to find my soul mate. The one person who is my other half, who makes me whole, who shows me what it means to love. That's why my relationships never last. Nothing has ever given me the feeling that it's forever. I've always been able to take or leave the women I've dated.

That's not the case at all with Becca. Even when she was stripping down and offering me her body, I chose to not sleep with her, just for the chance to continue being around her. I chose to be friends with her, instead of sleeping with her, even though she is the sexiest woman I've ever seen and she had me so turned on I thought my dick was going to bust out of my pants.

The drive home is uncomfortable, and no amount of rearranging my dick takes the pressure off. I should take off my pants, but it would be my luck to get pulled over and then arrested, and Denise would have to come bail me out of jail. I'll leave that kind of thing to Ryder. Denise has more than enough to deal with because of him, without having me add to it just because I have an uncomfortable erection.

Pulling into my assigned spot in the parking garage, I notice that Travis' truck isn't here. Again. I can't remember the last time we were both home at the same time, and we've only been back from tour for a little over a week. It's not like he should have that much on the go already. He was helping our parents out at their house a little these last few days, doing some repairs around the house because they refuse to let us hire someone, but he should be done with most of it by now.

Not like it matters. I'm a grown man. I don't need my brother around all the time. I can deal with this on my own.

Would have been nice to have someone to talk to, though.

I take the elevator up to our condo, a loft style penthouse with bedrooms on opposite sides of the living space, and head straight into the kitchen to begin my stress relief routine.

You might not know it to look at me, but I am a proficient baker. My mom taught me how to bake years ago, when it was clear I'd need something to keep me occupied, other than playing music. I got into a lot of trouble when I was a kid. Nothing bad, but I pulled a lot of pranks on my sisters and it was easier to redirect my energy than it was to punish me for it. I'm sure if I hadn't learned to bake when I was young, my pranks would have escalated and I could have hurt someone.

Probably me, when my sisters got their revenge.

By the time Travis gets home two hours later, I've already made several batches of cookies. I'm packing them into the bakery boxes I keep on hand for this reason when he walks into the kitchen. He stops dead in his tracks and gives me a look.

"What happened this time?" he asks, grabbing a beer from the fridge and sitting at the counter opposite where I'm working. "Let me guess. You didn't take my advice, and you talked to Alex before she was ready?"

I roll my eyes at him before turning to pull my last tray of cookies from the oven. "No, *Mom*. I didn't do that." I set the tray down on a trivet to let it cool and grab myself a beer before sitting next to Travis at the counter. "I kissed Becca at Connor's place earlier and she invited me over after."

Travis slaps me on the back. "That's great, man. Maybe she's the one after all." He smiles at me and downs more of his beer.

I run my hand down my face and groan. "Yeah, not exactly. Things were going great until she told me she would only sleep with me tonight, and then it could never happen again."

"Oh," Travis says, turning to face me better, concern splashed across his features. "So... what did you do?"

I snort a laugh. "What do you mean, what did I do? I told her that wasn't what I wanted, accepted her offer of friendship, invited her to come over tomorrow night, then came home and, well, you can see." I gesture at the kitchen and the stacks of bakery boxes filled with cookies. "Now I need to make a delivery to Aiden in the morning."

"That's the one good thing about your stress management techniques, hey? The kids at the shelter always have homemade treats to snack on."

"Yeah. At least someone benefits from my misery."

Travis reaches across the counter and steals a cookie from an open box. He shoves the whole thing in his mouth at once and grabs another before resting on his stool again.

"So what are you going to do, then? Are you sure you can just be friends with her?" Travis knows me better than anyone, and he knows how quickly I fall in love. He's been warning me to pace myself with Becca since we met her after the show last week, and I've all but planned our wedding already.

What can I say? I'm a hopeless romantic and a terrible listener.

"I'm going to try," I say with a sigh. "I'm going to talk to Alex, too. Maybe she can give me some insight into why Becca only does one night. Maybe I can be the exception to her rule."

Travis stands up, grabbing my shoulder and giving a squeeze. "Maybe. How could she possibly resist your charms? Incredibly successful guitar player, excellent baker, *and* looking to settle down? You're every woman's dream guy. She'll catch up, eventually." He gives my shoulder one last squeeze and walks to his side of the loft, apparently done with talking for the night.

I hope he's right, though. Maybe I can be Becca's dream guy, after all.

8

It's Moving Time

Becca

"He did WHAT? That fucking asshole. Be there shortly. I'll bring the bat." I jump up from the couch and throw my phone in my pocket while frantically looking around for my keys. "I gotta go. Connor ditched Alex at Rough Mix. He left with some chick."

Johnny sits there looking stunned. Whether it's at how quickly I'm racing around his loft, or at what Connor has done, I don't know.

The guys worked on the album today and when the rest of them went out, Johnny asked if I wanted to come to his place and hang out. The friend thing is starting well, but I haven't told Alex much about it. She's been too busy being firmly in the honeymoon stage of her relationship.

Until now, that is. Who could have guessed her honeymoon would only last one night?

"What? No. He wouldn't. I can't believe Connor would do something like that," Johnny says, finally getting up to help me find my keys. "He hasn't done anything like that in years. He doesn't bring women home anymore. Why would he do it now when he seems so happy having finally found Alex? It doesn't make any sense."

"Well, it might not make sense, but it's happening right now. I'm meeting Alex at Connor's place — Aha!" I throw my keys in the air and catch them. They were in my pocket the whole time. "Glad those boxes are still in my car."

"Do you want me to come with you? Help you pack up?"

I'm halfway to the door already. "No, that's probably not a good idea. I don't want to put you in a weird position. Connor's your friend. And you guys are in a band together. No sense in you getting mixed up in this."

"Fine. Promise you'll call if you need help, though. Okay?"

"Yeah, yeah. I promise," I yell as I get into the elevator and frantically stab at the close door button. "Ugh. Why do you have to live in a loft? It would be so much faster if I could run down the stairs."

Johnny's laughter is the last thing I hear as the doors close, and one last glimpse of his smile lights me up. I might be on the way to help my best friend after yet another boyfriend has cheated on her, but I still get a little rush when Johnny looks at me like I matter, like he really likes me. Or at least like he really did like me before I declared us to be only friends.

But now's not the time for that.

Alex needs me. Again.

How could Connor do something like this to her?

I make it to Connor's house in record time, with no memory of anything after starting my car. I'm lucky there were no police around, because I'm fairly certain I was going well over the speed limit.

I pull into the driveway and park in time to see Alex, Ryder, and Devon jump out of the Escalade the band usually rides around in. There's an unfamiliar car parked near the house, so close it's almost parked on the steps to the front door.

Seems like a bold choice, but okay.

"He's here?" The words tumble out of my mouth, going unanswered in the general confusion. But I know why I'm here, and it's not to ask questions. I reach into my back seat and pull out the bat I keep for these occasions. I toss it to Alex. "Time to play ball, girl."

Alex storms into the house with the three of us trailing along behind her. She drags the bat along the wall, knocking off pictures and banging it across door frames, before Ryder jumps in front of her. He tries to convince her not to go into the bedroom, claiming she doesn't want to see what's happening. He obviously doesn't understand the rage of a woman who's had many unfaithful lovers. He needs to get out of the way, but stay close enough to ensure Alex doesn't kill Connor.

The last thing she needs after another betrayal is to be sent to prison.

Orange is not her color.

In the space around Ryder and Devon, I see Alex pull some girl off of the bed by her and immediately start beating the crap out of her. This is getting weirder and weirder. Alex never blames the girl. She's never sought revenge on any of the women who've slept with her boyfriends before. The way she sees it, it's the man who is betraying her trust. The women rarely know that they're the other woman.

Connor is laying on the bed and even at this distance, I can tell he is out of it. It's not an excuse for cheating, but he must be completely out of his mind. He either drank a lot of alcohol or he's on something. There's no way he was in his right mind when he brought this chick home.

I pull out my phone to text Johnny.

Becca- He's here with a woman. But he seems trashed. Alex is beating the shit out of the chick and he hasn't even lifted his head off the pillow.

Johnny - He must be drunk.

Becca-That's no excuse.

Johnny - No, it's not. Still, something about this doesn't seem right to me.

Becca- We're heading to the pool house to pack up her stuff now.

Johnny - Need help?

Becca- Nah. Ryder's coming with us to pack up. That's one extra person than we normally have for a post-breakup move-out.

Johnny - Okay. Let me know if you guys need anything.

Ryder is already leading Alex out the side door toward the pool house while I get in my car and drive around with the boxes.

We pack up faster than we ever have before, partly because of Ryder's help, and partly because of the fully furnished nature of the pool house. When Alex accepted the job to be Connor's chef, part of the deal was that she would live on the premises and be available twenty-four-seven. She didn't even have to bring her own kitchen utensils because they set up the pool house and the main house with all the professional-grade equipment she could want. Her kitchen stuff is still in the boxes we packed it in during her last move.

We load everything into both vehicles, mine and Alex's, and she heads upstairs to double-check check we got everything.

"Devon wants us to bring Alex back into the main house. He says something is up and it's not what it looks like."

"That's what they always say," Alex says, coming down the stairs. "I can't do it. I'm really broken this time. I just want to go back to Becca's and drink all the alcohol, and forget I ever reconnected with Connor."

"Sure, babe," I say, wrapping my arms around her. "You know, I think this is a record. We just moved you in yesterday."

Alex snorts out a sound that's half laugh, half hiccup. "Yeah. Rock stars, am I right? It's all 'live, laugh, fuck' with them. I should have known he wouldn't be able to keep it in his pants."

Ryder snuggles in and wraps his arms around us both. "It's going to be alright, babe," he says into her hair. "You're way too good for him, anyway."

At least out of all this mess, she made another good friend. Ryder seems like a decent guy, and he is definitely on her side.

"Alright, enough of this mushy bullshit," Alex says, pushing out her arms and breaking out of the group. "Let's go home."

We all leave the pool house together. "See you at home," I tell Alex before getting into my car and leaving.

I don't know what's going to happen now, and it's probably selfish of me to think of myself, but I can't help but wonder where this leaves me and Johnny. Tonight was only our first night trying to hang out as friends, so I guess I haven't really had

time to get invested in the relationship. But if Alex is going to
be friends with Ryder still, then it should be okay for me to be
friends with Johnny. Right?

I race home and get my car unloaded before Alex makes it
back. After checking out my stash of hard alcohol to make sure
we'll have enough to numb the heartache, I go back downstairs
to wait for her to get here. While I wait, I pull out my phone to
send Johnny an update.

Becca- Back at my apartment now.
Waiting for Alex to arrive with
the rest of her stuff. I expect
she'll be blackout drunk soon.

Johnny- Fuck, that sucks. Is she
okay?

Becca- Kind of, I guess. This is
hitting her harder than any of
her other cheating boyfriends
did.

Johnny- Let me know if she needs
anything. Or if you do.

Becca- Will do. Thanks.

Johnny- I'll let you know if I hear anything from the other guys. This whole situation seems weird to me. Connor was saying the other day that he would propose now if he thought Alex would say yes.

Becca - Guys get dumb when their dicks do the thinking for them.

Becca - Gotta go. Alex just pulled up.

I stride straight to her and wrap her up in another hug as soon as she's out of her car. "Let's get the rest of your stuff inside so we can start drinking. I already emptied my car."

She sniffles a little, her eyes shining with tears, and nods. "Yeah. I could use a drink. Or maybe a dozen."

AFTER A FEW HOURS of drinking and listening to Alex cry, she finally has enough and goes to bed.

"Let me help you, girl," I laugh as she stumbles down the hall, whiskey bottle in hand. "You're too drunk to walk alone."

"*You're* too drunk to walk alone," she says, sloshing the whiskey as she points at me with the bottle. "But a little help would be nice. I can barely see anything. I think I lost my glasses." She squints at me.

I bark out a laugh. "Dude, you don't even wear glasses."

"I don't? Are you sure?"

I squint back at her. "Yes?"

She cocks her head, then laughs. "You had me going for a second. If you find them, can you bring them to me?"

"Sure," I agree, urging her to keep walking toward her room. "If I find the glasses that you don't wear, I will bring them to you."

"Phew. That's a relief. I don't think I could deal with a whole day of my vision being like this."

I help her stumble through her door, both of us giggling the entire time. I may be drunk, be she's drunker. More drunk? Dranker? Whatever. All I know is I'm not the one who thinks I wear glasses when I don't.

She makes it to the end of her bed before falling face down on top of the blankets. Luckily, I grab the bottle out of her hand before she dumps its contents into the middle of the mattress.

"Okay, Alex. Help me out here," I say while working her ratty old jogging pants off. "There you go. Get under the blankets. That's good." It's not good. She's not moving. Her bare legs are hanging off the end of the bed and she's making no attempt to move up.

"Come on, Alex. Let's go." I grab her legs and try to wheelbarrow her further onto the bed, rocking my body to get her to bounce forward inch by inch. The reflection in the mirror looks like I'm humping into her, and I burst out laughing. Good thing no one can see me right now. With only a little further to go, I climb up on the bed, straddle her legs, and use a bounce and push motion with my hands on her butt to move her the rest of the way. Hey, now that I've got the humping out of the way, I may as well get a handful of ass.

"You're lucky I love you," I tell her as I pull the blankets up. "Few people would go to the trouble to make sure you're on the bed. At least, not many people would do it for me."

Once I've tucked her in, I bring her a bottle of water and a bucket for beside the bed, just in case.

I should clean the living room a little before I go to bed, but instead, I grab my phone and do one of those things you should never do when you've had too much to drink.

I drunk-text Johnny.

9

Mission Accomplished

Johnny

Bzzzzz. Bzzzzz. Bzzzzz. Bzzzzz.

I crack my eyes open and strain to locate the source of the buzzing

Bzzzzz. Bzzzzz. Bzzzzz. Bzzzzz.

Where the fuck is my phone?

Bzzzzz. Bzzzzz. Bzzzzz. Bzzzzz.

I jump off the bed, shoving my pillows and blankets on the floor, finally finding my phone wedged between the mattress and the headboard. The time on the lock screen reads one-thirty-two. I only came to bed twenty minutes ago, after Devon updated me on the Connor situation and I finally gave up on Becca getting back to me.

After Becca left earlier today, I called my newest client, Lana, to see if she wanted to do some work on her tattoo. Lana used to babysit Ryder and Hunter when they were kids and their dad worked overtime. When she had a full double mastectomy and chose not to go with reconstructive surgery to replace her breasts, Ryder told her to call Hunter's shop and ask for me. We've been working on a large floral piece for the last week, and she's loving the results so far.

I worked on her for a few hours tonight, ears waiting to hear the buzz from my phone telling me I had a message from Becca. She didn't send one, though, so when I got home, I came to bed.

But here is a text from her now.

Becca- You up?

Becca- I had to put Alex to bed. She was too drunk.

Becca- She said I was too drunk, but I'm not. Well, maybe a little tiny bit.

I smile down at the screen, picturing Becca squinting at her phone, concentrating so she won't misspell anything so she can convince me she's not drunk. There's no way she didn't drink with Alex tonight. Not after how Alex found Connor. Devon's messages explained that the girl Alex saw had drugged Connor at the bar and then drove him to his place to sleep with him.
To rape him.
I should tell Becca right now, but I think that's news that would be better shared in person. And when all the parties involved are sober. But I'm still going to keep talking to her as long as she'll let me.

Johnny- A likely story. How much did you two drink? How is Alex feeling now?

Becca- She's passed out. But also she's hurt and mad.

Becca- Did I ever tell you how hot Johnny is? He is so hot. I'm pretty sure my panties melt every time he's near me.

I run my hand down my face, trying to wipe the grin away. I'm in bed alone, so there's no one here to see it, but I still feel funny about it. I shouldn't be enjoying her confession so much, since she's drunk and can't help it, but I like it anyway.

Johnny- No, you never mentioned that. I like the way it sounds, though. You should tell me again.

Becca- No way. I can't tell you how hot I think Johnny is. It's a secret. I'm the only one who can know.

Johnny- What if I promise not to tell?

Becca- Nope. Not good enough.

Becca- You can tell me a secret
first. Then maybe I'll tell
you.

She must really be drunk. Does she even realize she's talking to me right now? I thought she was kidding when she was saying my name like she was talking to someone else, but maybe she really thinks that. Can I use this to my advantage? If I tell her how I feel right now, she'll no doubt forget it by morning. I know I said we would be friends and nothing more, but I can't let this chance pass me by. I doubt I'll ever get another chance to tell her how I feel without scaring her off completely.

Johnny- Deal. But you need to
go first.

Becca- Okay. Johnny is literally the hottest guy I have
ever seen. Last night when we
almost had sex but then he ran
away nearly killed me. It was
so much like what happened with
Milo that all the memories came
flooding back.

Oh, fuck.

Why didn't she tell me she was so upset about that? And who the fuck is Milo? And how do I find him so I can teach him a lesson? That's something to talk to Aiden about one of these days.

Johnny- Who is Milo? And why
didn't you tell Johnny that he
hurt you like that? He would
never hurt you.

I would never. I could never do anything to hurt Becca.

Becca- Fuck Milo. Milo doesn't
matter. He was over twenty years
ago. Tell me your secret.

Johnny- Okay, here's my secret.
I really like you a lot, Becca.
I'm pretty sure I love you.

FUCK!

Just as I hit send, I realize it doesn't matter if Becca doesn't remember what I say. There will be a record of it in text on her phone.

"Fuck! Fuck, fuckity, fuck, fuck. What the hell, Johnny? How could you be so stupid? She's definitely going to run from you now."

How do I fix this?

A quick Google search tells me I am not qualified to do anything about it without the help of an expert hacker. I don't know any hackers, and I can't just find someone online. Imagine the field day that tabloids would have with that. I can see the headlines now:

Johnny Donovan, guitarist for Sleeping Dogs, pays hackers to delete evidence.

Johnny Donovan pays hacker to delete evidence of his freaky sex fetish.

What is Johnny Donovan hiding? What sort of depraved pictures does he to send to unsuspecting women?

They would make up any number of reasons. Actually, that part doesn't bother me so much. Tabloids print whatever they want, anyway. It's not like I haven't been splashed across their pages before. Usually, they're announcing that I'm dating one of my own sisters when they catch me out in public with one of them. That's one of the consequences of Travis and me having kept our family out of the spotlight. Everyone thinks our sisters are groupies or baby mommas.

What really bothers me is Becca finding out.

So why was I stupid enough to text it to her? I'm such an idiot.

Becca- Oooh, that's a good secret. I won't tell her. I promise.

She doesn't realize I'm talking about her. This is amazing. I might be able to salvage this after all.

Johnny- That's great. Thank you.

Suddenly it hits me: I have to delete the message directly from her phone. There's no other way. I throw my blankets around again, looking for the jeans and t-shirt that I left on the floor. I find them and pull them on, hopping my way to the kitchen as I do so. I stop to grab a box of my freshly baked cookies to give me a reason for showing up tonight before continuing to the door. After shoving my feet into my shoes and grabbing my keys, I jump into the elevator and punch the button to close the doors.

Becca was right earlier. It would be so much faster if I could run down the stairs.

SOMEONE HAS PROPPED THE door to Becca's building open with a rock. That's sort of annoying, not to mention unsafe, but it benefits me tonight. Right now, all I care about is getting to her before she goes to bed, and, most importantly, before she realizes it was me she was messaging the whole time.

I bang my fist against the door, a little too enthusiastically, and then wait.

And wait.

And wait.

Fuck. What if she's already asleep?

I knock again, this time with a more restraint. I'm not trying to wake up her neighbors, after all.

"Becca? You home?"

I listen with my ear to the door. I don't hear anything, so I knock again, louder this time.

"Becca?" I press my ear to the door again, finally hearing some movement. As the clinks and clunks of the door unlocking sound through the door, I add, "I have cookies."

The door flies open and if I'd still been pressed up against it, I'd be on my ass right now.

"Cookies? Yay!" She grabs the box from me, opening it as she turns around, motioning for me to come in. She's wearing the same tank and shorts she had on the first time I came here, but she's left off the worn out hoodie she had on over the top.

"I thought we could finish hanging out since you had to leave so quickly earlier. Plus, I thought you and Alex might like some cookies to soak up the alcohol," I tell her, glancing around for her phone. Getting inside was only step one of the plan. Step two is to find her phone and delete the message.

Shit, I don't see it anywhere.

Becca flops down on the couch, the cookie box in her lap. It doesn't look like she has her phone with her. Maybe it's in her bedroom?

"So, what have you been up to tonight? I'm sorry I had to leave earlier. I'm sure you get it." Becca stuffs another cookie in her mouth. "These are so good. Where did you buy these? I can't even believe how good they are."

I scan the room while walking to the couch. That fucking phone has to be somewhere. I can't just walk into her bedroom, though. Maybe if I say I have to use the bathroom, I can sneak into her room when she's not looking? That could work. I'm already by the couch now, though, and it would look weird if I turned around to use the bathroom now. I'll give a few minutes before I go.

Sitting down beside Becca, I reach into the box and grab a cookie. "I called a client and went to the shop to work on her tattoo."

"You went to get a new tattoo? Ooh, show me. Show me." Becca bounces in her seat. She's giddy when she drinks. It's cute when she lets her guard down.

"No, I worked on her tattoo," I tell her. "She came in for an extra appointment because I had some time available unexpectedly and I want to make sure I finish this for her before we go back on tour."

Becca turns to look at me, eyes wide. "You're going back on tour? Already? But you just got back." She throws the box of cookies down on the coffee table and tackles me to the couch, throwing her arms around my neck as we fall. "I don't want you to go yet. I'll miss you."

This is most likely the chance of a lifetime considering how skittish Becca is about being touched, so I wrap my arms around her as quickly and tightly as I can. I tip my face down, hugging her with my whole upper body, and inhale deeply. She smells a little spicy, like she did the night we met. I need to find out what shampoo she uses so I can smell it all the time.

No, wait. That's creepy. Isn't it?

"I'm going to miss you too, babe. But we're not leaving for a while. We're home for six months. We can still see each other all the time until then." I pull her against my chest, kissing her head. "And we can call each other text when I'm on the road. Maybe you can come out and visit for a while, too." I'm not sure how that will work if Connor and Alex don't work out this problem, though.

He was the one who was attacked, but with her history of breakups because of boyfriends cheating on her, I don't know if she'll have it in her to forgive him. I'm sure she'll want to, but with how much baggage she carries, who knows if she can? And then there's the mindfuck it would be for her to be with the lead singer of Sleeping Dogs. Connor has so many pairs of panties thrown at him when he's on stage he could open his own really gross lingerie store.

"You mean it?" She pushes herself off of me and reaches for the cookies again. "That would be amazing. I could get so many amazing shots of you guys. Do you know who you're bringing with you as an opener yet?"

I sit up again and snuggle right against her. "We're not sure yet. Denise is looking into it. I think it would be good to see what direction this album goes in before we commit to anyone. I always like it better when the opening act's sound vibes with ours, you know? It's too disjointed for me when the musical styles are complete opposites."

"That makes sense." She brushes crumbs off her shorts and stands up. "The guys you had at the last show were good. What were they called? *Lives that Cared?* I liked their sound." She bends and grabs my hand, pulling me up. Drunk Becca is not as hesitant to touch me as sober Becca was last night.

"Yeah, they're good guys. Young. A lot younger than we are. They're still in the partying it up every night part of their career. Some days I feel like we're winding down."

"I know what you mean," she says, dragging me around the couch. "I can't drink like I used to. I'm going to have a horrible hangover tomorrow."

"It might be time to admit it. We're getting old. Pretty soon we're going to turn into our parents," I chuckle.

"Eww, gross," she says. "Speak for yourself. I am never turning into my mother. She's literally the worst person on earth. I may get old lady hangovers, but I refuse to be like my mom."

"You never know," I say with a laugh when she glares at me. "Maybe you'll get a young lady hangover instead," I add with a wink.

Becca's been slowly dragging me along behind her throughout this conversation, and it appears we've arrived at our destination. Her bedroom.

What the hell?

I mean, yeah, I was trying to get in here to find her phone, but I didn't expect her to grab me and drag me here herself.

"Uh, Becca?" I ask before she pulls me into the room. "What are we doing here?"

She laughs. "Going to sleep. Attempting to avoid a hangover."

"Is that a good idea?"

"You got a better one?"

Shit, what am I doing? I need to get into her room to find her phone. I'll leave after. I'm not the kind of guy to take advantage of a drunk woman. Not more than letting her hug me and hold my hand, anyway.

"Nope," I say. "Lead the way."

Becca's room is spacious, with enough room for a couple of dressers and nightstands and a king-size bed. I can see her phone from here. Almost there. I can hang out until she falls asleep and then delete the messages and everything will be fine.

"I'm just going to brush my teeth and wash up. Make yourself comfortable," she says as she leaves the room.

Yes! Now's my chance. I wait until I hear the water running in the bathroom before I grab her phone, open up the messages, and then delete the one where I said I think I love her.

Relief washes over me, and I can finally relax.

I lay back on her bed for a moment, tempted to accept her invitation and stay the night, but I know she's not ready for that. And to tell the truth, neither am I. I think I proved to myself tonight that being just friends with Becca is going to be a lot harder than I thought.

"Becca?" I call out after knocking on the bathroom door. "I'm going to head home and let you get some rest. Be sure to drink some water, okay?"

"Oh, yeah. Okay," she yells through the door. "Thanks for the cookies."

"You're welcome. See you later."

I let myself out of the apartment, making sure the door locks behind me. Not quite the way I saw our first time hanging out as friends going, but it wasn't bad.

I still need to tell her about what actually happened to Connor. I'll have to find another time to do that, though. She's in no shape to process that mess tonight.

10

Greasy Breakfasts and Good Friends Becca

Becca

Johnny- Hey. How are you feeling this morning? Did you end up with the old lady hangover or the young lady hangover?

Becca- Is there such a thing as a middle-aged lady hangover? If so, that's what I have. I was up early and didn't feel too bad, but I do have a headache and I'm feeling slightly nauseated.

Johnny- Have you eaten yet? Want to meet up and get some breakfast? Bring Alex, too. I'm sure she could use some food.

Becca- Oh, yeah. A greasy breakfast sounds perfect. Alex is
still sleeping and I don't
want to wake her. She cried
a lot last night, so I'm sure
she's exhausted. I'll bet her
headache will be worse than
mine.

Becca- Meet me at Maggie's. You
know where that is?

Johnny- Sure do. See you soon.

SHIT.

Now I have to shower and actually get moving. I make quick work of it, dressing in baggy joggers and a loose long-sleeved t-shirt with my favorite hoodie over the top. I need to find myself a new comfort sweater one of these days. This one is nearly see-through because it's so worn out. That makes sense, though. I've had it for years.

On my way out, I notice another rock holding open the main door of my building. Seems like the landlord better get to fixing the buzzer properly, so that people will finally stop doing this. It shouldn't be that hard to leave a door closed. Everyone has cell phones now. Just send a text when you arrive if the buzzer doesn't work. Why would you just leave the building open to anyone walking by?

Some days, I really hate people.

It's not quite noon and traffic is light, making my drive to Maggie's nice and easy. I pull into a spot near the door and make my way inside.

I find Johnny sitting in a booth by the window. He couldn't have sat anywhere else, really. This restaurant is inside an old train car with windows all along one side and a counter and the kitchen on the other. *Every* booth is by the window.

"Hey," I say, sliding into the seat across from Johnny, taking in the way his shirt stretches across his chest muscles. "Sorry I'm late."

He waves me off, swallowing, and distracting me with the sight of his Adam's apple bobbing underneath all the ink on his neck. Jesus, does he always look this good? "I just got here. I had to drop off a few boxes of cookies to Aiden."

"Okay, good. I still had to shower and stuff when you messaged me." I pick up the menu, pretending to look at it so I don't have to look at Johnny. I remember very well how I tried to drag him into my bed last night, and how he turned me down. Again. I appreciate he did it, I guess, since we're trying to be friends, but rejection always stings.

The server shows up and asks for my drink order.

"Water and coffee," I say with desperation in my voice. "Two glasses of water and lots of coffee refills, please."

She chuckles and looks over at Johnny with a little smile. He's focusing solely on me, though, so he doesn't even notice. I doubt he's even noticed the phone number written on the napkin under his coffee cup.

"What are you getting?" he asks. "I can't decide between waffles or French toast."

"The answer is always waffles. French toast is soggy and gross." The server returns with two enormous glasses of ice water and a nice, big mug of steamy coffee for me. "Thank you so much, Ivy," I say, reading her name tag. "Now I will love you forever. You're a lifesaver."

She laughs. "Well, that's certainly the first time anyone has ever called me that while working this job. I gotta say, I like it much better than any of the other names I've heard."

"Hey, waiting tables is hard," I tell her. "Constantly running around, taking orders from people with no manners, on your feet all day, just trying to get people fed? It's a tough way to make a living. Never mind that people are never crankier than when they're trying to eat. The word 'hangry' exists for a reason, am I right?"

She chuckles politely, probably not wanting to mess up her tips from the tables on either side of us. I wasn't lying. Waiting tables is a tough way to make a living. I've done enough of it in my life to know that.

"Are you all decided? Or do you need a few minutes?" Ivy asks, turning on her server charm again.

"We are ready," I say, gathering up the menus. "I will have the full breakfast, with scrambled eggs, fried potatoes, extra sausage and extra bacon, and multigrain toast, please. And I think my friend here is having the waffles. Right, Johnny?"

His mouth is hanging open as he studies me. "Where are you putting all that? I thought you said you weren't feeling great?"

I laugh. "I said a greasy diner breakfast was just what I needed. For optimal grease, you need extra breakfast meat. Isn't that right, Ivy?" I look at her for confirmation and she nods. "Now, tell the nice lady what you want to eat so she can put in our order and get onto something else she needs to do."

"Oh, yeah. Sorry," Johnny apologizes to the server. "Waffles, please. And can I also get strawberries and whip cream on top? And a side of bacon?"

"Sure thing," Ivy says. "I'll be around with coffee refills shortly."

I watch as she walks to the counter to enter our order into the computer system.

"She's cute, isn't she?" I ask Johnny, torturing myself. Why would I want to know if Johnny thinks our waitress is cute?

I don't do more than one night, but this man across from me has more of my attention than any man I've met in a long time. Maybe that's why I'm trying to turn his attention to someone else?

If I were someone a man could actually love, I would be tempted to give it a shot with him. But as my mother likes to tell me, no one wants to wake up and look at me every day for the rest of their life. Better I cut it off after one night than risk getting too attached.

"Who?" Johnny asks, his head swiveling to see who I'm talking about. "Oh, the server? Yeah, she's cute, I guess."

"You know she gave you her number? On your napkin there."

He looks down at the napkin under his cup. "Yeah, I saw that. She does it every time I come in here. She does it to Travis, too. I don't take it seriously. Why? Does it bother you?"

I grab a couple of sugar packets and rip them open, focusing on dumping them into my coffee, rather than looking at Johnny. I don't know why, but it does bother me. It bothers me a lot more than it should for someone who doesn't do relationships, anyway.

"No, it's totally fine," I lie. "I was just making sure you saw it. Didn't want you missing out, in case you're interested."

"Thanks," he says through gritted teeth. "That was thoughtful of you."

"Hey," I say with a humorless laugh. "What are friends for?"

We drink our coffees in silence for a few minutes. Johnny alternates looking at me, with looking at his phone and typing messages. I chug back my first water and slowly sip on the second. The extra hydration already working to make me feel better. Maybe I have a few years of young lady hangovers left in me after all.

"So, listen," Johnny starts, and I have a feeling I know where he's going. "About last night. I—"

"Oh, don't worry about it," I rush before he can go any further. Embarrassment is already burning my cheeks and I'm wringing my hands like I can rub the shame away. I can't stand to listen to another apology, or worse, the reason he rejected me. It's best if we move on. "You have nothing to be sorry for. I'm the one who should be sorry. Let's just forget it, okay? I was drunk, and you are ridiculously hot. It was a moment of weakness."

Johnny looks stunned. His mouth is working, but nothing is coming out. Finally, he blinks several times and shakes his head, as if to clear it. He chuckles under his breath.

"Uh, that is not even close to what I was going to say, but I accept your apology. And I am sorry. I didn't want to stay, even though I was more than tempted, because I know it's not what you really want. I want more than one night, but since you don't, we're just friends. I was just trying to abide by the decision we made." His eyelids lower, and his pupils widen. "But trust me. Leaving you last night, after you invited me into your bed? That was the hardest thing I've ever done. My shower wouldn't get cold enough for me to deal with that aftermath if you know what I mean."

"Oh," I whisper, my breath quickening. I can feel the heat building in me. Just the mention of Johnny needing a cold shower because of me igniting lust like I've never felt before. "I... Hooo!" I finally say, fanning myself. "Is it hot in here?"

Johnny laughs, the tension broken. "No, that's just you," he says with a wink, pulling a laugh from me as well.

"But seriously," he begins again. "I wanted to talk about what happened last night with Connor."

I wince, not prepared for how much it hurts me to hear his name. Is it possible to have sympathy pains from someone else's betrayal? Because I think that's what this is. I'm feeling betrayed by proxy for Alex.

Johnny notices my reaction and reaches out to touch my hand. A tingle runs up my arm, making me raise my head and open my eyes. What the hell was that?

"It's good news," he says when the shock falls from his face. I guess he felt the tingle, too. Must be some electrical current thing. Like when you rub your feet on the carpet to shock someone. Except, instead of a shock, I felt a pleasant tingle. Strange. "Well, not really 'good' news. But not the same kind of bad news we originally thought it was."

Just then Ivy shows up with our food, arranging our plates in front of us. She ensures we have everything before leaving us to our breakfasts.

"So, what do you mean? How bad? And how good?" I ask, shoving an entire piece of bacon into my mouth.

Oh, yeah. That's what I'm talking about. Greasy diner food is the best cure for a hangover.

Johnny explains that what Alex and I saw was only part of what happened. We were there for the end of a disturbing attack on Connor. When Alex pulled that bitch off of him and beat the shit out of her, she was saving Connor from a rapist.

The texts Johnny has been getting the whole time we've been here have been updates on Connor's status. Drug-testing confirmed that someone had drugged him, and the woman eventually confessed to stalking him, leading up to last night when she finally got her chance to execute her plan of drugging him in an attempt to sleep with him.

"Devon says she's the one he escorted from the show last week. The one Connor found half-naked in the bathroom before he came back to the dressing room and discovered Alex. We actually saw her yesterday at a diner across town. We took a break from working in the studio and went for lunch and she was working there."

I finished my breakfast while Johnny explained the situation to me. Leaning back against the red vinyl of the booth, I grab my coffee in both hands and take a sip. Ivy must've come by and refilled it when I was listening to Johnny, so it's full again. Bless her.

"But how did she know where he lives? And how did she get him into the house?"

Johnny explained how she had apparently followed Connor home from the restaurant she worked at and stored the information away for a later date. That night at Rough Mix she saw her chance and slipped something into his drink before taking him outside. Connor was barely even conscious when we got there. Which would explain what appeared to be his extremely lackluster lovemaking. I didn't think Alex would've put up with someone who just lay there doing nothing. I know her exes haven't been great lovers, but come on. She has to draw the line somewhere and I'm sure participation is the bare minimum.

"And that's why she parked on the porch. He was still functioning when they got to the house, but he would have needed her support to make it into the house. They think she drugged him, then got him into the car almost immediately. Otherwise, he would have passed out in the car and she wouldn't have been able to move him at all."

I put my cup down. "Wow. That's just... just... What the hell, man? How can I be mad at him now?" I flop back against my seat and cross my arms over my chest. This isn't Connor's fault, so I can't continue to be angry with him. But now what?

"Yeah, I know," he says. His phone buzzes again and he checks the message. "It's Ryder. He wants to know if I know where you live?"

"What? Why?"

"He wants to go check on Alex. Can I tell him?"

I think about it for a moment. I could go home and check on her, and tell her everything Johnny just told me. But it might be better if it comes from Ryder, considering he stayed with Connor and Devon last night and knows more about what happened when we left.

"Yeah, tell him. Tell him not to tell Connor yet, though. She'll need time to digest the information and to figure out whether she'll even be able to forgive him. She's been cheated on so many times already, and rock stars aren't exactly known for their faithfulness. No offense. But she's probably going to want to really think about whether she can deal with everything that comes along with dating someone as famous as you guys are."

Johnny types a message into his phone before placing it face-down on the table again.

"Now, what should we do for the rest of the day?" Johnny asks. "I don't think you'll want to be back at your place if Alex eventually forgives Connor. I doubt your walls are thick enough to block out the noises they'll be making." He laughs and mimes humping the table.

I burst out laughing. "You're probably right. Let's go find something to do."

"I know just the thing. I'm going to take you on a date."

11

Not-a-Date

Johnny

"TA-DA!" I SAY AS we approach the door to Ink Revival, the shop where I work on my clients. "What do you think?"

Becca looks at the door, and at the logo on the big picture window of the shop.

"I think it looks closed," she says. "What are we doing here?"

"Well," I say, pulling my keys out of my pocket. "I figured I could show you one of my many talents, and maybe teach you a couple of things. Welcome to our first ever not-a-date."

She watches me skeptically, her eyebrows drawn and her mouth scrunched to the side.

"Come on in." I hold the door open and motion her inside, flicking the lights on so we can see. The privacy film on the window blocks quite a bit of the light from outside, making it hard to make out the details of the room without the interior lights on.

"Are you supposed to be here?"

I hang up my jacket at the door, and Becca does the same with her sweater.

"I have keys, don't I?" I laugh. "I only work on clients when the shop isn't open. If Revival is closed, Hunter expects I might be here. Plus, I texted him and told him I was coming in."

"Okay," she drawls, looking around, examining the large framed artwork on the walls. I wonder if she can see the signatures on them well enough to tell that some of them are mine?

The shop isn't what most people think of when they think of tattoo shops. While they also take on everyday clients looking to get some art on their skin, what Hunter and the rest of the team specialize in is tattooing over scars. The shop is relaxing, and looks more like an art gallery than a traditional tattoo shop. Each artist has a private room to work in, including me, even though I'm almost never here. Each artist also has a type of scar they have a soft spot for, and will always volunteer to work on. Mine are mastectomy scars.

My mom and my sister were both diagnosed with breast cancer in the past, and luckily they've both made it through. Mom was my first experience with tattooing mastectomy scars. My sister Rose was my second. Since then I've tattooed at least a hundred breast cancer survivors, mostly women, but there were a couple of men who came to me too.

"I thought you could tattoo me," I say, turning to take in her reaction. "I have some available skin and I thought it might be fun for you to try your hand at it. Unless you're already an accomplished tattooer?"

"What?" she blurts out. "I can't tattoo you. I have no idea what I'm doing. I'll hurt you."

I have to chuckle. "Have you seen me?" I lift my shirt and turn around slowly, giving her a chance to take it all in. "I think I can handle it." I'm covered nearly head to toe in tattoos. I've felt every kind of pain tattooing offers. "If I was worried about it hurting, I wouldn't have suggested it."

She takes a seat on the dark green velvet sofa in the waiting area. I thought Hunter was crazy when he bought it because it's nearly an exact color match to the paint on the walls, but it looks great in the space. I guess it's safe to say interior design isn't one of my many skills.

"So you brought me here to tattoo you?"

Uh-oh. Seems like my idea isn't the hit I thought it would be when I first came up with it at the diner. I drew some sketches up for her the other night and today is too good of a chance to pass up. We could get a few hours in before anyone noticed we weren't around. But maybe I was wrong in assuming that Becca would enjoy seeing the shop just because she has a lot of tattoos of her own. Maybe she hates her tattoos and wishes she never got them.

"Well, that, and I thought you might let me tattoo you. Only if you want, of course, and you would have final approval of the design." I run my fingers through my hair, no doubt causing the blond curls to fluff up. "We can leave and go do something else if you prefer."

She puts her hand on my knee, and my pace quickens. How does she affect me this much with the barest touch?

Just friends, Johnny. You're just friends.

"I didn't say that," she says, giving my knee a pat before taking her hand away. I wish she would leave it there, but I can't exactly tell her that, can I? "This is all a bit of a shock to me, is all. I didn't even know you could tattoo. Now here we are, in a shop you mysteriously have the keys to, and you're suddenly an artist? Look at how gorgeous these are," she says, standing up and moving closer to one of my paintings. "You're an artist, and you tattoo, and you're in a famous band? Is there anything I'm missing?"

I cough and mutter, "The cookies."

"Excuse me? What was that?"

"I said you missed the cookies." I laugh at the look on her face. A cross between frustration, awe, and, well, probably more frustration, with just a hint of irritation thrown in for good measure.

"What about the cookies?" she asks, as she grinds her fists into her hips and takes a step toward me. "Where did you get those cookies, Johnny?"

Laughter escapes me, and I hold my fist to my mouth to get it under control. Seeing her, short, angry, and confused, has me bursting out in an uncontrollable fit of hysterical laughter.

"Johnny," she says, her voice taking on a dark tone. "Tell me about the cookies, Johnny."

She's saying my name too much, and it's making me laugh harder. She's trying so hard to be intimidating and it's having the opposite effect. More than ever, I want to wrap her up in my arms and kiss her senseless, taste her breath, feel her body against mine, hold her and never let go. If I could see this level of anger every time I irritated her for the rest of my life, I could die a happy man.

I've nearly calmed myself when she taps her foot, sending me off into another fit of giggles. This one is easier to control, luckily, and I easily catch my breath enough to talk to her.

"I baked the cookies, Becca. The other night when I left your place. I bake when I'm stressed, or need to calm down."

She throws her hands up in the air. "You bake, too?" she yells. "You are going to make some lucky girl very happy one day, Johnny Donovan."

Hearing her say I'll make someone else happy knocks the breath from my lungs. I don't want to make someone else happy.

I only want to make you happy, I tell her silently.

"Okay, so let's get to it then, shall we?" she asks, a smile on her lips. "Where am I tattooing you? And what am I doing?"

I stand up and walk past her, motioning her to come with me.

"Allow me to show you to my lair," I say, walking her past the front desk, to a common space lined with light boxes and other materials the artists use when designing tattoos and making transfers. At the end of the common space is a hallway with three doors on either side. "These are the artists' rooms," I say, leading her to the last door on the left. "And this one is mine."

I open the door and motion for her to go ahead of me.

She steps into my room and spins in a slow circle, studying her surroundings. More framed art lines the walls here, some of it mine, some of it belonging to other artists I've worked with over the years.

"This is nice," she says, sitting on one of two stools in the room. "How often do you come in?"

"Only as often as I'm needed. I only work on a particular type of client, so unless one of them needs me, I stay away."

Becca laughs. "So when the sexy babes with big titties need tattoos, it's Johnny to the rescue?"

I choke on a laugh. If only she knew the actual story, she'd see that's pretty much the exact opposite of what I do. "Yeah, something like that."

I take a step past her and begin setting up my workstation. I've had the tattoo I wanted to give Becca mapped out in my head since that first night at her place. I saw so much gorgeous skin available on her left leg, my hands started itching to put my mark on her. It's not like I'll write my name or anything, but she and I will both know I was there. When I went home that night, and after my marathon baking session, I sketched out several ideas for her to look at. I think I know what she'll like the best, but there's always the possibility she'll surprise me. She is a surprising woman.

I pass her the packet of papers with the transfers I've already prepared. "Here are some ideas I drew up for you," I say. "Does anything catch your eye?"

She takes her time flipping through the papers, carefully examining each one before placing it on the convertible chair where my clients sit. Her eyes linger on one drawing in particular, but I notice she's also set another one off the side.

"Why'd you draw this one?" she asks, holding out the horror themed stencil. "Why this collection of horror movie villains?"

I'd drawn horror movie villains in a similar style to the large Freddy tattoo she has on her right thigh, but instead of each face being complete and distinct they almost flow together, like each villain melts into the ether before transforming into another, more evil villain.

"Oh, yeah," I snicker. "I didn't expect you would pick that one. It just didn't seem fair to me that Freddy got such prime real estate on your thigh and the rest of these guys got nothing. He's getting so much focus, like there is too much importance placed on him."

Becca stares at me without blinking for what feels like minutes. My eyes feel sandy from keeping them open to look back at her. I wish I could tell what she's thinking. I wish *she* would *tell* me what she's thinking. But something about this feels personal, private, as though I'm witnessing an internal struggle.

God, this woman is fascinating. I want to know everything about her.

"Okay, yes. This one," she says, handing me the transfer. "It's time Freddy shared the spotlight. I can't let him run the show anymore."

I exhale a slow breath. "I didn't even realize until just now that's what I was hoping you'd say. I'm sort of partial to these guys. This was the first sketch I did for you."

"I love it," she says. "Freddy was actually my first tattoo. It's time for him to relinquish his throne."

My eyebrows shoot up, surprise coloring my face. "Really? That's a bold choice for a first tattoo. Not to mention, many people find the thigh to be incredibly painful."

"Don't remind me," she laughs. "That piece you're doing for me can only fit in one spot, you know." She slaps her left thigh, one of the few remaining spots of ink-free skin she has.

"Well, in that case, let me apologize in advance for causing you pain." I grin, enjoying being in her company, even if it's just as friends. "And might I suggest you tattoo me first? That way, when we're done with you, I can take you home so you can relax?"

"Excellent idea," she says with a gleam in her eyes. "I know just what I'm going to do. The only question is, is there enough space on your body for it?"

"Oh darling, you're in for a treat when it comes to that." I wink at her and laugh, before adding, "But first, let me give you a little lesson in how to do this. Then you can jab me with pointy needles all you like."

"Muahahaha," she says, sounding like her own version of an evil villain. "Remember this moment when I bring the pain. You asked for it." She mimes petting a cat, an evil grin taking up residence on her face. "This is the best not-a-date I've ever been on. None of my past dates ever let me stab them. They're always all 'ow, why did you do that?' and 'that's it, I'm calling the police'. You're so fun to be with."

My stomach drops. I am fun to be with, and one day, hopefully, I will get to show her that for real. For now, though, stabbing each other on our very first not-a-date is the best I can do.

12

Tiny Cameras and a Vagina Sex Bathroom

Becca

JOHNNY HOLDS HIS SHIRT up as he presses his hip closer to the mirror, trying to get a better look at the tattoo I gave him. It's small and in a weird spot, so it's hard to get a good look at on his own. After debating for a moment, while enjoying the last few minutes of unrestricted access to a view of his abs and amazing Adonis belt (seriously, it should be illegal to be that sexy), I pull out my phone and take a picture.

Tattooing him was both easier and harder than I thought it would be. I didn't really want to hurt him, and I didn't want to give him a terrible tattoo, either. That's part of the reason I chose the design I did. From what he'd said about the location, I thought I'd be doing some upper thigh or incredibly intimate butt-cheek work, but Johnny was only joking about me having fun with where I was tattooing him. He had a small spot near his right hip where the pieces that he has on his back and stomach don't meet, that was available.

"Here," I say, handing him my phone with the picture on the screen. "This will be easier to see."

He lets his shirt fall and grabs my phone.

Damn, back to a fully clothed view. At least his jeans are still open for now, giving me a glimpse of skin and sexy black boxer briefs. I suppose that will have to do.

"It's a camera," he says, smiling up at me before looking at my phone again. "Lines look nice, very smooth. And you did a great job fitting it into the space. It clearly doesn't match what's on my front and back, but somehow it still looks like it was meant to be there."

"Thanks," I say, taking the phone back when he offers it. "It's my logo. You've been branded. Johnny Donovan is now the property of Becca Morris Photography. It's a pretty big deal." I laugh. I know he's not my property, but I can't lie and say I don't like the idea of having my mark permanently on his body. "Now you can avail yourself of such benefits as helping me carry my equipment, accompanying me to shoot locations, being a snack bitch for my clients, and other assorted tasks as required. It's a very prestigious position to be in. Highly coveted, you know."

Johnny laughs, his eyes crinkling. "Well, I'm glad to be of service. And thank you for the privilege of being your unpaid assistant." He starts cleaning up the equipment and swapping out supplies for the tattoo he has planned for me. "Now, take this," he says, tossing me a large, thin towel, "and go through the door just outside this room. It's the bathroom. Pants off and... what kind of underwear are you wearing?"

I spin around to face him. "Excuse me?"

He gives me a small smile and steps close to me. "I figured we could place the tattoo from about here," he says, placing a hand just below my hip bone, "to about here." He trails his fingers from my hip to my lower thigh, igniting a trail of sparks on my skin.

My breath escapes me in a whoosh, and I drop the towel, the sudden rush of heat in my lady bits surprising me. "I... umm... uh... what was the question?"

He turns me slowly, walking me to the door, his hand on my lower back. "Panties. If they go up high on the side, leave them on. If they don't," he whispers in my ear, "well, then they'll need to come off."

I stumble into the hallway, tripping on the tiniest bit of trim in the doorway, before lunging for the bathroom door at the end of the hall, throwing it open, and jumping inside. What the hell was that? "Keep it together, Becca," I tell myself. "Johnny is a love and marriage kind of guy and no one wants to wake up to someone who looks like you every day for the rest of their life," I say, parroting what my mother has said to me countless times. "Yes, he is sexy as hell. No, you can't have him."

Now that my pep talk is out of the way, I strip off my pants and underwear and come to a horrifying realization. I mean, I already knew about it, but still.

My panties are wet.

"Shit, shit, shit," I whisper, holding my underwear and spinning frantically, looking to the bathroom to give me some answers. I could just hide them in my pants, like so many women do at the doctor's office, but I can already picture Johnny bumping my pants onto the floor, bending over, picking up my wet panties, and giving me that look. You know, the one that says he knows I want him, even though I already shot him down? Ugh, I can't deal with that. So what am I going to do?

On approximately my eighth or so spin in place, I spot my salvation. This bathroom has an air dryer to dry your hands with.

Yes! I'll use the hand dryer to dry my underwear. Problem solved.

I smash at the start button with the side of my hand and fan my underwear into the air coming from the nozzle. If only I were paying closer attention, I would have noticed that this is a hot air hand dryer and while it is drying my underwear, it's also sending a very distinct scent into the air.

The smell of arousal.

The smell of vagina.

The smell of S-E-X.

"Fuck!"

I've never been concerned about the smell of my vagina. It's always smelled perfectly normal and healthy. Then again, I've never had a sexy man that I'm supposed to be just friends with cause a flood in my panties, which I then heated with a hand dryer.

Tap, tap.

Johnny knocks softly on the door. "You okay in there, Becca? Did you forget something?"

The towel. I forgot the fucking towel.

I spin around frantically, full-on Winnie the Pooh-ing it, shirt and no pants, hoping the towel will magically appear.

It doesn't.

"Oh, yeah, haha." I close my eyes and lean against the door. "I'll just come back and grab it. Be right there." *Please leave, please leave, please leave.*

"Here, just open the door a crack and I'll pass it to you," he says from the other side of the door. "I've got it right here."

Of course he has it. Why wouldn't he bring it with him? He's a nice guy. He would have seen I forgot it and brought it to me. That's a totally normal thing for a nice person to do. "It's okay. Really. I'll be out in a second. I can come grab it."

"Seriously, Becca. I have it in my hand right now. Just open the door a bit and put your hand out and take it. I'll close my eyes and look away if you're worried I'll see something a friend shouldn't see."

Ha! If he only knew why I'm actually worried.

Should I just open it? What if the smell of my vagina seeps out into the hallway, like some olfactory beacon of my desire, and he figures out how turned on I am? Or worse, what if he thinks I've been in here masturbating while he waits to tattoo me? Fuck. I need to open the door.

"Okay, I'm opening the door," I say, opening it a crack and poking just my hand out. "Give me the towel. Quick."

Johnny laughs. "*Now* you're in a hurry? You've been in there for ages playing with the hand dryer and now you're concerned about time?" He puts the towel in my hand and I pull it inside with me before shoving the door closed with my body. "What have you even been doing in there?"

"Definitely not masturbating, if that's what you're thinking," I blurt before slamming my hands over my mouth. *What the fuck was that, Becca? He obviously thinks you're masturbating now, if he wasn't thinking it before.*

"What?" he yells just outside the door, a laugh at the edge of his voice.

"I mean, haha, that would be hilarious, right?" I wrap the towel around my waist and grab my underwear and pants. I can do this. Deep breath.

It still smells like vagina and sex in here.

I open the door and step out into the hall, closing it behind me as I walk through. Maybe if I can minimize how long the door remains open, the smell will dissipate before Johnny smells anything.

"Hey, head on in, and I'll be right there. I just need to go to the bathroom and wash up."

"NO!" I yell, grabbing his arm to stop him from opening the door. "I mean, no," I add smoothly. "You, uh, you can't go in there yet. I..." I search around in my brain, praying for a reasonable explanation to reveal itself to me. I find one, but it's not much better than the truth. Fuck it, I'm going for it, anyway. "That diner breakfast did a number on me," I say, rubbing my stomach to really sell the lie. "After what I just did, you're going to want to let it air out in there for a while." I'm cringing on the inside. Of course, everyone poops, but it's not something I would normally announce to a good-looking man while I'm standing half-naked beside him. The only good thing about it is after this there's no way he could ever be attracted to me again.

Friend zone locked and loaded. Johnny will forever remember me as the woman who stunk up his bathroom at the tattoo shop.

Awesome.

And then the strangest thing happens. Johnny laughs. An honest-to-goodness laugh, too, not one of those uncomfortable I'm-trying-to-be-polite laughs.

"Don't even worry about that," he says. "This place is practically swimming in disinfectant. It's the only thing anyone can ever smell in here. I'm sure it's fine. Be right back." And before I can pull on him again, he slips out of my grasp and goes into the bathroom, shutting the door behind him.

The sex bathroom. The attraction bathroom. The bathroom that still smells like my vagina.

Well, that's that I guess.

I'll just go lay on the tattoo table and die of embarrassment. I hope Alex convinces my mom to cremate me and spread my ashes somewhere with an amazing view like I've always wanted.

13

All Lined Up

Johnny

"Definitely not masturbating, if that's what you're thinking,"

The memory of Becca's words rings through my head as I finish washing up in the bathroom. Her description of her stomach issues prepared me for an entirely different smell, despite what I said about disinfectant, but when I walked in here, all I could smell was sex.

And pissing with the hard-on it caused was not fun.

"She couldn't have been masturbating in here, could she?" I whisper to myself. "Why would she do that?"

She seemed a little flustered when I ran my hand down her side, showing her where the tattoo would go. It was probably overkill, but I couldn't resist the chance to touch her a little. I'll be touching her a lot over the next few hours, what with the size of the tattoo we're doing and all, but I wanted to touch her without also causing pain at the same time.

So, did she like it when I touched her? Is that what her stuttering declaration and overall awkwardness were about? Or am I seeing things I want to see and hoping she's starting to be interested in me?

Wait, that's not quite right, anyway. She was interested in sleeping with me two days ago, so she might still be. I'm the one who called it off. I'm the one who decided we'd just be friends.

Maybe she just came in here to take the edge off? She was trying to respect my wishes to just be friends?

Fuck, being friends with someone I'm interested in is hard. *So hard.*

And so is my dick.

I pull out one of my trustworthy old visions of Ryder's Gran to help with that situation. I'm all for people exploring their sexuality no matter how old they get, but having an eighty-year-old woman and her similarly aged friends discussing their sex lives in detail right in front of me is a little much. But it works wonders for making my dick soft. A few minutes recalling their 'teeth in or out' debate, and I'm ready to head back to Becca.

I tap on the door to my room before opening it, in case Becca isn't covered up, and then I step inside.

"You all set?"

"Ready when you are, captain," she says.

She's laying on the table, on her back, towel over her hips and legs, and her arm thrown over her eyes. I know she's not feeling sick, but she seems a little out of sorts.

"Do you still want to do this? Are you feeling okay?"

"Oh yeah," she says, taking her arm off her eyes. "I want to do this. Freddy needs to be kicked off his throne. This is probably the best thing that could happen to me."

I step closer to the table, sitting on my stool and pulling over the cart with my tools. "Okay, great. Then let's get you on your right side." I hold the blanket up, keeping her covered while she rolls. "Perfect. Okay," I say, handing her a corner of the blanket, "tuck this corner under your body, and take this part and pull it up between your legs. That should keep you covered enough that you don't get cold."

She arranges the blanket like I've instructed, adjusting her body to get comfortable, and tucking her arm up under her head. "So," she says, pausing a moment before continuing. "You know I'm not paying you for this, right?"

I choke on a laugh. "Yeah, I'm aware. I wouldn't ask you to." I want to tattoo Becca more than anything. My artwork on her beautiful body is more payment than I deserve. Knowing she has a piece of me inked into her skin for the rest of her life is better than anything she could give me. Well, almost anything.

"Okay, good. So long as we're clear on that. I've run into a slight problem with my photography business and there's a chance it could get much worse."

"Oh? What kind of problem? Tell me about it." I pull on my gloves and spray green soap onto Becca's thigh to clean it. I wipe the soap off and grab a disposable razor to prep the area before I put the stencil on. "Maybe I have some ideas." I shave the area while she explains.

"Ugh," she groans. "I had a wedding booked last weekend and the mother of the bride canceled on me when I showed up at the venue. Like, I walked in carrying all my equipment, and she told me they no longer required my services."

"What a bitch." The blanket has shifted and is covering part of the area where I want to place the stencil, so I move it, accidentally brushing the skin on her ass cheek while doing so.

Becca's sharp intake of breath mimics my own.

I doubt her dick gets hard like mine does, though. Considering she doesn't have one. At least, I couldn't feel one when she was straddling me a couple of nights ago.

"Sorry," I say, reaching for the deodorant I need to transfer the stencil to her skin. "So, why do you think it might get worse?" *That's it. Change the subject. Move on. Don't acknowledge the bulge pressing against your zipper.*

"Oh, umm. Well, she asked me to refund her deposit, and I refused. She wasn't happy about it."

"Why would she expect a refund? She canceled when you got there to do the work. It's not like you could have just booked another wedding on such short notice. People aren't usually hiring their photographer at the last minute." I slide the deodorant over her skin and line up the stencil, pressing it down gently.

"Yeah, that's what I said. Plus, she signed a contract that stated the deposit was non-refundable. People try it every once in a while, but this is the first time anyone has ever canceled the day of the event and *expected* a refund."

"Do you want to check out the placement? I can step out so you can look in the mirror."

She waves me off. "I trust you."

She really does. I don't know why. I haven't shown her any of my work. For all she knows, I could be the shittiest tattooer of all time. I'm not, but she doesn't know that.

I won't take her trust lightly.

"Anyway, that woman is well-connected in Westborough society circles and this could come back to bite me in the ass. I was hoping to make some contacts at the wedding and maybe book out the rest of the year. So I lost out on those possible bookings. And if she retaliates, it could be bad."

"What will you do if she retaliates?"

I keep the conversation going as I start the tattoo. This is going to be a large piece, in full color, so I expect it will take many hours to complete. I might need to get Becca to come back here with me a couple more times to finish working on it. But I don't mind. Anything that lets us spend more time together is fine by me.

Becca hardly notices that I've started, not even moving a muscle as I begin the line work.

"I'll have to look into offering other services, I suppose. Maybe family shoots, or boudoir. I'm not sure yet. I'm hoping this all blows over and she lets it be."

I hum a reply, just a noise to let her know I heard. She could be in trouble if this woman is as well-connected as Becca says she is. A woman like that might ruin Becca's career with gossip and lies.

"But enough about her. I want to know more about you. We're going to be here a while, so I might as well learn a little more about you while we're at this."

I spray her leg and wipe her down, removing blood and ink so I can see what I'm doing. Tattooing is messy work, but it can be so rewarding.

"Okay, let's see. You've met Travis, my brother. Did you know that I have five sisters too? That surprises most people."

"Five? That's a lot of estrogen in one place. It must have been interesting growing up in your house." Becca laughs. "How many times were you given a makeover? Be honest."

I spent much of my childhood in my sisters' dresses with poorly applied lipstick on my face, but that's not something I want Becca to know. At least not yet. I'm sure she'll see pictures if she ever meets my Mom.

"Umm, yeah," I chuckle. "More times than I'd like to admit. Travis and I both had it rough, what with being the only two boys and the youngest of all of us."

"You and Travis must be pretty close. How'd you guys get to be in the band together?"

I stop for a second and think. "You know, I don't know that it was ever a conscious decision. I started playing guitar and met the rest of the guys, and Travis just sort of tagged along. He picked up a bass somewhere and taught himself to play."

"That seems a little strange," she says. "Did he show any interest in music before that?"

"Now that I think of it? Not really. When we were younger, he loved working with my dad in his shop. He loved building stuff and fixing things. I can't even recall him listening to music before we started the band."

I used to spend hours drawing, and Travis spent the same amount of time building stuff. I'm not entirely certain how either of us found music, let alone wound up being in a successful band.

I wonder if Travis is even happy?

"Well, it sounds like your family is nice, at least. And big. I can't imagine what it would be like to have such a big family. It's been just me and my mom for as long as I can remember. If I saw my dad walking down the street, I wouldn't even recognize him. I can't remember what he looks like and my mother didn't keep a single picture."

"Shit, that's depressing."

"A little. But I'm used to it. It's all I've ever known."

We've been at this for a while and I've finished the line work already. One reason I get as many clients as I do is that I work quickly without sacrificing the quality of the tattoo.

I spray down Becca's thigh and wipe it clean again.

"I don't know about you, but I'm starving. Want to order something and keep working after? Or have you had enough already? I can wrap you up and we can continue another day."

Becca twists her body to look at my work so far. "I want to keep going, but I'm also starving and desperately in need of coffee."

"Here," I tell her. "I'll step out and bring some of this stuff to the autoclave for cleaning. You get up and have a look in the mirror and when I come back, I'll wrap you up so we can get something to eat."

She nods and I take what I need to and leave the room. It only takes a few minutes to get everything into the autoclave and set the cleaning cycle, but I take my time with it so Becca has some privacy.

I head back to the room and knock before I enter.

Once she's wrapped up, I clean and sanitize the parts of my machine that don't go into the autoclave while Becca orders food.

"Food should be here soon," she says, walking into the hall-way. "I'm going to sit on the couch."

I finish cleaning and sterilizing everything, putting everything away in case Becca changes her mind about continuing with the tattoo today. When I go to the front of the shop, I find Becca examining one of my paintings. It's impossible to tell from the painting, but it's the design I tattooed on my mom after she got breast cancer.

"I'm still a little shocked to find out you're such a talented artist," she says without turning to face me. "You keep surprising me."

"It's something I've always done. When the opportunity came up for me to start tattooing, I jumped on it. I'd been doing it for a few years when my mom got sick, and it all just came together. That painting is of the tattoo I did for her after she had a double mastectomy."

Becca spins around, her mouth hanging open. She blinks rapidly but makes no sound. I walk to the other side of the waiting room and point to another of my paintings.

"And this is the one I did for my sister Rose after she had her double mastectomy."

Becca thumps down on the couch, her mouth still open. "You tattooed over their scars?"

"Yes," I say, running a hand through my curls. "Shortly after I tattooed Rose, Sleeping Dogs started touring, so I didn't get into the shop much. After the first tour, I decided to only take breast cancer survivors and mastectomy patients. I volunteer my time and the resources to do it. None of my clients pay me." I laugh. "I'm sorry I didn't tell you that you're not the first."

I can see the wheels turning in Becca's head, like she can't imagine the Johnny she knows is also the Johnny who also does this work.

"Are you okay?" I ask.

"Why do you do it?" she asks, brows drawn. "Why do you cover these women's scars? What do you get out of it?"

"Why do I do it?" I've thought about this a lot, but I've never told anyone else before. I can feel that Becca *needs* to know, so she will be the first person I tell. "It's the one thing that makes me feel like I'm doing something worthwhile. Seeing the faces of the women, and sometimes men, that I tattoo when they look in the mirror for the first time after we're done... there's nothing else like it. Helping a woman find her beauty and femininity after losing something that had been such a large part of both? That's the best feeling in the world.

"Better even than being on stage, if I'm being honest. Performing is a rush, and the feeling of adrenaline coursing through my body as thousands of fans chant my name is amazing. But watching the tears of gratitude and acceptance when a woman sees how beautiful she still is after cancer has ravaged her body? Knowing *I* helped put that look back on her face? Nothing can compare to that."

14

Getting a Little Too Friendly

Becca

"...BUT WATCHING THE TEARS of gratitude and acceptance when a woman sees how beautiful she still is after cancer has ravaged her body? Knowing *I* helped put that look back on her face? Nothing can compare to that."

Hearing Johnny's explanation of tattooing mastectomy patients, of helping them reveal their beauty despite their scars, has heat flooding my body. Especially knowing he does it for free and supplies all the materials to do it. All my desire from earlier comes rushing back, making me rash, impulsive. Before I know it, I'm up off the couch throwing myself at Johnny, arms wrapping around his neck, lips smashing into his.

I hear Johnny gasp, feel his sudden intake of breath against my mouth, but it only takes him a moment before he's shoving his hands into my hair, tilting my head, deepening the kiss. When he parts my lips with his tongue, my knees go weak. A tingling sensation in my chest threatens to steal my breath. Johnny fists his hands in my hair, gently tugging me this way and that, changing the angle of our kiss.

"Fuck Becca," he pants, his breath ragged as he kisses my cheek, my jaw, my earlobe. "I've been wanting to kiss you all day."

He drags his mouth down my neck, licking and sucking the tender flesh before kissing his way to my mouth again.

I let my hands fall from around his neck, snaking them around his waist, feeling the smooth skin under his shirt. He lets me push his shirt up and over his head. I take it and drop it to the floor at my feet, reaching for him again. With my hands on his chest, I slowly back him up against the wall. Johnny raises his hands, hesitating slightly, before reaching forward and grabbing my ass, pulling me against him. He's touching me.

He's touching me and I don't hate it.

I actually love it.

His hard length presses into my stomach, and a groan escapes his lips. I trace the lines of his abs, trailing my fingers down, down, stopping when I reach the waist of his pants. I begin by undoing first his belt, then the button and zipper of his jeans, before finally reaching into his boxers and wrapping my hand around him.

"Oh, fuck," he groans and thrusts against my hand. I stroke slowly, savoring the noises he makes, loving the feeling of his hard length sliding in my grip.

Suddenly, Johnny pulls my hand free, moving me and dropping me into a chair made of the same green velvet as the sofa and just as soft.

"What…" I try to ask what he's doing, but my answer comes when he kneels in front of me, pulling my joggers down carefully, avoiding both the fresh tattoo and touching my skin too much. He had his hands all over my leg when he was working on me, but he's still trying to be mindful of my touching issues.

I don't think I could find him hotter than I do at this moment.

"I'm going to touch you a little," he whispers, thrusting his left hand behind my back, under my ass, pulling me to the edge of the seat.

"O—O—Okay," I stutter, watching him study me. His eyes are darker than I've ever seen them, only a sliver of light brown iris remaining to be seen. He's looking at me like my pussy is the only thing he's ever wanted to eat. "You don't have to do this," I whisper.

He looks up at me with black eyes. "Oh, yes, Becca. Yes, I do have to do this. I think I might die if I don't do this," he growls and dips his head, his first tentative lick sending sparks up my spine. "Fuck, babe. You taste so good."

Johnny buries his face in me, kissing me with abandon, feasting on me. He guides my legs onto his shoulders with his free hand before sliding it under me, lifting me closer to his mouth. Looking up at me, he groans and locks on to my clit, sucking the sensitive bundle of nerves into his mouth. Each suck couples with a flick of his tongue until I'm climbing higher and higher, closing in on that peak, ready to fall over the edge. I close my eyes, and Johnny stops moving, letting me go. I open my eyes to see what's going on.

"Eyes on me, Becca. I want you to watch me when I make you come. I need you to see, to believe, how much I enjoy this." He boosts me up, sliding an arm under me again, and he lowers his mouth to devour me once more. I stare into his eyes as he pushes me to the edge, forcing me toward my climax once more. My eyelids drift lower until a humming 'unh unh' sound vibrates against me, a warning from Johnny to keep my eyes on him.

"Johnny," I whimper. "Please."

I feel him chuckle against me, but he continues his efforts, intent on making me come like he said he would. He moves his arm and I feel him press a finger inside me, which he soon replaces with two.

"Oh, yes," I moan.

Johnny pushes his fingers into me, stroking and massaging the upper wall of my channel. Pressure builds inside me, winding me higher, and my hips buck wildly until I'm fucking his face. His answering moans hum against my clit, throwing me over the edge.

Sparks fly up my spine and take over my sight, fireworks exploding with each pulse of my orgasm. Johnny's licks and flicks continue, extending my climax, making it go on and on and on, pleasure verging on pain. A feeling so good, I don't know how I'll be able to survive it.

A feeling I've never had before. Certainly not like this.

As the shocks of pleasure subside, Johnny pulls his fingers from me. I watch as he licks them clean, his eyes never leaving mine. A shiver runs up my spine. No one has ever done something so erotic in front of me. With me. For me.

Bang, bang, bang.

A knock on the glass door.

"Shit. The food," I mumble in response, still unable to form words.

"I'll grab it," Johnny says, jumping up from his knees. He leans over and kisses my lips. "That was... something else."

Holy shit. I think that's my line. My first orgasm from oral sex? That's something else alright. That's a miracle.

Wait. Was that a bad something else? He hesitated. Maybe he hated it. Did he mean he hated it or that he liked it when he said it was something else?

Johnny goes to the door and opens it a crack, grabbing the bags of food without exposing me to the delivery guy. He comes back over to me, dragging an end table over from the corner to put the food on. He looks down at me splayed out in the chair, legs still made of jelly, body still too floppy from the best orgasm of my life to stand, and smiles.

"Let me help," he says, kneeling in front of me again. Just as gently as he removed them, he slides my joggers back up my legs. It's harder to get them up over my ass than it was to get them down, so he takes my hands and helps me stand up before pulling them up the rest of the way.

"Thanks," I say, looking down.

"I'll go wash up and then we'll eat?"

I can only nod. He smiles, kisses me on the cheek, and turns to walk away. As soon as he's out of sight, I pace the waiting room, chewing my thumbnail as I walk.

What the fuck did we just do?

This can't happen.

Can it?

No.

We can't do this again. Things would get way too complicated. We're just friends. We need to stay just friends.

Why did I start that, anyway? Oh, right. His confession. He sounded like he really believes the women he tattoos are still beautiful with their scars. How could I not kiss him after that?

I wish someone thought the same thing about me. But I know better. Having scars over much of your body is way different from having scars in a localized area. Especially when those localized scars are from something as fierce as kicking cancer's ass.

I didn't exactly kick that pot of soup's ass. More like it kicked mine.

"So I was thinking—"

"Ahhh," I squeal, nearly jumping out of my skin. I spin around to see Johnny right behind me. "Why are you sneaking up on me?"

Johnny chuckles. "Sorry, didn't mean to scare you."

I take a seat near the end table and open up the food. We ordered tacos from my favorite Mexican restaurant. A girl can never have too many tacos. I open up one box and squeeze some lime onto them. I pick one up, take a huge bite, and look at Johnny.

"Anyway, like I was saying," he says, opening one of the other boxes. He pulls out a taco and fidgets with it, not adding anything to it, but also not biting. I'm finished with mine in just two more bites. "Umm, what we just did was great..."

Oh shit, here it comes. He's letting me down gently. At least I can be glad he's not taking my picture and calling me Freddy, I suppose.

"But we said we would just be friends? We probably shouldn't do it again?" I rush to fill in the blanks for him. "I'm glad you think so too." I take another taco and stuff half of it in my mouth, so I don't blurt out that he's the only guy to ever make me come like that. It's not like it's ever happening again, so he doesn't need the ego boost. "It's too complicated, anyway," I say, mouth half full of chewed taco. "Even if I didn't have my one night rule, two of our best friends are in a relationship. Probably. If Alex can get over what happened last night. We need to be around each other without any weirdness."

"Exactly," he agrees. "I'm so glad we can be cool about this. And I'm sorry if I pushed you, if I made you uncomfortable."

"Oh, no. I'm pretty sure I started all—" I wave my napkin around in the air. "—that. Whatever it was."

"Okay." He puts his hand out to me. "So... friends?"

I place my hand in his and give it a firm shake. "Friends."

He grins at me and takes a bite of his taco. "So friend, are we finishing up this tattoo today? Or should we work on it another day instead?"

"I'm good to keep going if you are."

"Alright. Eat up and then we'll keep going."

15

Advice from the Old Dog

Johnny

"Knock, knock. Cookie delivery," I yell as I let myself into Aiden's house. He gave all the guys keys years ago when we did all of our rehearsing in his garage, and I kept mine. Aiden never answers the door, anyway. He is usually playing drums in the garage and can't hear you knock. Or he's playing video games and doesn't want to get up.

"Hey man," Aiden says without looking away from his game. "What are you doing?"

"I baked last night, so I have some cookies for the shelter."

That gets his attention, and he pauses his game and comes to the kitchen. He opens one of the boxes I've deposited on the counter and grabs a couple of cookies before heading back to his chair. I help myself to a cup of coffee and go have a seat on the couch.

"Do I want to know why you were on a baking kick last night?" Aiden asks, wiping crumbs off his shirt before grabbing his game controller and playing again. "Or is it safe to assume I already know what's up and it has something to do with Alex's friend Becca?"

I huff out a laugh and shake my head. "Am I really that transparent?"

"Well... yeah, you're completely transparent. I figured you'd fall in love with her from the minute we saw her after the show."

"Yeah, yeah. You know me so well."

"So, what's the problem? Not sure if you should do it because she's Alex's best friend or...?" Aiden holds up the controller in a silent request to play the game with him, but I shake my head no.

"Can't. Promised Mom I'd come over and help her with something. With how much time Trav has been spending over there, I'm surprised there's even anything left to do. He should have been able to fully renovated their house by now." I take a drink of my coffee. "But back to your other question. The problem is that Becca is not interested in a relationship. She invited me over after we all had dinner at Connor's place a few weeks ago, but she said she only does one night."

He pauses his game again and looks at me. "What do you mean 'one night'?"

"She said if we slept together it would only be that one night, and then never again. I told her I didn't want that and together we decided to be friends."

"Okay. So be friends and that's it."

"Yeah," I drawl. "About that. I picked her up the day after Connor's attack. We had breakfast and then decided we needed to find something to do so Alex and Connor would have more time to talk."

"Okay? What's the problem, then?"

I take a deep breath. I don't normally kiss and tell, but Aiden is the most level-headed guy I know, and I could really use some advice. "Well, when I was at her place that first night, I noticed her left leg wasn't as tattooed as the right. She has a huge Freddy Krueger on the front of her right thigh and its prominence made me think of a tattoo featuring a bunch of other horror movie villains. So I drew it for her."

"And what? She didn't like it?"

"No, man. She loved it. I took her to the shop after our late breakfast and let her tattoo me, and then I tattooed her with the design. She said Freddy had had the spotlight long enough."

"Wait." Aiden drops his controller and turns to look at me. "She tattooed you?"

"Yeah," I say, trying to hide my smile. I love that she tattooed her logo on me. It feels like she claimed me. "She gave me a little line art camera. Here, I'll show you." I stand up and pull down the side of my pants so he can see the camera on my right hip. "She said it's the logo for her photography business."

Aiden gives me a smirk. "She branded you, man. Now you're hers."

Fuck, I wish that was the case. My life would be a lot easier right now if Becca felt the same way about me as I do about her. As it is, it's hard to maintain our just friends status when I spend all my time thinking about how amazing she is or fantasizing about her hot body and the way she responded to me when I went down on her at the shop.

"Yeah. Well, see, that part is fine. It's what happened after I did the line work on her tattoo that has me all fucked up. I was telling her about the work I do on mastectomy patients and out of nowhere, she grabbed me and started kissing me."

"Okay? So you're together now?"

"No, but things went a little too far. Afterward, I was going to say that maybe we could try dating casually since we seem to get along so well but before I could get the words out she jumped in with how it was a mistake and we need to put it behind us so we can stay friends."

"Ouch," Aiden presses a hand over his heart. "Sorry, man. That sucks."

"I guess I should have expected it. She made it clear that she only does one night. We didn't actually have sex, but maybe it was enough to qualify as the one night."

"So, what are you going to do now? Are you guys still trying to be friends?"

"I'm trying. We grabbed coffee a few times since then and it was a little awkward. It'll get better, I'm sure. But I don't know if I can be just friends with her, man. She's so fucking hot. And the more time I spend with her, the more amazing she gets. She's funny, smart, cool, and hot. She's the one man. I just know it."

Aiden lets out a long, slow exhale and I prepare myself for the lecture I can feel coming. Aiden is older than the rest of the guys in the band by a few years, and he's been completely on his own since he was eighteen, so he's more mature than the rest of us, too. He's always taken on a more serious, older brother-type role with the rest of us, and that's how I know he's preparing himself to have a weighty conversation with me. I've been on the receiving end of a few of Aiden's "talks" and he's normally right on in his assessment of a situation.

"Let me have it," I say.

"I'm not going to give you shit about this, Johnny. I'm going to ask you to be careful. If she only does one night, it's for a reason. You are looking for love. The two of you couldn't be more at odds with what you want from a relationship. That you want one and she doesn't, for example."

I know he's right, but I can't shake the feeling that Becca is meant to be more to me than only a night or as only a friend. I've never been more sure of anything in my life. I'm going to marry this girl. I can't explain that to Aiden, though, without sounding like a lunatic.

"Yeah, you're right. I'll be careful." I stand up and bring my cup back to the kitchen, putting it in the dishwasher. "I better head out now though, or mom will send a search party. The last thing Westborough needs is the pack of wild animals known as my sisters running around town trying to track me down. Who knows what kind of destruction they would leave in their wake?" I chuckle when Aiden visibly shudders.

Aiden met my sisters many times, so he knows exactly what I'm talking about. They're not exactly sweet and innocent bastions of femininity, at least not in the traditional sense. They're more likely to crush your hand with a firm handshake than to offer you their fingers to kiss. My sisters are tougher than anyone else I know, and that includes Devon, our head of security.

"Get the fuck out of here, then," he says, his voice taking on a slightly higher pitch. "Last time your sisters were here looking for you, they took my shower lube and spread it all over my toilet seat. Next time I went to use it, I slid right off the seat and got myself wedged between the toilet and the wall."

I burst out laughing at the memory. Luckily for Aiden, Devon and I had let ourselves in not long after he got himself stuck. We got him loose without needing to call the fire department, a fact which he always forgets when he tells this story. It could have been a lot worse.

"It's your own fucking fault for having shower lube in the first place," I splutter through my laughs. "Who the hell has special lube for the shower, anyway?"

"Hey, I refuse to jerk off with shampoo. That shit's not made for such delicate skin. Lube is. Why wouldn't I have shower lube?"

"Have you ever thought of maybe having sex? Then you wouldn't need to jerk off so much that you need special lube in the shower. Just a suggestion." I chuckle as I walk to the front door.

"Here's a suggestion: get the fuck out of my house," Aiden yells as I open the door. I shake my head. Pretty touchy about the shower lube subject.

"Yeah, yeah. See you tomorrow at Connor's? We're doing some work on the album, right?"

"Yes, fine. See you then."

I close the door behind me and hop into the car. My parent's place is just a few blocks over so I'm there in no time. I notice a few extra cars at the house, Travis's truck among them, and I wonder what Mom needs me for if he's here already. She probably just misses me.

I am her favorite, after all.

16

Hideously Disfigured

Becca

"No! No, no, no, no, no!" I cross off the entry in my agenda with aggressive strokes, black ink spreading, and the tip of the pen ripping the paper. Throwing my pen across the room, I lean back in my chair and push my palms into my eyes, harshly rubbing away the wetness building there.

I didn't think much of it when the first cancellation called me. That happens sometimes with weddings. Someone gets cold feet, someone cheats, or someone dies. I've heard it all before, so I'm rarely surprised when I get one or two cancelations a season.

Six cancelations in the last month, though? That's something to be concerned about. It appears as though my run-in with Mrs. Carmichael was not without immediate consequences, after all. The weddings that have canceled on me so far have all gone out of their way to say they're friends with her. Not only did that incident destroy my chances of booking up solid next year, but it's also quite possibly destroyed my entire career as a wedding photographer.

Fuck.

I'm going to have to get a regular job. Ugh. I really don't want to do that. Not only am I not qualified for anything remotely interesting, but now that I've worked for myself, I don't relish the thought of working for someone else.

Maybe I can advertise for some family portrait sessions to tide me over until I book some more weddings? There has to be something I can do to make this work. I've already given up what I really wanted to do with photography. I can't let my backup plan fail, too.

My mind made up, I pull my laptop closer to me. I spend about an hour making some new graphics advertising the family sessions and updating my website. Once I've got them posted to all my social media platforms, and my scheduling link is up and running, I close up the laptop. Leaning back in my chair, I close my eyes and throw up a little request to the universe to let this plan work out. I can use all the help I can get.

Leaving everything where it is on the kitchen table, I get up and head to the shower to get ready for my day. I stupidly promised mom I would go over and help her with something. I don't know what she has planned for me, but I know whatever it is, I hate it already.

When I pull up to mom's house, I see there are two other vehicles parked there already. *I wonder who's here?* When I walk up the steps and open the door, I hear loud laughter coming from the back of the house. She must not have chores for me to do if she's entertaining guests right now. Something tells me that's no better than chores, though.

I find mom and her guests out on the back patio, enjoying the late summer sun.

"Oh Rebecca, there you are. Come here, darling." Mom motions me to where she's sitting on the far side of the table. "I have someone I'd like you to meet."

Uh oh. Something feels weird about this. Mom never introduces me to people. She's avoided it ever since I was old enough to stay home alone and she no long had to take me out in public.

"This is Jeff," she says, indicating the older man sitting directly across from her. He holds his hand out for me to shake, but I just give him a little wave instead. "And this is Jeff's son, Roger." She gestures to the other, slightly younger man in the seat opposite to the empty chair meant for me. A strange gleam appears in her eye, and she smiles at me.

Fuck. She's trying to set me up. What the hell is she thinking?

"Mom? Can I speak to you in the kitchen for a minute?" I grab her elbow and drag her along behind me, pulling her through the French doors into the kitchen before shutting them on our guests. I turn a glare on my mom. "Um, what the hell are you thinking?"

She has the audacity to look offended, like she isn't the same person who's been telling me all my life it's better to rely on myself than to worry about trying to have a man around. She has drilled it into me since I was four years old that no man would want to tie himself to me, so I shouldn't even bother.

"Well, Rebecca, it's occurred to me recently that maybe you're lonely. I thought you might still try to find a partner, even with your... disfigurement. Love is blind, after all." Mild disgust paints her features, as though the idea that love is blind leaves a bad taste in her mouth.

"Okay, great. Wonderful," I whisper, not wanting to be rude to the men outside, even if I have exactly zero interest in seeing either of them ever again. "What does that have to do with you? And, more importantly, what does that have to do with Jeff and Roger out there?"

She brings a hand up to rest her palm on her chest. "Well," she huffs. "I thought I was doing you a favor. But I see how ungrateful you are. Just like you are about everything else I've done for you all your life. This is just another thing to add to the list of sacrifices I've made for you. I suppose I should have known you would have this reaction. After all, when have you ever appreciated anything I've ever done for you?" She sniffles, her eyes shiny with unshed, and almost certainly fake, tears.

Great, here comes the guilt trip. I swear my mother should win an Oscar for how well she guilt trips me. Even when I know that's what it is. I know it's all an act, and yet I always end up falling for it. Just like I am now.

"I'm sorry, mom. I know you're just trying to help. You sur-prised me, that's all. If I'd known this was a date, I'd have dressed a little nicer." I wave my hand, gesturing to my scruffy-looking outfit of jeans and a long sleeve t-shirt with a threadbare sweatshirt over it. "This isn't exactly my nicest date outfit." I smile, trying to bring her around. If I can't get her to cheer up now, I'll be sucking up for days, maybe even a week.

"Hmph." She crosses her arms and turns away from me, leaving me scrambling to get in front of her so she'll look at me.

"I mean it, Mom. Thank you for thinking of me. I'm sorry I reacted so poorly to the surprise. Will you forgive me?" Please, please, please, forgive me. "Can we go back out to the deck now? It would be rude of me to detain you, and to make those gentlemen wait any longer."

She spins around and walks back to the French doors, throwing them open with a flourish. "Boys, so sorry to keep you waiting. Rebecca wanted to apologize for dressing so atrociously today. She's not very fashionable, as you can see." She glides back to the tables and slips into her seat. "But what can you expect, really? There's not much she can do about it when the poor dear has to keep her hideously scarred body hidden from innocent eyes."

Oh goody, we've progressed to the 'discussing Becca's hideous body' portion of the conversation already. I might just make it home in time for dinner. In fact...

"Before I forget," I say with as much false remorse as I can muster as I lower myself into my seat, "I promised Alex I would help her with something at her new place later this afternoon. She's promised me dinner in exchange."

"Well, of course, dear. Such a good friend Alex has been to you all these years. And so selfless of her." She gives me a pat on the leg, with enough force to be just shy of a slap. Yup, she's mad. She leans conspiratorially across the table, whispering to the men. "Alex is a truly beautiful girl. She could have been the most popular girl at school, but her heart is so big she befriended my poor Rebecca instead. Why, if it weren't for Rebecca, I'm sure Alex would have been prom queen, maybe even dated the captain of the football team."

The guys are nice enough to snicker politely at mom's story, but they still look uncomfortable. At least they have enough awareness to realize my mother's behavior isn't kind. I don't give a shit about that though, since they're taking turns looking at me with the morbid curiosity one would expect to see expressed at an old-fashioned circus sideshow, not at a relatively normal looking person who's sitting right in front of them.

Well, normal looking enough when my skin is fully covered, anyway.

I may not be as hideously disfigured as my mom thinks I am, but I'm certainly no porcelain skinned goddess either.

I have a feeling the next few hours are going to drag.

17

Johnny, Put the Kettle On

Johnny

"Honey, I'm ho—" I'm cut off when a herd of children barrels into me, tackling me to the lawn in front of my parent's house. I let out an exaggerated groan of pain and roll over, getting to my feet and keeping a low fighting stance. I'm staring into the faces of seven wildly grinning children, only four of whom I recognize as related to me.

"Who are you?" I lift my chin to the three kids I don't know. "I need to know the name of my enemies before I take them down." Really, I don't much care who they are. If they're hanging out at my parents' place, they're fair game. That, and they took part in sneak attacking me when I opened the front door, so they started it.

Not that I'd actually hurt children. It's play-fighting, and it's all in good fun. Mostly. They still need to be taught a lesson.

My nephew, Tyson, answers. "These are the new kids from across the street. That's Braden, Sarah, and Austin. Braden is in the same grade as me and is going to come to my school."

"That's awesome, kid." I tell him. Tyson has had a hard time making friends. To put it more accurately, his bright red hair has made him the butt of many 'kick a ginger' and 'ginger's have no souls' jokes. Kids can be little dickheads. Hopefully, this Braden kid will stick by him once school starts. "Now, who's ready for a battle of epic proportions? I won't take it easy on you because you're just kids. Keep that in mind, noobs." I point at the three neighbor kids. "I'm Uncle Johnny and I am going to take you all down. Show no mercy!" I yell, beating my chest like a gorilla.

The older kids giggle and the youngest of those present, Jack, my sister Ava's four-year-old, breaks ranks and runs right for me. I make the critical error of not paying attention to him, because hey, he's four, what kind of damage can he do? Turns out, it's a lot.

He can do *a lot* of damage.

While I'm distracted watching the older, bigger kids rally, Jack runs as fast as he can, coming straight for me. I look down at the last second, and see he has his head down, intent on using it as a battering ram. Realization dawns on me too late, when his fully formed, incredibly hard skull rams full speed into Little Johnny and the Twins.

"Aieeeee." I let out a high-pitched keening noise that sounds suspiciously like a teakettle, and drop to my knees, tears already forming in my eyes, as the contents of my stomach, the cookies and coffee I had earlier at Aiden's, attempt to stage a comeback on the grass in front of me.

"Gotchu, Unca Johnny, I winned. Nana, did you see? I winneded Unca Johnny." If I had room in my brain for anything other than pain, I'd correct him for saying 'winned' instead of 'beat' or 'defeated' but all I can think of is my poor, mangled testicles, and all the little babies I'll never be able to have now. "I hitted him, Poppa. I hitted him right in da nuts."

With blurry eyes, I can see my parents, and some sisters, maybe, standing in the doorway. My ears are working perfectly, though, and I can hear them all trying so hard not to laugh when I finally give up the fight and tip over face first into the lawn, hands still covering my dick.

"Alright kids, everyone get into the backyard. Let's give Uncle Johnny a few minutes to catch his breath." My mom takes over, herding the kids back through the house, and my dad comes over to help me up.

"Well, wasn't that a bit of good fun on a Sunday afternoon, eh?" Dad says with a smile, pushing me onto my back with his slippered foot. "That Jack, you got to watch him."

"Yeah. So fun," I groan, still holding my dick, rolling side to side just a little. "Thanks for the warning, Dad. Don't you think maybe it would have been better to warn me before he took away my ability to procreate?"

"Oh, I don't know about that now," he chuckles while he pulls me from the ground. For a man in his sixties, he's still incredibly strong from working with his hands his whole life. "It gave the rest of us a good laugh. Did you hear the noise you made when you went down? I called out to your mum to make me a cup of tea because I thought she'd set the kettle on."

I dust off my jeans, ridding myself of dirt and lawn clippings before walking through my mom's house. If I track dirt on her freshly mopped floors, my squashed berries will be the least of my worries.

"Come on, Johnny," Mom calls from the kitchen. "I made you an ice pack. Now, here you go." She fusses over me when I get to the kitchen, leading me to a chair and forcing me to sit, dropping a bag of frozen peas in my lap.

"Ice your nuts, son. I'll grab you a beer." Dad wanders to the garage, to one of his special beer fridges. He loves beers as much as I do and he keeps a couple of mini fridges at different temperatures for different brews. "I got a new one you're going to be really keen on, I think."

The house continues to bustle around me, kids, adults, and even a dog or two, running here and there, all speaking loudly, laughing, and just generally contributing to the feeling of home.

There's nothing quite like being home surrounded by a family that cares. I could do without the headbutt to the junk, but even with it, there aren't many places I'd rather be. Maybe here, but having my own wife and kids with me, that's about the only thing that would make this better.

Mom sits across from me, her cup of tea in hand, and pats me on the hand. "Now, are you going to tell me about this girl who's got you all tied in knots? Or am I going to have to get Jack back in here to take another run at your manhood?"

I snort a laugh. "I give. I'll tell you. Don't bring in the big guns." Dad comes back in and hands me a beer, before disappearing out to the backyard with the rest of the family, leaving me alone in the kitchen with mom.

"Travis says you've been spending a lot of time with this girl?"

"Ha! What would Travis know? He's always over here helping you guys with stuff. I can't even remember the last time I saw him at our place."

"Hmm, is that so?" Mom takes a sip of her tea. "Well, I can't say he's been here *that* much. I have seen him helping that nice young lady from across the way once or twice, though. Have you met Finley yet?" I shake my head no. "Well, she'll be joining us for dinner tonight. You met her kids outside when you arrived, I think."

Maybe that's where he's been. Has Travis gotten himself entangled with a single mom? I'll have to ask him about it next time I see him. If I can get him away from the rest of the guys, that is. I don't want to broadcast his business in the middle of the studio with everyone else there to give their opinion. He's my brother. I'll give him shit but I won't out him to anyone.

"Enough about Travis. What about this girl? What's her name?"

"Her name is Becca. She's a photographer, and we first met after the last show we did. She was there to shoot the special meet and greets set up by the radio station."

"Travis says she has nearly as many tattoos as you. Is that why you liked her at first?"

"I'm not sure, Mom," I say, taking a long drink of my beer. Dad did good with this one. I'll have to grab some for myself later. "She was taking photos from the floor when I was on stage.

I saw her and it was like lightning struck me. I couldn't look away after that."

"Oh," Mom squeals and claps her hands together. "When can I meet her? When will you propose? Oh, my goodness. More grandkids. I can't wait!"

"Mom!" I yell to get her attention. She's off in her own little world, painting nurseries, making baby clothes, and planning a wedding. "We're not dating. Becca doesn't date. That's the problem."

"She doesn't date? Why?"

I let out a disappointed sigh. "I don't know. She wouldn't tell me. She shuts down when we talk about that or when we talk about her family too much. But we've agreed to be friends. I'm trying to forget I have the feelings I do, but it's so hard, Mom. She's amazing. Funny, smart, and driven. Not to mention she's so beautiful. We've been having a lot of fun together. I'm trying to let that be enough for me." I knock back the last of my beer.

"Oh, honey. I'm sorry. Out of all my kids, you've always been the one who feels the most. You've been looking for true love since you were a little boy. Of course, back then, you were positive you were going to marry me." She smiles wistfully.

I was far too old when I finally conceded that I would, in fact, not be marrying my mom. That was probably my first broken heart. She's such a wonderful mom. I just figured she would probably also be the best wife. My dad agreed with me. She is the best wife, but she's his wife, so he's allowed to think that. But she's right. Ever since I recovered from the childhood disappointment of learning that I couldn't marry my mom, I've been looking for my own true love.

And now that I've found her, I'm afraid she doesn't want me.

18

Two Months Wasted

Becca

MY DATE AND I are saying goodbye outside of the restaurant where I just sat through the least exciting two hours of my life. This is the eighth date my mom has set me up with and it's my eighth strike out. If I were a baseball player, the fans would be getting angry. But I'm not, and the only one getting angry is me.

After nearly two months of shitty dates, you'd be getting angry, too.

"Well, Troy," I say, "it was... interesting to meet you. Thank you for dinner." He'd insisted on paying even though I'd made it clear I was perfectly happy to pay for my own meal. Even if the rest of the date had been good, the manner in which he'd rudely insisted he would pay would have turned me off of him. He was almost aggressive in his insistence.

"Yeah, sure. You bet. So... should I follow you home, or what?" Troy asks, leering down the front of my dress, not even attempting to hide the way he's staring at my boobs. "Or do you want to come to my place?"

I snort out a laugh, turning it into a cough at the last second when I realize he's serious. This guy thinks I'm sleeping with him? What date was he on? We barely spoke, and when we did, he was trying to mansplain photography to me. A man who admitted he'd never even touched a camera tried to explain how cell phone cameras were just as good as any DSLR on the market, and that only suckers would pay a photographer to take pictures of their events when they could just ask their guests to all take photos on cell phones and get the same results.

Yeah, I'm sure you can guess how impressed I was. I mean, yeah, you can take some decent pictures on cell phones these days, but that doesn't mean my skill set and chosen profession is obsolete.

"Sorry Troy, it's not going to work out. I don't think we have any chemistry. Goodbye." I turn and hurry to my car, not letting him get another word in. I know I'll hear about this from my mom, but I can't care about that right now. This guy was a nightmare.

Cell phone cameras? Is he serious? What the hell is wrong with this guy? How could he think telling me my job was unneeded and could be done just as well by any idiot with a smartphone was a good idea?

I lock the doors as soon as I get into my car, just in case Troy takes offense to being shot down. He seems like one of those guys who would follow a woman just to yell at her about what she's missing out on. I don't think he'd get violent, but better safe than sorry.

I listen to a little Sleeping Dogs on the way home. It's hard to believe the lead singer of the band is the same guy who broke Alex's heart all those years ago when we first met. And it's even harder to believe they've reconnected and are now more in love than ever.

Thinking about Alex and Connor has me thinking about Johnny. He sure is persistent, but he's kept his word and is just being a friend. He's actually become my best friend other than Alex. We've hung out so many times since that day at the tattoo shop. Sadly, there's been no repeats of that amazing orgasm he gave me, but that's for the best. We also see each other at least once a week at Alex and Connor's place for family dinners on Sundays. He hasn't brought up the thought of us being together again, so I suppose he really is content to just be friends.

Although, sometimes I catch him looking at me with puppy dog eyes.

I kind of like it when he looks at me like that.

I almost regret telling him about my one-night-only deal. Like maybe I should have given him a shot or something. Plus, I missed out on what I think would have been the most amazing sex of my life by telling him that. I wouldn't have tricked him into it, or anything, but it would have been nice to get him into my bed. I'm sure it would have been something I'd never forget.

My phone rings before I'm even home.

Mom's calling.

Looks like Troy has already tattled on me. What I don't need after yet another shitty date is a lecture from my mother, but I don't think I'll have much choice. I should have turned my phone off right away because now that she knows it's on she'll keep calling until I answer.

"Hi Mom," I answer as soon as I pull into my parking spot at the apartment. "I was driving. Sorry I didn't pick up."

"I thought I told you to get that Bluetooth thing to connect when you're in the car. Why didn't you listen to me?"

"I have Bluetooth, Mom. It just didn't connect this time."

"Well, fix it. I can't have you ignoring my calls."

"Sure thing, Mom. I'll get it looked at tomorrow." No, I won't. I don't want to answer the phone when she calls any more than I have to. A few minutes in the car is all the reprieve I get unless I'm doing a shoot.

"Troy called me. He said you were very rude to him."

I roll my eyes so hard I see my brain. "Is that so? Well, I thought it was rude when he told me any person with a cell phone could do my job better than me. Or when he expected sex because he paid for my dinner after I said was happy to pay for myself."

"Oh, honey. You know you can't afford to be so picky, not with the way you look. Not a lot of men are going to want to lie next to that every night, you know."

"Yes, mother. So you've said."

"Don't take that tone with me. I'm just trying to help you. That's all I've done my whole life. Ever since that accident, I haven't been able to sleep a wink thinking that you'd be alone for the rest of your life. And imagine how I felt when your father left because he couldn't look at you? And forget about me ever finding someone else. No man would want a woman with a child, let alone a child with such a grotesque disfigurement. So I've been alone all this time, too. I've given up everything in my life for you, Rebecca. I would think you would be thankful for having such a dedicated and loving mother."

I cover the mouthpiece on my phone and exhale loudly through my nose, a scream building behind my clenched teeth.

She tears me down to feel better about herself. I know this. But it hurts when she does it just the same. I don't know the real reason my dad left, but it wouldn't surprise me if it was because of her, not me. There's always a little voice in the back of my head telling me it's my fault, though. Funnily enough, the voice sounds just like my mother.

"You're right. I'm sorry, Mom. I must just be disappointed the date didn't go well. Maybe you should just give up now? You've introduced me to what, eight or nine different men? I probably am meant to be alone after all, just like you always said." I send up a silent prayer that she'll give up. I don't know how much longer I can do this before I murder one of these losers she sets me up with. She's scraping the bottom of the barrel and expecting me to be grateful for the scum she finds there.

"Oh no, Rebecca. I know we can find someone who will put up with your appearance. And look on the bright side. It's not like your scars are genetic, so any babies you have will be normal. Unless, of course, you're just as clumsy as you were as a child and you have another accident like you did then."

"That sounds great. Let me know when you've found someone. I've got to go now, Mom. I'll call you in a couple of days, okay?"

"Why don't you just go ahead and come over tomorrow afternoon, around three? I'm sure I can find someone else for you to meet by then."

"Sorry, Mom. I can't. Remember? I've got a full day of family shoots planned for tomorrow. What about next week? Maybe Friday?"

I hear the frustrated breath she releases because I've dared to inconvenience her. Like going on dates arranged by my mother every weekend for the last two months hasn't inconvenienced me?

"Fine Rebecca. I'll call you with the details."

"Sounds great. Talk to you then."

I hang up without letting her get any more words in, poking at the end call button with as much force as I can muster. Some days, I really miss landline phones. Hanging up on my mother would be so much more satisfying if there were more of a physical component to it. Pushing an icon is not the same as slamming the handset down in the cradle.

Sometimes I wonder if having her in my life is worth all this. Every time we talk, I end up feeling like complete shit. And now with this whole setup plan she has, I feel even worse. Seeing the types of guys she thinks I should settle for is doing terrible things to my self-esteem. But she is my only family, even if she doesn't always act like it.

I miss Uncle Silas and Uncle Patrick. If they still lived here, at least I'd have someone telling me that my mother is full of shit. The way it is right now, all of her bullshit goes unchecked and burrows its way into my head. It's like a parasite feeding on any self-esteem it finds, leaving me with a head full of shit that looks and sounds exactly like the things my mother says to me.

Maybe I should call them? Not tonight, but soon.

Tonight, I'll call Alex and tell her about yet another bullshit date. I know she'll agree with me about the cell phone camera thing. She'll share my outrage at his dismissal of my chosen career. Well, my second choice career, anyway. Fine art photography is harder to get into than I thought when I initially started out, but wedding photography pays the bills.

At least it did before Mrs. Carmichael had me blacklisted.

That bitch. I'm the one suffering because she didn't read the contract. Maybe I should have just refunded her deposit? I wouldn't be in the shit I'm in now if I had. But I couldn't let her get her way like that. So my pride came before my fall. Typical. As soon as I start to feel like my life is going alright, something comes along to shit all over me.

19

Evil Genius

Johnny

"So what? You guys just hang out?"

"Yes, Ryder. We just hang out." Ryder is having trouble understanding my new relationship with Becca. He doesn't see how I'm able to be friends with her when I'm so clearly in love with her at the same time.

"Yeah. I don't get it." He shakes his head, pulling the guitar's strap over his head and setting it in the stand. "You say you love her. And you just... drink coffee and watch movies and stuff?"

I shake my head and roll my eyes at him, not bothering to give him an answer. I know what I have with Becca isn't conventional, but when she offered me friendship as the alternative to her one night only rule, I jumped on it. I'd rather be friends with her than acquaintances who fucked one time. Besides, we do way more than just drink coffee and watch movies. We talk all the time. She's told me a little about her childhood and I've told her all about mine. She loves to hear me talk about my family. Her laughter at stories involving my nieces and nephews is always so loud and innocent. Especially if the stories involve me getting hurt in some way.

Most of them do, of course, because Uncle Johnny is the man to come to when you want an epic battle. It's my job to play fight and run around with all the kids until they're so tired they fall asleep as soon as their heads hit the pillow. My sisters may not like it when I get the kids riled up, but they sure love how easily they fall asleep the nights after they've played with me. I take my favorite uncle status seriously. I'm not happy with anything less.

Something about the way Becca listens to my family stories so intently cements the knowledge she didn't have as wholesome an upbringing as I did. From what little she's told me, I know her father left when she was very young and her mother can be a little hard to deal with sometimes. She shuts down when we talk about her family, though, so it's rarely a topic of discussion.

She doesn't seem to have anyone in her corner other than Alex, and with how busy she's been with Connor lately, she hasn't had anyone. Until now.

After that day at the tattoo shop when I tasted her for the first and last time, I've been nothing but a good friend. The best friend. We've done coffee, movies, long phone calls, text conversations, and just about anything else there is to do in Westborough. We've even talked about the dates her mother insists on sending her on. Those conversations aren't the most comfortable for me.

I've also offered to help her set up a photo shoot tomorrow. She told me she'd rented a vintage couch from a prop shop, but she didn't have any way to transport it to the location and I jumped at the chance to volunteer my services.

And Travis' truck.

And Travis.

He didn't mind.

Much.

"She needs a friend right now," I say. "And since she isn't interested in more, I'll gladly fill that position. She's cool, and I enjoy spending time with her. We always have something to talk about, and we always have a great time. Would I rather be with her? Yes, of course. But she doesn't want that. So I will keep it in my pants, and I will be her friend."

"Yeah, because friends always volunteer to drive couches out to the middle of a field and then back again." Travis laughs as he packs up.

We've been in the studio today, working on the album. He's used his weird mind-reading power on me again, so he knows that I'm still hopelessly in love with Becca. He's only giving me shit about it right now because he has to help move the couch tomorrow. But when he's finally interested in a woman, and he needs help to do something for her, I will be right there. We may not always agree, but we're still family, and that's what family does.

"Yes, Travis. That is exactly what friends do. They help each other."

He laughs, knowing full well he'd do the same thing if one of his friends needed help.

My phone buzzes in my pocket, and I jump to grab it, knowing it's Becca. Everyone else who texts me is here right now. She's the only other person it could be. I don't even try to hide the ridiculous grin that stretches my lips when I look at the screen and see her message.

Becca- Hey, what are you up to?

Johnny- Just leaving Connor's place. You?

Becca- Ugh. Just got back from the worst first date ever. My mom is still trying to fix me up with someone.

"Fuck." Okay, so maybe there are some parts of being friends with Becca that aren't that great. Hearing about her dates is one of those things. Hearing that her mom is still trying to fix her up is another. But it does give me an idea.

Johnny- I'm coming over.

Becca- *Bring beer.*

Being reminded of Becca's love for beer has me smiling again. I wonder what kind I should bring her tonight? She's liked almost everything I've brought before now, but it will have to be something pretty special this time if I'm going to convince her of my plan.

"Uh-oh. What's that smile for?" Aiden asks from behind his drum kit. He's still messing around while the rest of us pack up. I'm sure he'll play here for a bit longer and then go home and play some more. Drumming is his form of stress relief like baking is mine. "You look like you're up to something."

"Huh? Who? Me?" I point to my chest and swivel my head around, pretending to look for someone else he could be talking to. "I'm not up to anything."

"Yeah, sure. That's why you grinned at it like an evil genius just now?" Ryder asks.

I chuckle and shake my head. "Fuck off, Ryder."

"Okay, assholes. That's enough talking. Get the fuck out of my house. It's date night and Alex is going to walk me through cooking dinner." He rolls his eyes. "As much as I love helping her in the shower, I really can't wait until the damn cast comes off. She needs to demonstrate the cooking skills to me. My lack of basic skill in the kitchen causes her to channel her inner rage chef, turning her into a sexy female Gordon Ramsey. I swear when she was teaching me her recipe for French toast she was this close," he holds his finger and thumb so close they're nearly touching, "to holding slices of bread up against my ears and calling me an idiot sandwich."

"Oh, poor baby," Ryder laughs. "The love of your life breaks her hand, saving you from a would-be rapist, and now you're sad you have to help with dinner? Order takeout, for fuck's sake. Problem solved."

"Fuck off, Ryder. The problem isn't that I have to help. The problem is that she's trying to teach me certain techniques and when I don't understand her instructions, she gets irritated. It's cute, but she doesn't need the frustration. It would be easier if she could show me how to do these things, rather than trying to instruct me verbally." Connor explains. "But yeah, takeout would solve a lot of problems. Too bad Alex has her heart set on teaching me how to cook."

"Well, good luck with that," I tell him, on my way to the door. "See you Sunday. Can't wait to see what you're making us for dinner."

"Ha ha, funny. Maybe you should come over and cook instead?"

"Yeah, that could work. I don't mind helping."

"I'll hold you to that. Don't mind if Alex is in there with you, though. I think she misses cooking."

"That's alright, I'm sure she can teach me a thing or two. I've never cooked with a professional chef before. I wonder if she'll call me an idiot sandwich?" I give them a wave and then leave with the sound of their laughter flowing along behind me.

I'm eager to see Becca.

If she likes my plan, it will solve all of our problems at once. Now, I just need to convince her that having me as her fake boyfriend is the perfect plan.

20

The Man with a Plan

Becca

A KNOCK AT THE door tells me Johnny is here, and that someone must've propped the front door open again. It's like the other people who live in this building have never heard about security before. We have security doors for a reason. Just answer your buzzer if you don't want to go down and let someone in. It's not that hard.

"Hey. I brought you a gift," Johnny says with a grin, presenting me with a big rock. "It was holding open the door again. You should talk to the building owner about that. Maybe install some extra locks on your own door, so at least you know you're safe if someone leaves the main door open."

"What I should do is stand there with my bat and show people the awful shit that could happen if just anyone could get in the building. Starting with breaking their fingers. That's what I should do." I step over and put the rock on the bookshelf.

Johnny laughs at my threats of violence. He knows the bat has only been used to threaten Alex's cheating ex-boyfriends. Even if the people leaving the main door open are being idiots, that's no reason to use my bat on them. It's only for special occasions. Maybe I should take his suggestion of adding an extra lock to the door. This isn't the worst area of town, but it's not the best either. It helps that I live right next door to the gym Alex's Pops owns. If anything happened, he'd have a crowd of trainers and fighters up here faster than I could snap my fingers. But his gym is not open twenty-four hours, so I still need to take care of myself for the night shift.

"Cream ale," he says, placing the six-pack on the kitchen counter. He's been here a few times now, so he feels comfortable making himself at home, and that's how I like it. If my guests aren't comfortable enough to get their own drinks, then they'd better not come over. I don't invite people over so I can wait on them. Fuck that.

"Hmm, it's been a while since I've had a good one. What's this one all about?" Finding someone who appreciates craft beers like I do has been amazing. I've tried so many new beers since Johnny and I became friends, and so has he. It's like we've both had different favorites and now we can show each other something new.

"I'm embarrassed to have to say it, but I wasn't feeling all that inspired today, so I called Dad and he recommended this one. I don't know anything about it. So we're both virgins." He smiles and waggles his brows at me suggestively. *Good lord. He even looks hot when he's trying to look stupid.* Who knew being friends with a sexy man would be such a hardship?

But it is hard. No, that's not right. It's extremely fucking difficult. You try keeping up with day-to-day conversations when dirty fantasies about the person talking to you are playing on a non-stop reel in your head. It's no easy feat. Not even a little.

"Your dad?"

"Oh yeah. I think he loves beer more than we do put together. He's converted the garage into his beer cave. He's so proud of it that he talks about it like it's his eighth kid."

It's hard to forget that Johnny comes from such a big family sometimes. I've only ever met his brother Travis, but I'd be interested to see what his five sisters are like. I wonder if they're all tattooed like Johnny? Or maybe they're more laid back, like Travis? Johnny looks like a rock star. Travis looks like he wandered on stage on his way to the hardware store, picked up a bass, and start playing. Sleeping Dogs is lucky to have both of them, but I wonder how that works in their family. How are they so different? What are their sisters and parents like?

"Beer cave? That sounds amazing. You'll have to show me sometime."

Johnny inhales sharply and thinks for a moment.

"Yeah, that would be nice," he finally says. "So tell me about this horrible date. What was so bad about it? And why is your mom trying to set you up in the first place? You don't even want a relationship, but if you did, you certainly wouldn't need any help to get a man's attention. Guys are constantly checking you out."

It's cute how Johnny thinks guys check me out. I mean, yeah, they look. But they're not looking because they are checking me out. They're looking because they can see my scars. They're looking because they know I'm Freddy Krueger. They're not looking because they think I'm attractive. It's because I'm a freak show that their eyes are drawn to me. My tattoos, while beautiful on their own, can only hide so much ugliness.

Ugly is like a train wreck. People just can't look away.

"She's gotten it into her head that I'm going to be alone forever," I tell him, without adding the reason she thinks that. "And, for some reason, she thinks she's the one to solve that problem. But the thing is, she has terrible taste in men." I'd never expect her to choose those same men for herself. She is, after all, attempting to get me to *settle* for someone. She doesn't think a quality man would want me, so the men she finds for me are not quality.

"Well, can't you just talk to her about it? Let her know that you're fine and happy the way you are?"

My shoulders drop as a sigh escapes me. I know from past conversations that Johnny is close with his family. They talk to each other all the time. They see each other frequently. They take each other into consideration. I don't know how to explain it's not like that with my mom. She'd probably prefer not to consider me at all.

"My mom and I... well, we have different ideas about how involved she needs to be in my life. And very different ideas on how grateful I should be about her involvement. Sometimes it's easier to just go along with her than it is to argue. She's a master at manipulating me and making me feel guilty."

Johnny nods knowingly. "Ah, yes. Guilt, a mother's favorite weapon. I'm familiar with that as well."

I'm having a hard time reconciling what he's told me about his mother with the kind of manipulation and guilt my mother is a fan of wielding, but I take his word for it. I can't explain how my mother is probably so much worse without going into the details of what she guilts me with, and I refuse to do that. He doesn't need to know how I drove my father away. Or how I ruined my mother's life with my clumsiness.

"Yup, so I'm just dealing with it as best I can. I'll go on the horrible dates, and hopefully, someday soon, she gets over this need to see me paired up and she'll let me get on with my life."

Johnny finishes his beer, and cracks open another.

"Okay, hear me out. What if there was a better way than 'wait and see'?" he asks. "I think I have an idea, but it's a little out there. It will work though, and it will probably be a hell of a lot faster than going on these dates while you wait for her to lose interest."

"Oh, yeah?"

"What if you already had a boyfriend?"

I snort out a laugh. "I'm sorry, what? I never want to see any of those guys again, let alone allow one of them to be my boyfriend." Johnny must be drunk if he thinks I'd allow any of those guys into my life.

"No, not them. Me. Let me be your boyfriend." He looks sincere. And eager. It's those puppy dog eyes again. I'm so weak against his puppy dog eyes.

"You want to do what?" I splutter, so shocked I can feel the look of it on my face. "I thought we agreed that we were just going to be friends?"

Johnny came in here tonight, bouncing around like a puppy, and now I realize it's because he was all excited about this plan he'd cooked up that he says will solve the problem I have of my mom setting me up on dates. And it solves the mystery of his very effective puppy dog eyes. They work because he's part puppy.

"Let me clarify. I'll be your *fake* boyfriend," he says. "We'll just tell her we're together and continue doing what we already do. We're friends and we're together often enough it shouldn't be hard to fake a relationship."

We're sitting on the couch, drinking the beers he brought over while some superhero movie plays in the background. We'd barely finished our first beers before he spat out this plan, so it's safe to say he caught me by surprise.

"My fake boyfriend? That sounds like a disaster waiting to happen." I don't know why, but I'm picturing costumes and some sort of juvenile shenanigans.

And lots of fantastic sex.

My cheeks suddenly feel like they're on fire and I hope the lamp light is dim enough that Johnny can't see how red I'm getting. "Isn't that going to hold you back from finding the love of your life?"

Johnny has opened up to me about wanting to find his other half, his soul mate. He's the most romantic person I've ever met. He's the adult male version of little girls who play princesses and plan out their weddings. I'm sure he wouldn't admit to having his future wedding planned, but I'd bet good money he already has his eye on a venue and a color scheme in mind.

"No, I'm taking a break from that for now," he sighs, finishing his beer and opening another. "I've been looking for her for years with zero success. I think maybe it's time to sit back and wait for her to come to me."

When we met, Johnny had thought that I would be that person for him, but now he knows that's not something I do; I only do one night and then I walk away. I still feel a little embarrassed when I remember how I was straddling him on this couch, shirtless, and he lifted me off of him and told me he would want more than one night with me. This is exactly why this fake relationship thing could prove to be a disaster. He's going to catch feelings and I'm going to have to hurt him.

That, and he makes me want to break my one-night rule. I can't tell him that, though. It wouldn't be fair to give him that kind of hope, knowing that once he knows more about me, he'll want nothing to do with me.

"I don't know, Johnny. It seems with how you used to feel about me that this could be a bad idea." A bad idea that I suddenly want more than anything.

"I won't lie to you, Becca. I think we've become good enough friends to tell you I still feel a little something more than friendly toward you. You're the sexiest woman I've ever seen; I'd have to be blind not to notice. But this fake relationship could work out the best for that, too. I've never made it past a couple of months with a woman, no matter what I thought I felt for her at the start. Maybe this is a way to get it out of my system while helping you with your problem at the same time?"

When he says it like that, it almost makes sense.

"We would need to have rules." I find myself saying, my heart desperate to agree to the plan when my head knows it's not a good idea. "Things we can and can't do. That sort of thing."

"Of course," he says. "And I'd need to meet your mom too, I'm guessing, or she won't believe you?"

Ugh. Of course, I forgot about that part. What are the chances that my mother could behave in front of Johnny and not give away how disgusting she finds me? Probably not very good. But if I want her to stop setting me up with these losers, this is my best chance. It might even be a good way for Johnny to get over me. If he knows that even my own mother thinks I'm unlovable, he'll be ready to move on to someone more suitable for him. Like a supermodel or something.

"Okay. Let's do it." I blurt out before I can change my mind.

Johnny's eyes light up and an enormous smile splits his face. "Alright. Let's make some rules."

Rules for a Successful Fake Relationship

<u>Rules for a Successful Fake Relationship</u>
- Don't fall in love.

- Don't let our friends know.

- Only show affection in front of Becca's mom.

- NO SEX.

- No relationships with other people while we're dating.

- Don't do anything that will jeopardize the friendship.

True Story

Johnny

"Yeah?" I'm trying to contain my excitement, but I just can't. Becca agreeing to be my girlfriend, even though it's fake, is the most exciting thing that's happened to me in months. Since the day at the tattoo shop, to be honest. Thank god I was honest when I said I still had some feelings for her, or my level of excitement right now would probably seem a little crazy. "You won't regret this. Aside from solving your problem with your mother, you're going to enjoy having me as your boyfriend. I've been told I'm excellent at it. Well, for as long as it lasts, I am." Until I realize the woman I'm with isn't my other half, that is.

Becca laughs, grabbing herself another beer. "Well, I have nothing to compare to, so I'm sure I wouldn't know the difference, anyway."

Did I hear that right? Becca hasn't had many boyfriends? I find that hard to believe. This woman is a walking wet dream. Soft and curvy, with an uncomplicated style. Aside from her perfect eyebrows and bright lipstick, she's about as low-maintenance as a woman can get. Every time I've seen her she's been in jeans and t-shirts with that nearly worn-out hoodie she loves thrown on over top. She's that perfect girl next door with tattoos and a bit of makeup to give her a little edge. She has this innocence about her that makes me want to protect her and dirty her up at the same time.

"Well, I will blow all your past boyfriends out of the water," I say. "I must warn you, that after this is all over, I will most likely have ruined you for other men." And I really hope that's true, because if this goes the way I hope, then I will be the last man she ever needs to be with. The last man she ever *wants* to be with.

"That won't be too hard. Milo is the reason I don't do relationships. It should be easy to be a better boyfriend than him."

"Milo?" Sounds like a douchebag. Wait. That's the guy she mentioned in her text that one time, isn't it? The guy that hurt her.

"Yeah, Milo Mathews. He's the closest I've ever had to a boyfriend. I was fourteen."

"Oh." I don't even know what to say to that. How can this amazing, sexy, smart, hilarious woman not have had a relationship since she was fourteen? What did this dickhead Milo do that was so bad she swore off relationships forever?

"I've never told anyone this, but it's something you'll probably need to know as my fake boyfriend." First order of business? Figure out how to get her to drop the 'fake' when she calls me her boyfriend. She takes a deep breath and closes her eyes, exhaling roughly before she begins. "I don't want to get into it too much, but you need to know a little so I can tell you the story properly."

"Tell me whatever you think you need to, Becca. I'm here to listen. You don't owe me anything."

She takes a huge breath, closes her eyes, and begins. "When I was four, I had an accident at home. I pulled a pot of soup off the stove and burned most of the right side of my body and a little of the left side." I suck in a breath, the thought of tiny Becca being burned with boiling liquid sending pain shooting through me. Becca slides off the sleeves of her ever-present hoodie, showing me her arms. "It's a little harder to see the scars through the tattoos, but they're still there."

"I kept to myself throughout my school years. I wore long pants and turtlenecks with long sleeves year round. I was the ugly, weird kid, and I had no friends. One day, when I was fourteen, Milo sat next to me in the library.

"Milo was the exact opposite of me. He was good-looking, popular, and played on the baseball team. I thought he sat next to me by mistake, but he'd done it on purpose.

"He spent months gaining my trust, becoming my friend, until, eventually, near the end of the school year, he said he liked me, that I was his dream girl." She scoffs. "It felt like everything I'd ever wanted had come true. I was on top of the world.

"But of course, it wasn't like that.

"One day we were making out at his place and he convinced me to take off my shirt. He took a picture of me and my scars and showed the entire school. He was never my friend. He was faking it the entire time."

Rage flows through my veins, burning me from the inside out, blinding me. I'm going to find this Milo character, and I'm going to make him bleed. How dare he do this to Becca? How dare he destroy a child like that? Never mind that he was technically a child, too. The guy was a dumb fucker, and I'm sure he still is. I force my breath to steady. Becca needs me to listen right now, not go off acting crazy and looking for revenge.

But that doesn't mean I'm not tracking this asshole down later.

"After that, the kids at school started calling me Freddy Krueger." She looks, and realization dawns on me. "But it wasn't a complete disaster. That's also when I started getting these tattoos. I ran into a relative of Milo's when I sprinted out of his house that day. A relative who just happened to agree that Milo was a little prick. He helped me out with all the tattoos and became like an uncle to me. He's one of the best men I've ever known."

"Holy shit," I say. "The Freddy tattoo."

She nods. "Remember how I said it was my first tattoo? I got it as a fuck you to Milo. I was fourteen."

"Fourteen?" I'm shocked. I can't even decide what to say about it. "Wow. That's... I don't know what to say."

"Once I started getting all the tattoos, and stopped wearing clothes that covered me head to toe, the other kids stopped calling me Freddy. Eventually. Except for Milo. He was an asshole right until the last time I saw him." She chuckles a little. "But yeah, that's why this horror villain tattoo you designed for me is perfect. It's the only choice I could make. Freddy has had his day. I can't continue to give him, and Milo, so much power over my life."

She takes a drink of her beer and dabs at her eyes. I don't see any tears, but it looks like she got a little misty while telling me the story. I want to hug her, but now I understand why she doesn't really like to be touched. The last guy who touched her betrayed her trust in the worst way. It's no wonder she doesn't want people to touch her.

"Anyway, that's why I've never had a boyfriend. And why I don't let anyone into my life in that way anymore. But since you're my friend first, and my fake boyfriend second, I think I can trust you not to take naked pictures of me to flash around, or to start calling me Freddy." She laughs a little, the sound more sad than mirthful.

"Well," I drawl. "I still might want some naked pictures, but I'll be damned if I ever show them to anyone. And if I give you a nickname, it will be something that actually suits you, like 'beautiful', or 'gorgeous', or 'sexiest woman on the mother-fucking planet'." That earns me a smile, but I can tell she doesn't believe what I'm saying. She knows I won't betray her, but she doesn't believe that she's beautiful. Fuck this Milo guy. "On a totally unrelated, and not at all revenge-motivated note, where is Milo these days? Did he leave town after high school? For educational purposes, of course."

"Oh, yes, of course. *Educational purposes.*" This time her laughter is real, and it helps to quell the raging fire in my blood. A little, but not much. "I don't think I should tell you that. I know what happened to Alex's cheating ex-boyfriend Derek, and Denise's dickhead ex Andrew. I don't think I could have your incarceration for assault or manslaughter on my conscience. Plus, visiting you in prison would be too much of a bummer."

"Hmmm, you might be right. I'm too pretty for prison. Plus, you just agreed to be my fake girlfriend. I'm not ready to give that up just to be someone's real girlfriend in prison. No promises about what I'll do after we convince your mother to butt out of your love life, though. I've seen those prisoners looking for love websites. Some of those guys are hot. And jacked!"

That gets her laughing, a proper belly laugh. The tears spring from her again, but this time they're from laughter instead of sadness.

Now I have two missions: make Becca my girlfriend for real, and help her understand that she's truly beautiful, scars or no scars.

No. Wait. Three missions: I also have to find Milo Mathews and break his legs.

23

Picture Perfect

Becca

I'M STANDING IN THE sunshine, in the middle of a field of wildflowers, watching two sexy, shirtless guys manhandle a vintage couch off the back of a truck and into position for me. Not a bad way to spend a Saturday, if I do say so myself. And with the added weightlessness I feel in my chest from telling Johnny about Milo and my scars, this day is just about perfect.

If I didn't have another of my mother's dates set up for tonight, it probably would be perfect. It's too late to cancel, though, so I'll just have to tough it out. I may have a fake boyfriend now, but I still have manners. Even though I'd rather do anything at all with my fake boyfriend than go to dinner with whichever loser my mom has picked for me this time.

"How's this?" Travis asks.

Johnny pulls his t-shirt from where it was tucked into his back pocket and uses it to wipe the sweat from his face. It has me thinking decidedly unfriendly thoughts about the man who is supposed to be just my friend. By my choosing.

True to his word, Johnny has turned out to be a great friend. Who else but a friend ropes his brother into moving a couch in the sweltering heat of a sunny afternoon? No one, that's who. It's a good thing we're friends now, too. I'm sure Alex and I wouldn't have been able to manage the couch, but I don't think the families I have booked for photo shoots today would appreciate me being a sweaty, disgusting mess, either.

But no matter how much I appreciate all the work they've already done for me, I still need them to move the couch a little. I spotted a small clearing with a dense crop of wildflowers about fifty yards away and I need the couch over there.

"Actually," I say with an apologetic grimace, "Can you move it just a little more that way?" I point over to the crop of wildflowers. "To the middle of that dense grouping of wildflowers? The colors will photograph beautifully."

"Of course we can," Johnny volunteers. "We're at your service today. Right, Travis?"

Travis laughs and shakes his head. "I can help you move the couch over there, but I have to run soon. I promised Mom and Dad I'd go over and do some work outside while the weather is still nice."

"Oh, you're leaving that soon?" Johnny asks. He turns to look at me. "Do you mind if I hang out here with you?"

I hadn't actually thought about it, but it's probably a good idea if someone stays here with me. I'm out in the middle of nowhere meeting people I've never met before. That's the start of a horror movie if I've ever heard one.

"Yeah, that would be great, Johnny. You can be my assistant. But what about the couch? How will we get it back if you leave with the truck, Travis?"

"Here, catch," he says, tossing me a set of keys. "I'll drive your car and you guys can keep the truck. Your car will be at our parents' house for you to pick up later."

I throw him my keys. "Perfect. Let me make sure I have all of my equipment out before you leave, though. I'd hate for you to have to turn around and come back right away."

Johnny helps me unload the last couple of items from my car and then Travis is on his way.

My first clients arrive shortly after Travis leaves, and the afternoon proceeds smoothly. Johnny has to put his shirt back on when the mother in the first family can't stop ogling him. I'm not sure who was madder, me at the woman for looking at him, or her husband at Johnny for looking so good shirtless that his wife couldn't keep her eyes off of him.

Johnny is the perfect assistant. He delivers cold, bottled water to the clients as we work, helps position them properly, moves props, and even fans them while I'm shooting. He's been recognized a few times, but everyone is respectful, and besides asking for autographs, and one family begging him to pose in one of their family pictures, there are no incidents or mishaps. His request that they not post about it on social media until later in the evening is heeded and we're able to finish all the appointments without being mobbed by fans.

Afterward, while we're packing up my equipment, I can't help but think how lucky I am that Johnny agreed to be my friend even when he'd wanted more. We've texted constantly since that day, and he's always been so kind. He's never even asked about my scarring, not that I'm too surprised. It took Alex twenty years before she asked and I don't think Johnny would have been much different. If I hadn't told him about it last night, to help this whole fake relationship we're having, I probably never would have told him.

And he never would have asked.

Once we've finally finished wrestling the couch back into the back of the truck, we sit on the open tailgate for a minute to catch our breath. Well, so I can catch my breath. That couch was a lot heavier than I expected. They really built things to last back in the day. No wonder I was able to rent it from that prop company. One day, when I have enough room to store my own props, I'm going to have a couch just like this. Maybe more than one, for different seasons.

"What are you up to tonight? Want to grab dinner or something?" Johnny asks.

"Ugh." The groan escapes my lips before I can stop it. "My mom is setting me up on another date and I already agreed to it before you and I came up with our plan. I'm sure this one is just as much of a loser as the last guy. She doesn't seem to get that I don't want to date."

He bumps his shoulder into mine. "You mean you haven't told her about your one-night rule?" He chuckles. "Or your new boyfriend?"

"Yeah, no. She wouldn't be understanding of that. At all." Considering I never told her about what happened with Milo in high school, she really wouldn't understand at all. "My mom is... let's just say she's not a very nice person. It's easier to just go along with her plans sometimes than it is to resist and put up with her guilt trips and manipulation. But having you as my boyfriend will help, I'm sure." My therapist doesn't agree with my methods, but it's what works for me, so it's what I'll do until it doesn't work anymore, I guess. "She'll need to see you in person, though, or she probably won't believe you're real."

"That sounds shitty," he says. "Didn't you say it was just the two of you, too? Your dad left when you were little? It's got to be hard enough with a single mom, but I can't imagine what it would be like with one who isn't even motherly."

"Well, that's how you get someone like me. Completely messed up, just a little nuts, and probably not very well-adjusted." I laugh. "But it is what it is. That's all I know. I probably wouldn't even know what to do with a motherly mother. It would be strange, for sure."

Johnny hops off the tailgate and holds out a hand to help me down. Just like any other time we touch, almost always accidentally, tingles shoot through my hand and up my spine, leaving me with a pleasant buzz in my body. Johnny feels like what I imagine a proper home would feel like. Warm, welcoming, caring. Makes me wish I could hold on to him, keep him for my own. But I already know that someone like him isn't meant for someone like me. We may look like we're similar on the outside, but on the inside, he's mushy and loving, and I'm broken and hurt. Johnny can only ever be my fake boyfriend. Certainly not my actual boyfriend, let alone anything more.

"Well then, let's get your car back so you can get ready for this date."

"Great. Can't wait," I snark. Johnny laughs and makes his way to the passenger door, holding it open as I climb in.

Sexy, loving, and a gentleman. Johnny is going to make some woman very happy one day.

If only it could be me.

24

Family Matters

Johnny

THE CARS LINING THE street at my parents' house show that at least some of my sisters are here. Great. I'll never hear the end of it if I don't bring Becca in to introduce her to everyone, especially since both Travis and I helped her today.

I had hoped I'd be introducing Becca to my family under different circumstances, like we were dating or having a baby or something like that, but introducing her as my friend is going to have to do. I certainly can't tell my family about the relationship we're faking so her mother will stop setting her up with horrible guys. I couldn't handle their pity if they knew.

I take a deep breath and jump into it. "So my family is here and because we helped you today, they're going to want to meet you. And we can't tell them about our arrangement. They'll fall in love with you and be heartbroken when we stage our breakup."

"Okay," Becca drawls and looks out the truck's window toward my parents' house. "And? What's the problem? You don't want them to meet me?"

"What? No! Are you crazy? You're the best." I grab her chin and turn her to look at me, thankful that the more time we spend together, the more of my touch she can tolerate. "My family is... a lot to handle. I don't know exactly how many people are in there right now, but I can tell you, no matter how many people there are, it's going to be loud. And chaotic. Possibly even painful, but that part is mostly for me. I want you to be informed before we head in there. You say it's best to go along with your mother's plans because of guilt and manipulation? Well, imagine that, but from a loving, smothering mom, and five nosey older sisters. And all of their kids." I sneak a peek at the house and sure enough, a couple of my sisters and my mom are standing in the doorway, and a few kids out on the lawn, waiting for us to get out of the truck. I sigh, my shoulders dropping. "It's too late to turn back now, anyway. They're watching us."

Becca turns back around and looks out the window. "That doesn't look so bad. There aren't too many of them."

"Yeah. Right." I agree, knowing she doesn't see any of the others who are staring at us from all the windows on the front of the house. "Let's get this over with, then. We don't want you to be late for...? What's your date's name?"

"Ugh, don't remind me. I think his name's Mike. Or Mark? Maybe it's Mac? I don't even know. She has them meet me at her house so she can introduce us, and play interference to explain my hideous disfigurement."

"Your what?" I ask, just as her door opens from the outside. I know she said she had scars, but they're not even noticeable. Did she actually just refer to them as hideous disfigurements? What the hell?

My sister, Millie, is standing at Becca's door, holding it open. "Hi, I'm Millie. That idiot's sister. You must be Becca. I've heard so much about you. We weren't sure if Johnny would be brave enough to introduce us to his new girlfriend, so they elected me to come get you." She holds an arm out, inviting Becca to get out of the truck. "Come on in, then. Mom's been dying to meet you."

Becca looks back at me, eyes wide. "You were serious?"

"Yeah. Sorry about this. I'll get you out of here as soon as possible." I hop out of my side and run around to Becca's. It took a little longer to drop off the couch than expected, so it's already coming up on dinner time. If I can't get Becca out of here quickly enough, she's going to get invited to have dinner with my family, and by invited, I mean trapped. Mom and Dad Donovan are not to be denied when it comes to invitations to dinner.

"Oh, Mom. Becca doesn't like to be tou—" Before I get the warning out, my mom has her arms wrapped around Becca and she's hugging her like they're long lost best friends. "—ched."

I can't be sure, but it looks like Becca *almost* melts into the hug. I wonder if she's as uncomfortable with being touched as she makes out? Seems like Mom's hug has gotten through her defenses a little. It's taken ages for her to trust me enough that I could touch her hand and help her down from the truck earlier today, and here Mom has her wrapped in an enormous bear hug.

Go Mom.

"Becca, it's so good to finally meet you," Mom says, still not letting her go. "Johnny has told us all about you."

"Yes, he certainly has," my dad says from the open doorway. "But he understated how pretty you are. Oh, my girl, you're a right stunner, you are. Isn't she a stunner, Agnes?"

Mom holds Becca by the shoulders and leans away to put her at arm's length. I see Becca flinch when Mom first touches her shoulders, but the look is gone almost as soon as it appears. "Oh yes, Dennis, she certainly is. Imagine the beautiful grandbabies these two will make? Oh, my. It's enough to bring a tear to my eye."

"Mom!" I yell. "Boundaries, please. You can't go talking about grandbabies the first time you meet a girl. And like I told you before, Becca and I are just friends."

"Oh, poo. You're no fun." Mom says to me. She loops an arm through Becca's and leads her to the house. "Come now, Becca. Let's get you inside and get you something to drink. You can tell us more about yourself, yeah?"

Dad follows along behind Mom and Becca. "Johnny tells me you like a good beer. I can't wait to show my special fridges in the beer cave."

"Wait," I hear Becca say as she disappears into the house. "You have more than one beer fridge? Let's go look now."

Dad's and Becca's laughter waft out as he shuts the door. Well, looks like I'm no longer needed. Becca seems to hold her own, even with having her personal space invaded and her future procreation possibilities commented on.

"Is that your girlfriend?" my nephew, Mark, asks. "She has lots of tattoos like you, Uncle Johnny."

"No, she's not my girlfriend, buddy." *I just wish she was.* "We're just friends."

"How come you brought her to dinner? Is it because she's so pretty?" This from Drew, Mark's little sister. "Do you want her to be your girlfriend? Nana made a cake for dessert. I bet Becca would be your girlfriend if you gave her some cake," she adds helpfully, before skipping away to find something more interesting to do. She'll probably go find Ariella and Arianna, Millie's twin girls, to see if they'll get off their phones and play with her. It's highly unlikely, I'd say. I haven't seen their faces since their twelfth birthday a couple of years ago, when they got their first phones.

"Mark, go on in and see if Nana needs any help, okay? I need to talk to Uncle Johnny for a minute." Millie sends Mark off to join everyone else and soon it's just the two of us left standing in the front yard.

"Well?" she prods. "Is this the one?"

I roll my eyes. I brought this on myself. I've spent so many years thinking every girl I met was the one that my family is always giving me shit about it.

"I thought she was," I say. "But she's not interested, so we're just friends." I don't let on that I'm still holding on to hope we'll be something more one day. It's not like I'm expecting anything from Becca. I'm just hoping in the future, if she ever reconsiders her position on relationships, maybe she'll see me as an option.

"Bullshit."

"Excuse me?"

"You heard me," she says. "I said bullshit. You've got it so bad for that girl."

"She's not interested."

"But you are?"

I walk over to the front step and sit down. Millie isn't going to let this go until she gets something out of me, so I might as well get comfortable.

"Yes, I am. I've never felt this way before." She raises her eyebrows at me. I get it. I'm like the boy who cried wolf, but instead of a wolf, I keep saying I've found the one. "I'm serious. This is nothing at all like any of the other times. I saw Becca from the stage for the first time when she was shooting our last show, and it was like I'd been struck by lightning. I couldn't fucking look away. Every day I spend as just her friend kills me a little more inside. But that's all she wants, so I'll take it."

Millie wraps an arm around me and gives me a little squeeze. "Come on. We'd better go in and make sure she's alright. She looked a little shell-shocked when Mom hugged her like that. Something tells me she's not used to having a lot of family around."

I laugh. "You're right about that. It's just her and her mom. And her mom is something else, from what she tells me. It wouldn't surprise me if Becca said she'd never been hugged before and that's why Mom's affection surprised her so much."

"What on earth have you done to that poor girl by bringing her here? The neighbors call the cops on us when we have family barbecues because we're so loud and crazy. She has no idea what she's in for." Millie laughs, shaking her head as she opens the door to let us in the house. "She's going to know the meaning of 'touched out' before she gets out of here tonight. Mark my words. Most women don't learn about that before they have babies climbing all over them."

I can't even argue, because as soon as we get inside, I look over to the living room and I find Becca sitting on the couch. She has my mom snuggled up to her on one side, my sister Rose snuggled up on the other side, and she's holding both Jack, the four-year-old junk ruiner, and his little sister Allie, the baby who just recently turned a year old. And she's laughing at some story my mom and Rose are telling her.

From the looks of it, it's a descriptive retelling of Jack's triumph over me and my testicles last weekend.

Outstanding.

25

Fitting In

Becca

"OH MY GOD, THAT'S amazing." I have tears in my eyes from laughing so hard. "I can't believe he hasn't been walking with a limp all week. You have a rock-hard head, kiddo." Jack spins around and smiles at me, proud of the little head-butting stunt Rose and Agnes have been telling me about.

I don't know how long I've been sitting here, the filling in a Donovan sandwich made of four different members of Johnny's family, but it took next to no time at all for me to feel comfortable with this much physical contact. I've never wanted to call my therapist in celebration before, but I feel like I should at least call and leave a message about this. This is huge. His Mom even hugged me. Like, really hugged me. I almost cried right there in the front yard. My mom hasn't really hugged me since before the accident, so I forgot what a true hug felt like. I didn't even know enough to know I missed it.

And now I know I really missed it.

"You doing alright in here?" Johnny asks from across the room. He must've just come in with his other sister, Millie, the one who opened the truck door for me when we arrived. "Do you need to get going soon?"

"No," Mom says, disappointment coloring her voice. "You don't need to leave, do you? Say you'll stay for dinner."

"I'd love to stay for dinner," I hear myself telling her, not at all surprised to find that I mean it. I would love to stay. So I will. "Thank you."

Johnny raises an eyebrow at me, silently questioning whether I'm actually okay with staying or if I'm trying to be polite. I give him a slight nod and then gently squeeze Jack and Allie before passing them off to the ladies on either side of me.

"Johnny, can you take me to find your dad? I believe I was promised a beer and a tour of his beer haven in the garage. I got distracted by these adorable kiddos when we walked in and he slipped away from me."

"Sure thing," Johnny says, crossing the room in three long strides and holding a hand out to help me up. I think I'm almost as shocked as he is when I grab it and don't let go once I'm up.

"I'll be back soon, Agnes. I can help you in the kitchen if you like, as long as you show me what to do first."

"Oh no, dear. You're our guest. We have more than enough kids around here to help. You enjoy your beer with the boys. Lord knows they're going to be beside themselves with excitement to have a new person to talk to about hops, and brewing, and barley, and all the other nonsense that goes along with that stuff they drink."

I chuckle at her description of our beers. Sounds like she is not a fan. She would get along great with Alex, I'm sure. Alex has never been interested in my beer talk, either.

"Well, that's very kind of you."

Johnny pulls me out of the living room and past the kitchen to an empty mudroom. With having this many kids around, it makes sense the Donovans would have a huge back entrance like this. I can't imagine trying to get everyone in and out of the front door in the middle of winter, never mind where you'd keep everyone's coats and boots. If I ever have a house of my own, I want a mudroom like this. Johnny drags me further into the room, closing the door behind me.

"Are you okay?" he asks, worry lines between his eyes. "I know you're not a big fan of touching and you've just had a lot of physical contact. Do you need a break or a glass of water or something?"

I smile and shake my head. It's sweet that he remembered I don't like to be touched, but I feel good about what happened. "I think... I think I'm fine. Maybe your mom's hug broke me? Or fixed me? I'm not really sure. All I know is I froze up for a half second when she hugged me and then I just melted into her embrace. Is that what hugs are supposed to be like? I have very little experience with hugging."

A look of concern crosses Johnny's face before quickly lighting up with a grin. "Mom's hugs have always been pretty special. And she's had lots of kids and grandkids to practice with over the years."

"Well, she is fantastic at it." I let out a long, shuddering breath. I've never let myself think about it, but I didn't realize until now how stressful it is being around my mother. From the second Johnny's sister opened the truck door, I've felt nothing but welcome here. Exactly as I am. Whether that's because they don't know about the scars I'm hiding remains to be seen. For now, I'm going to allow myself to suck up all the good vibes I can, because I feel better right now than I ever have.

"Becca?" Johnny's hands have found mine again, and he's holding my fingers while his thumbs barely whisper across my knuckles, tickling me.

I'm looking at our hands together, the way he seems ready to stop at any moment if I were to tell him to. But I don't want that. For the first time since Milo, I want a man to touch me. I want to feel Johnny's hands in places where, until now, only my hands have been. I want him to kiss me like he did before. Like I was the only woman he'd ever wanted.

"Johnny," I say, forcing him to look me in the eye. "Kiss me?"

So much for that rule. We'll have to amend the list.

His eyes widen in surprise for just a moment before he wraps his arms around me and slams his lips to mine. I open my mouth and our tongues immediately tangle together, sliding over each other's lips and mouths, taking as much as we give. My stomach fills with butterflies and I can't believe I haven't been kissing this man all along.

This kiss surpasses those others, by far. Being held in Johnny's arms while he kisses me is better than I could have ever imagined. He takes a couple of small steps and nestles me against the door, pushing his hips into me, his hard cock pressing into my belly, and I groan into his mouth. I feel the scrape of Johnny's fingers as he runs his hand up through my hair, grasping the back of my head, and tilting my mouth away. He leaves a flaming trail of kisses along my cheek, my jaw, and my earlobe until he finally reaches the little hollow behind my ear. The tip of his tongue tentatively strokes me there, sending shivers up my scalp, and intensifying the feeling of his hand gripping my hair. He kisses his way down my neck, agonizing me with how slowly he moves, while he slides the hand not in my hair down my back until he's gripping my ass so hard it almost hurts. He takes my mouth with his again, his tongue laving mine, exploring, caressing, and kissing with what feels like a single-minded determination to kiss me more thoroughly than anyone has ever kissed me before.

Noises I didn't know I could make escape my throat, a mewling, whimpering sort of sound that belies a need for Johnny so strong, and so right, I'm not sure how I fought it for this long.

We've already broken the rule about only showing affection in front of my mother. Maybe we can break the one about no sex? Maybe I can change my one-night rule for the duration of our fake relationship arrangement? Right now, with how this kiss is making me feel, that sounds like the best fucking idea I've ever had. I slide my hands under the hem of his shirt, feeling the ridges and divots that make up his hard abs. I move to pop open the button on his jeans and Johnny stops me.

"Becca, wait," he whispers against my lips. "We can't do this. We shouldn't break any more rules."

I cup his dick through his jeans, forcing a groan from his lips. "This doesn't feel like 'can't'. Fuck the rules." I say. "I want you, Johnny."

"Oh god, Becca. You have no idea how much I want you. No idea how much I want to say fuck the rules and take you right here against this door. I want to strip your pants off, pull my cock out, and thrust into you so I can feel just how hot and wet you are." Oh fuck, I want that too. So much. Johnny releases a disappointed groan when I nod excitedly, kissing me deeply before letting me go. "But we're in my parents' mudroom. There are kids running around all over the place, and my dad is waiting to show you his beer cave. If we hide out here any longer, they're going to send out a search party."

Shit. He's right.

"Fine," I say, heaving out a huge sigh. It's probably better this way. Changing the rules would complicate things too much. But maybe, in this situation, complicated isn't such a bad thing? "But before we leave this room, can I ask for one more thing?"

"Anything," Johnny promises.

"Will... will you hug me?" I look down at the ground, old feelings rushing in, fear of rejection flooding my veins.

Strong arms wrap around me, pulling me close, leaving no space between us. Johnny guides my head to rest on his chest. I wrap my arms around his waist and hold him tightly, afraid to let go. His heartbeat in my ear calms me, and soon I'm pulling away from the hug.

"Thank you,"

He tucks my hair behind my ear and cups my face, a smile on his lips. "Anytime, beautiful. Anytime."

26

Take Me Home

Johnny

"THANK YOU SO MUCH for dinner," Becca says to my parents on our way out. "The only time I eat this well is when my friend Alex invites us all to her place for dinner. Otherwise, I'm strictly a takeout and microwave dinner kind of girl."

A comically exaggerated look of disgust crosses my mom's face, her nose and lips scrunching up, before her eyes light with mischief. "You know, Johnny is an excellent cook. He'll just have to be in charge of dinner when you two get married."

She knows Becca is not my girlfriend, but she can't stop herself from trying. To be fair, even though I've always thought whichever girl I was with was 'the one', I'd never brought any of them home before. This is the first time my mom's really had an opportunity to embarrass me in front of a woman. I think she's enjoying herself a little too much.

"Don't worry about that now," Dad offers. "Come back to see us and we'll feed you. And then you and I can talk beer some more."

"It's a date." Surprisingly, Becca hugs them both goodbye, and after she's checked to make sure we've transferred all of her camera equipment from Travis' truck back to her car, we're on our way.

We haven't had a chance to discuss the kiss at my parents' place, nor have we addressed her new level of comfort with hugging. Hell, I don't even know if she's planning on taking me home or if she's driving me to her place in a bid to get me out of my pants.

I really hope it's the second one.

But not if she's still thinking it can only be one night. After seeing her with my family tonight, laughing, joking, playing with the kids, and seeming like she belongs there, I want her even more. This is the reason I've always been looking for my other half. I want someone to join my family. Someone to help *me* join my family.

My family loves me, I know that, but I've always felt a little outside of it all. I know that having a partner to be with me in my family will help me feel more accepted. It has never passed my notice that I'm not the same as the rest of them. For one thing, I'm the only one with tattoos out of them all, including Travis. Other than the tattoos I did for Mom and Rose, the rest of them are clean slates. And I'm certainly the most artistic out of all of us. The rest of the family is much more practical, choosing stable careers that provide benefits and a decent paycheck. Sometimes I think even though Travis is in the band with me, it's more to keep an eye on me than because of a legitimate desire to make music.

When we were kids Travis would be out in the shop working on something with Dad and I would be in the house, or in the yard, or at the library, sketchbook out, drawing everything I could see or imagine. That's why I apprenticed at the tattoo shop. It was all about the art for me. And even now, with the volunteer work I do there, it's about art and giving back. I think Travis would have been just as happy joining my dad in his carpentry and woodworking business as he is being the bass player in Sleeping Dogs.

So Travis fits in, and I don't. But with a girlfriend like Becca, I'd be another Donovan with a family. And then I'd fit in too. Before that can happen, though, I need to make her my actual girlfriend, not my fake one.

I'm so lost in my thoughts, I don't even notice that we've arrived at Becca's place. Looks like she's taking me home after all.

"Ugh. Hold on one second," she says, placing a hand over mine to stop me from getting out of the car. "I have to turn my phone back on."

"Oh, sure. Okay." I don't know why I need to stay in the car for that, but it doesn't really matter. Whatever Becca needs from me, I will give her.

"I bet I have at least twenty voicemails," she says with a sardonic little smile. "No texts, though. At least not from my mom. Luckily, she hasn't figured out how to work texting yet."

Twenty voicemails?! That's insane. Why on earth would she leave more than one voicemail? Does she not trust Becca to get back to her when she's available?

"I canceled the date I was supposed to go on tonight to be with you and your family, and I'm sure she's already heard all about it. The dates she sets me up with are fans of telling on me when I don't live up to their expectations."

"Telling on you? Are they children? Or do they think you're a child?"

"I don't even know," she says. "I gave up understanding my mother years ago. Oh, I was wrong." She tilts her screen in my direction, showing me the total number of voicemails. "Twenty-seven. That's a new a record."

Twenty-seven fucking voicemails?! This woman must be insane.

She holds her phone down by her lap, allowing the voicemail to start. She pushes the delete button repeatedly, not even listening to the messages. I can hear her mother's voice through the speaker, but I can't make out any words. She sounds like she's screeching, though, so it's a safe bet that she's not impressed.

"I have to call her," Becca says, looking over at me. "Do you want to head in without me, or are you good to wait here for a few minutes?"

"I can wait for you." To be honest, I'm more than a little curious about what her mom is going to say. What can she say? Becca is a grown ass woman and if she wants to stand up the date her mother made for her, that's her choice.

"Hi, Mom," Becca says into the phone.

"*Where... how... embarrassing.*"

"Yes, Mom. I know. I'm sorry. I was with my boyfriend." She looks over at me when she says boyfriend, and my heart beats a little harder.

"*No... who? Where... him,*"

"Yes, I do, Mom. His name is Johnny. Alex introduced me a few months ago."

"*When... tell... you know... probably... for you.*"

"Okay, thanks Mom. Yeah, gotta go. Johnny's here now. Yes, at my place."

"*What... this... night?*"

"Okay, that's enough. It's none of your business. I'll talk to you later. Goodnight."

Becca pokes at the screen on her phone, hanging up on her mother. I would never hang up on my mother because she'd bring the wrath of all the gods down on me, but I can see why Becca would hang up on hers. I couldn't hear most of what she said, but what I heard didn't sound good at all.

"So," I say, getting Becca's attention. "Seems like that went well."

She laughs. "It wasn't as bad as I thought it would be. Come on. Let's go in."

We get out of the car and gather up Becca's camera and equipment before making our way to the entrance of the apartment.

Becca stops suddenly. Someone blocked the door open again.

"Fuck!" Becca yells. "These assholes keep doing this. Why can't they just use their buzzers? It's not that fucking hard.

It's the same as a fucking doorbell. I bet if they had their own houses, they wouldn't just prop the doors open with rocks." She kicks the rock out of the way, ensuring it rolls into the gutter. "If I didn't have my hands full, I'd throw that rock farther so they couldn't find it."

I juggle the bags I'm holding and go to the gutter, stooping to pick up the rock and tuck it under my arm. "We'll put it with the other one in your apartment," I explain. "That way, they'll never find it, and you'll have it to remember me by."

She smiles and holds the door open for me to slide through, then waits for it to click closed behind her before starting up the stairs. Following her up the stairs has quickly become one of my favorite things. I could watch her ass sway back and forth with each step until the end of time and never get bored.

It seems to me there might be a little more swing in her steps tonight, and I can't help but wonder if her newfound comfort with being touched has something to do with it. If it does, I hope to be touching her a lot more tonight.

27

One Night

Becca

I CAN'T BELIEVE I spoke to my mother like that. Then again, I also can't believe that I canceled that date with only an hour's notice, with a text message. But, hey. At least I canceled. I could have stood the guy up.

Not that it made much difference. I was right; the guy told on me as I thought he would.

What an asshole.

I also can't believe she accused me of making up a boyfriend. And then had the audacity to tell me I wasn't allowed to have him over at my apartment this late. And to ask what I planned to do while I had him here. Like I'm not a grown-ass woman capable of making my own decisions about who shares my bed.

"How about here?" Johnny asks, placing the door rock on the bookshelf near my kitchen table. "I think it really makes the color of these books pop."

And just like that, I feel better. Somehow, with one cute comment, he took the shadow Mom placed on this day and replaced it with sunshine. That's what it feels like when he's around. Like I'm finally able to feel the sun on my face.

Like I get to be happy.

And I'm going to hold onto it for as long as I can. This may be a fake relationship, but since it's the last one I'm ever going to get, I'm going to milk it for all it's worth.

That starts right now with throwing my one-night rule out the window.

"Johnny?"

He comes over to me. "Becca?"

"No one is going to come looking for us now." My breath comes faster. God, I want this man so badly. Now.

"Thank fuck," he says, grabbing me roughly by my hips and pulling me close. "I've been so fucking hard for you all day."

I slip my hands up into his hair and drag his lips down to meet mine. This is what I've been waiting for since that first night. Since I saw him on stage and I stopped fucking breathing when he winked at me. His tongue licks into my mouth, his teeth graze my lip, and I can't stop my hands from roaming all over his body like I want to touch him everywhere at once. His skin is fire under my fingers and I can't get enough.

"Please don't turn me away," I say, stopping our kiss to rip my shirt off. "I just about died that first night."

"Never," he murmurs against my mouth. "That was the hardest thing I've ever done. But I know now that I need to have you. If you'll let me."

I step away from him and slip my pants down my legs, kicking them off my feet. Standing in only my underwear now, I reach for his shirt, pushing it up and over his head.

Good lord, all that ink is making me dizzy. I need to spend hours mapping out all the art on his body, touching every line etched in his skin. I can't focus on any one spot for long, my eyes longing to drink in every inch of him, to memorize it all. I wonder if he'd let me photograph him? A body as beautiful as his needs to be photographed, cataloged in a museum somewhere, preserved for future generations to wonder at.

"You are so beautiful," I whisper, the words slipping from my mouth in awe. "How are you allowed to exist?"

He chuckles, stepping closer, sliding a bra strap down my left shoulder, kissing the spot it leaves bare. "If I'm beautiful, then you are radiant. Angelic. Pure perfection." He punctuates each compliment with a kiss down my arm. His hand cups my breast, his thumb brushing over a pebbled nipple, sending shocks of pleasure to my center.

I pop open the button on his jeans and slide the zipper down. My hands find his hips, slide under the waistband of his jeans, and push them down to the floor, leaving him standing in his boxer briefs, joining me in my near nudity.

Johnny bows his head to my chest, sucking a taut nipple into his mouth through the lace of my bra, teeth barely grazing the flesh. The moan that escapes me sounds inhuman, and I can't even care. How did I ever think I could live with having Johnny for only one night? We've barely begun, and he's already the best I've ever had. He teases and licks at my nipple with his tongue, his hand circling around my back, and with a flick of his fingers, he unhooks my bra. When he moves his head to allow it to fall to the floor, I see his eyes widen, his pupils darken, and he licks his lips in appreciation.

He likes what he sees.

"No, darling," he says, correcting the thought I must have unknowingly voiced, "I love what I see. You are more beautiful than I imagined. How could a man ever be satisfied having only one night with you?"

My breath catches in my throat, the feelings of inadequacy swelling and threatening to overwhelm me. When this fake relationship ends, it's going to destroy me. But I can't stop.

I grab his hand and drag him to my bedroom. Once inside, he slides his hands around my waist and walks me backward to my bed. I sit and slide my way to the middle of the bed, leaning back on my elbows for support. Johnny's hands slide into the top of his boxer briefs, inching the waistband down, exposing his skin sliver by sliver. The tattoos don't end. He has tattoos all the way down to the base of his cock.

"The rumors aren't true," he says with a small grin. "I could never bring myself to tattoo my dick."

"Pretty damn close," I force out, without looking away from where his dick is hidden by his underwear. "I can't imagine it would hurt much more than being tattooed right at the base like that."

"Oh, no. That's not why I never got it tattooed." He pushes his underwear to the floor. "This is why."

His dick is hard, standing at attention, and all along it are little silver balls, lined up in pairs of two.

Hold the fucking phone.

He's pierced. He has a Jacob's ladder piercing with six barbells, and there's room for several more if he ever felt so inclined.

Several. More.

"Holy fuck," I say, staring, while liquid heat melts my panties. "Ho-ly fu-uck."

He chuckles a little but looks nervous. "I can't tell if that's a good 'holy fuck' or a bad 'holy fuck'. It doesn't scare you, does it?"

"Honestly? A little." He winces. "But I'm so damn turned on right now. I once told Alex the only way I'd ever cheat on her was if some sexy, tattooed guy waved his huge, pierced cock in my face, and well, here you are." I gesture to his dick with its many piercings. "Did you really think you could show me that ladder and expect that I wouldn't want to climb it?"

He laughs. "Becca, you are the most amazing woman I've ever met." He kneels on the end of the bed, before crawling his body up over mine. "Not to mention the sexiest." He slides his tongue up the side of my neck, stopping with his mouth by my ear. "But if you think you're climbing this dick before I taste this pussy again, you're fucking crazy."

He slides back down my body, pulling my underwear along with him, throwing them aside once he's pulled them over my feet. He settles his body in between my legs, grabbing a pillow and sliding it under my ass.

"I've been thinking about this every day since we did our tattoos," he confesses, trailing kisses along my inner thighs. "I've had an intense craving for the taste of you and no way to satisfy it."

I'm a little nervous this time about how close his face is to the scars on my right leg. At the tattoo shop, everything happened so quickly that I had little time to worry. But now he's right near the scars that I hate the most. I've always thought they were more prominent that the scars anywhere else. Probably because they didn't receive as much aftercare as the ones that my mother believed were more visible, and therefore more important. But Johnny doesn't seem to notice, or if he notices, he doesn't mind. And that just makes me want him more.

He trails kisses closer to my center, to the blazing heat that I desperately need him to extinguish. A whimper escapes me, and I wiggle my hips to get closer to his lips.

"What's this now?" He asks, blowing softly on my clit, making me squirm. "Did you need something, babe?"

That fucker. He knows what I want.

"Tell me what you want, and I'll do it," he says. "Just say the word."

"Put your mouth on my pussy. Make me come." My voice comes out in a whine when I meant for it to sound frustrated. But it works.

Johnny flicks his tongue and licks my clit with tiny pulses. Electric sparks shoot through my body, my orgasm hovering just out of reach. He switches to long, slow strokes of his tongue, finishing each stroke with a little wiggle right over my clit, building me up higher and higher. When he slides an arm under me, hugging my ass and pulling me into his face, I nearly come undone. He's touching me, and I love it. I want more. But it's when he slides a finger in, and then two, finding that spot inside, stroking in time with his tongue, that my orgasm rips through me.

I ride through the waves of my climax, Johnny coaxing it from me, making it last longer, pulse stronger, and feel better than it ever has before. Light flashes behind my eyes as I arch off the bed.

My breath comes in ragged gasps as I writhe under his tongue. As the pulsing slows and then stops, so too does Johnny, his tongue strokes languid, his finger strokes mere caresses. When he finally pulls away, when I'm wrung out, exhausted, and don't think I can take anymore, he looks at me with lust-filled eyes.

"You look so beautiful when you come," he says with a grin. "I need to be inside you." All I can do is nod, the words stuck in my throat. "Here?" He leans over to my nightstand, opening the drawer.

Somewhere deep in my brain, I understand that he's looking for condoms, so I nod. He finds the box and puts it on top of the nightstand, pulling a condom out and ripping it open. I lift my head with what little energy I can muster and watch and he rolls it down over his cock, over those little barbells, and I draw in a quick breath. Fuck, that looks so hot. I can't believe this sexy man just gave me the best orgasm of my life and wants to do it again. I must've done something right in a past life.

Johnny crawls back over me, settling his big body in between my legs, his cock nudging at my entrance. He takes my lips in a soft kiss, and slowly, inch by inch, he fills me.

"Oh god," I whimper as I adjust to his girth.

"Relax, baby," he whispers. "Just breathe."

I didn't even notice I was holding my breath, so I exhale and concentrate on relaxing. He groans obscenely as he slides all the way in. He pumps his hips, and because I'm still on the pillow, his pubic bone rubs against my clit with every thrust. My orgasm roars back into existence, crashing into me with no warning, and I clamp down on Johnny's dick with a gasp.

"Oh god, you feel so good," he groans in my ear. "So fucking hot and wet. I can still taste you on my tongue and the way you're squeezing my dick..." He slides into me, and I feel the pulsing of my walls around his dick. "I don't know how long I'm going to last, babe."

"Oh, fuck, Johnny," I moan. "Fuck. Don't stop."

He rolls his hips, pushing into me deeply, filling me, stretching me. He's shaking with the effort of holding himself back. My second orgasm wanes but doesn't stop completely.

"Fuck me," I whisper, grabbing his hair by the handful and thrusting my hips up. "Harder, Johnny. Fuck me harder."

That's all the permission he needs. He pulls back and slams into me, harder and deeper than before, forcing a scream out of me. Again he pulls back, and again he slams into me. Again, and again, and again. I feel the tension building, the tightening in my belly, the tingling in my clit, and then another orgasm is crashing over me, through me, surrounding me, and I'm screaming Johnny's name and he's screaming mine, and I'm no longer sure if that's my pulsing orgasm I feel or if that's Johnny coming inside me I feel. Again and again, he thrusts, slowing to pump us both through the last of our orgasms until we're both sweaty, panting messes.

He rolls to the side and slides the pillow out from under me, throwing it to the floor. "We should go pillow shopping tomorrow," he says, disposing of the condom in the wastebasket by the bed. "We've made a real mess of that one."

A hysterical laugh bursts out of me, and I roll to face Johnny. He pulls me close, wrapping his arms around me and tucking me into his chest. He kisses my head and squeezes me tightly while we both chuckle, our tired bodies relaxing into each other.

The last thing I remember thinking before I fall asleep is, *one night could never be enough.*

28

A Good Sign

Johnny

DID THAT ACTUALLY JUST happen?

Becca is still asleep on my chest after the best night of my life and I am in so much trouble. There's no way it won't destroy me if I ever have to let her go. She trusted me enough last night to let me in, finally, and now I'm laying here with my arms wrapped around her.

More than the sex, it's her trusting me enough to touch her that's making me realize how much I feel for her.

And I don't think I can ever let go.

So much for not letting my feelings get involved. But as long as I can keep her from finding out, everything should turn out fine.

How long can I lie here without my bladder exploding? It's been about an hour since I woke with the need to take a piss, but I couldn't bear to move, so I've been trying to deny the urge. But an hour is a long time to hold it and I'm now faced with the choice to either get up and take care of it or stay here and piss myself.

Clearly I can't choose to piss myself, but just as I'm about to get up and take care of it, Becca stirs. No, wait. She doesn't stir. She jumps out of bed and heads to the door.

"Oh my god, why did I wait so long?" she says as she shuffles along with tiny steps, still completely naked. "I have to pee so bad."

I stifle a laugh and look away. She looks so sexy as she hustles away that my dick gets hard. I really need to be able to piss without difficulty, and pissing with a hard-on is anything but easy.

Think unsexy thoughts, think unsexy thoughts, think unsexy thoughts. Ryder's Gran immediately comes to mind. She's the craziest little old lady you'll ever meet, and her best friend Gladys is a geriatric lady horn dog. Picturing her coming on to Ryder, trying to make him show her his dick, is enough to destroy my burgeoning erection.

For now.

I hop out of bed and pull on my boxer briefs, an extra layer of protection against denying my need to piss and just falling into bed with Becca again as soon as she reappears. But as soon as I take care of my bladder, that's exactly what I plan on doing.

Becca comes back wearing a silky little robe, and it's almost worse than watching her walk away naked. It skims over her skin, accentuating rather than hiding her curves, and comes to a stop just below her ass. My dick tries to get up to its old tricks.

"Do you wan—"

"Be right back." I yelp, running for the bathroom. Pissing takes forever, relief washing over me like I'd waited days, instead of hours. When I'm done, I wash up, use her toothpaste to brush my teeth with my finger, and head back to the bedroom. But Becca isn't in there anymore.

Without getting dressed, I wander out to the living room, finally finding Becca in the kitchen, getting coffee ready. Walking up behind her, I wrap my arms around her waist, slowly so she has plenty of time to adjust to my touch, and rain kisses down the side of her face and neck. She flinches slightly when I get to her neck.

"You okay?" I pull away and ask. "Is it okay if I do that? I should have asked first. That was stupid of me. I'm sorry."

She spins around and surprises me by wrapping her arms around my waist, burying her face against my chest. I feel her inhale deeply like she's smelling me, and I have to smile. If she knew how many times I've wanted to do the same thing to her, she'd be shocked.

"No, it's okay. You surprised me is all. And that was my bad side. I'm still not used to being touched, especially being touched there. But I... I think I like it when you touch me."

A rush of anger rises in me. "You never told me if that Milo asshole is still around."

She laughs. "He's old news." She waves her hand as though she's waving him away. "So listen," she says, changing the subject. "I've already decided I need more than one night with you."

I pull away and look into her eyes to see that really she means it. She wants more than one night with me. There's something else there that she's still not telling me, but she is telling the truth about wanting more. My dick twitches in response, getting ready for another round.

"Please tell me that includes mornings, too," I tilt her head up, skimming her lips with mine, breathing a soft kiss to her mouth. "Because I don't want to leave yet."

She rises on her tiptoes, wrapping her arms around my neck, fusing her mouth with mine. Looks like she doesn't want me to leave yet either. I slide my arms down her back, over her luscious, firm, *naked* ass, and grip her thighs, lifting her up and directing her legs around my waist.

"Fuck yes," I groan into her mouth, as she locks her ankles behind me. "Hold on tight. I'm taking you back to bed. I haven't had enough of you yet."

I take her down the hallway, setting her on her feet in her bedroom. Instead of getting on the bed like I assume she's going to, Becca drops to her knees in front of me. She smirks up at me, reminding me of when I saw her for the first time at the show, and hooks her fingers in the waistband of my underwear. My dick twitches.

"Anything I should know?" She's asking about my piercings.

"Just do whatever feels comfortable for you," I choke out.

She smiles up at me again before wrapping her hand around the base of my dick and I nearly come from the contact. She licks her lips, her pink tongue poking out, and then she leans forward slightly and licks a trail from the base to the tip of my dick, right up the center of the barbells, giving a little flick at the head, and sending a jolt straight through my entire body. This already feels too good. I'm about to blow and all she's done is lick me. She keeps on that way, licking me base to tip, base to tip, cupping and rolling my balls in one small hand, gripping my dick with the other. She works me into a frenzy. My balls tighten, as does the base of my spine, and I know I'm about to come.

"Baby," I groan. "You gotta stop."

She lets me go and sits back on her heels, looking up at me with a pout.

"Robe off. Get on the bed," I say through gritted teeth. "And grab a condom." I close my eyes and take deep breaths, willing myself to calm down, to step back from being on the verge of coming. Once I've calmed myself, I open my eyes.

Becca's on the bed like I instructed, naked, condom package on her belly, staring at me with so much heat in her eyes I'm lucky I don't combust. It's then I know she wants me as much as I want her. No matter what she's said about one night only, or not having boyfriends.

She. Wants. Me.

I crawl over her on the bed, lowering my body gently, kissing her. I lick and suck her lips, her neck, her breasts. Becca opens the condom and pushes me back so she can roll it on me, then pulls me down and lines me up with her entrance. She's slick and hot, and so ready for me. I slide inside her with one long thrust, both of us releasing moans as I bottom out deep inside her. I roll my hips, pulling out slightly before sliding back in, pushing against her clit with my body.

"That feels so good," Becca whispers in my ear. "Keep going."

I continue to roll my hips, Becca's hands on my ass pulling me in and dictating the pace. I feel her tightening around me, her breaths coming faster, and she rocks her hips more fervently.

"Right there," she moans, "Don't stop. Yes, Johnny. Faster."

I thrust faster, still rubbing against her until I feel her spasming around me, milking me, urging me to come. I pull out quickly and flip her over onto her stomach.

"Ass up, babe," I growl, grabbing a pillow and shoving it under her hips. *I really do need to buy her more pillows.* She scrambles to get her knees under her, arching her back and sticking her ass out, putting herself on display for me. I can't help myself. I bend over and give her a lick, shoving my tongue in her pussy before kneeling behind her.

"Fuck. You taste so good, Becca." I run my hands up the backs of her thighs, grabbing her ass and spreading her wide with my thumbs. "Everything about you is perfect. This ass, this pussy," I slide the tip of my dick through her folds. "The way you look, the way you taste. I can't get enough of you."

I rest my dick at her entrance, teasing her, and myself, with tiny little pulse-like thrusts, not quite entering, until she slams herself backward, impaling herself on my cock. Her pussy is still fluttering with aftershocks from her orgasm, and I lose all control. I thrust into her wet heat again and again, harder, faster, until her moans and mine are mingling in the air.

"Yes, Johnny," she screams, as her pussy clamps down on me, shocking my orgasm from me, freezing me in place. The fluttering of her orgasm prolongs mine as we sit there, frozen together, both of us only moving where we're connected, until finally, we fall apart at the same time, exhausted, spent, thoroughly wrung out.

I take care of the condom and roll over, pulling her to me, her back to my front, and I kiss her shoulder. When she flinches, I kiss her shoulder again. I leave a trail of kisses from her neck all the way down to her wrist, before rolling her to face me and kissing her deeply. I cup her face in my hand and look into her eyes.

"You don't have a bad side, Becca. You're perfect everywhere."

Her eyes get shiny, but before she can cry, she buries her face in my chest. I think I hear her whisper, *I can't get enough of you either,* but it's probably just a dream.

When I wake up a short time later, Becca is already out of bed. A look at the alarm clock on the nightstand tells me if I don't get moving, I'm going to miss my tattoo appointment. My clothes are laid out on the end of the bed. Becca must've collected them from the living room when she woke. I hear more than one voice coming from outside the bedroom, so I figure I should probably pull on my clothes before I leave the room.

I open the bedroom door quietly, not wanting to interrupt Becca's conversation. I hear her voice carry down the hall, and she's obviously upset.

"I don't care what you think, Mom. Johnny is my boyfriend. I won't go on any more dates."

"Oh, Rebecca. You're being ridiculous. Of course you will. Just this last one. Next Friday at Club Redemption. You'll meet Chris, have a drink, have a dance, and who knows? Maybe you'll like him more than this Johnny character, and then you can let him off the hook."

What the fuck? This woman is really something else. Showing up at Becca's place in the morning to force her into going on a date she doesn't want? What a bitch. And what does she mean by "let me off of the hook"? I'm exactly where I want to be.

I choose that moment to come out into the living room, immediately walking up to Becca, pulling her into my arms, and kissing her soundly. "Morning, babe. I missed you just now when I woke up alone. You should have woken me when you got up." I turn to face her mother, holding out my hand. "Hello, I'm Johnny, Becca's boyfriend. You must be her mom. She's an amazing, beautiful woman. You must be so proud."

She shakes my hand, giving me a look like she thinks I'll get her white suit dirty, or mess up her manicure. "Yes, I'm Rebecca. I'm sure you've heard all about me." She gives Becca a look that I can't define, but whatever it means, I know I don't like it. Also, did she just say her name is Rebecca? So she named Becca after herself?

"Actually, I've heard very little." I turn to Becca, dismissing her mother by turning my back. "I have a tattoo appointment, babe. Will I see you later?"

"Oh, yeah. Sure. Of course," she says, sounding a little flustered.

"Great. I'll text you when I'm done." I kiss her again, wrapping my arms around her, and she hugs me back. Her mother makes a gasping noise behind me somewhere, and I take that to be a good sign. If she's surprised to see Becca hugging me, maybe she'll believe this relationship is real and back off and leave Becca alone.

I let go of Becca and head straight for the door. When I have it open, I turn to look at Becca one more time. "Love you, babe. See you later," I say, and then I close the door.

I chuckle to myself as I walk down the hallway.

That was an impactful exit, but now I have another problem. Becca drove last night. I need to find a ride to the shop. Oh well. The look on her face when I said 'love you' was worth it. She smiled. I'll take that as a good sign, too.

Things are looking up.

29

Do You Dara Mia Two?

Becca

THE BIG DUMB GRIN is still on my face when I turn back to look at my mom.

"You can't believe he really means that, do you?" she scoffs. "I mean, look at him. He's a very good-looking man, dear. He should be with someone who is equally good-looking, don't you think? It would be quite embarrassing for him to be with someone who isn't on his level."

I sigh. Of course, seeing me with Johnny once wouldn't be enough for her. I knew this would happen, but it still stings. It probably hurts more because he just said he loved me.

Does he love me?

No, of course not. That was just part of the act. Wasn't it?

But my mom's right. I'm not on his level. He's being a good friend. A good friend with great benefits, but still just a friend.

The way he turned his back on my mother and acted like I was the only person in the room. Like I was important. Well, let's just say it was difficult for me to stop myself from dragging him off to the bedroom again.

I felt beautiful this morning.

Now? Not so much.

Mom has that effect on me.

"You should consider one of the more appropriate men I've chosen for you, Rebecca. Any of them would be a far more suitable match for you. Don't hold on to a man who deserves more just because you're selfish." She walks to the door. "Next Friday. Eight o'clock at Club Redemption. Chris will meet you outside." And with that, she opens the door and leaves.

My breath escapes me in a rush.

That bitch!

She might be right, and Johnny does deserve better than me, but she's still my mother. She shouldn't get such joy from saying so. Or be saying it at all.

I find my phone on the counter and open my contacts. I've been meaning to call Uncle Silas for a while. I just need to hear his voice right now, to help get my mother's voice out of my head.

On the third ring, Uncle Silas answers.

"Becca, sweetheart. It's so nice to hear from you, darling. How are you?"

Uncle Silas' voice is a little strained, but it soothes me instantly.

"Uncle Silas. I've missed you so much. When are you going to move back to Westborough?"

"Come on now, darling. Do you really think I could give up the glitz and glamor of Las Vegas to come back and live in boring old Westborough? Besides, Uncle Patrick's show is here. I couldn't ask him to leave the Dara Mia Two Revue behind."

Not only is Uncle Patrick Uncle Silas' husband, he is an accomplished drag performer who goes by the name Dara Mia.

The story goes that when Uncle Patrick was in film school, a local drag club had an amateur night with a cash prize, and one of his friends said he should do it. Uncle Patrick said he'd do it, but only if 'you dare me' to. And that's how the Dara Mia character was born. He won the cash prize at amateur night and was invited to be part of the regular show at the drag club.

That's where he met Uncle Silas. He went in with a bunch of friends and it was love at first sight. They've been together ever since.

Years later, when Uncle Patrick was invited to Vegas to head-line his own show at a small club, he named it the Dara Mia Two Revue. I'd never begrudge his success, but it's been bittersweet because that's what forced them to move away in the first place.

"Ugh, I know. I just miss you both so much. And it's been too long since I've seen you."

"Tell me about it, honey. When can you make it out for a visit? I'll bet you need a break from your mom, don't you? Come to Vegas and stay with us for a while."

"I'd love to, Uncle Silas, but there's a lot going on right now. Mom's been trying to set me up with a guy. You'd die if you saw the guys she's picking out for me. I don't know where she finds them, but she needs to put them back."

"She's always had... interesting taste in men. Worse than that, though, is how she's always had such a skewed vision of you. You are an amazing woman, darling. You deserve a man who worships the ground you walk on, one who would give you the world. Like me and your Uncle Patrick, but, you know, less gay." He laughs, but it turns into a cough.

"Not feeling well? It's probably all that desert air," I tell him. "You should consider a more temperate region. Like maybe... Westborough?"

"Hilarious. It's just a little cold. Nothing to get upset and relo-cate over."

"Damn, I thought I had you that time." I laugh. "It's so nice to hear your voice. It's been a rough day."

"Tell me all about it, darling."

So, over the course of the next couple of hours, I tell Uncle Silas everything. Including what's happening with Johnny and my newly confused feelings about him. Well, everything aside from my new tattoo. Uncle Silas is the one who did all my other tattoos, and I think he's a little protective of me in that regard. He probably wouldn't like to hear that I allowed Johnny to tattoo me without having him properly vetted. By him and Uncle Patrick, of course.

"Well, that all sounds rather exhausting, Becca. Your mother sure has a way of turning your world on its ear, doesn't she? But this Johnny, he sounds nice. Are you sure he's just a fake boyfriend?"

And that's the real question, isn't it? Last night and this morning sure felt real, but was it really?

"I don't know, Uncle Silas. I'm not even sure I want him to be a real boyfriend. You remember what happened with Milo. I couldn't bear to have Johnny run from me when he realizes I'm not good enough for him."

"First off, you are more than good enough for any man. Johnny would be lucky to have you. And second, my nephew sure was a little dickhead, wasn't he? I've never regretted for a minute choosing you over him."

Uncle Silas might think I'm good enough for Johnny, but he doesn't know the reality. He's dated actresses and supermodels. I'm not exactly in the same league as them. Besides, it wouldn't look good for him to be with someone like me. He's a celebrity and I'm a would-be wedding photographer. What would people say?

"Thanks, I'm glad you chose me too. You're like the father and mother I never had all rolled into one handsome package."

"Oh, honey. If I'd ever had a child, I'd have wanted her to be just like you."

After a few more minutes of small talk, and some updates on the Dara Mia show, we say our goodbyes, with a promise from me that I'll visit soon.

Talking to Uncle Silas always makes me feel better. I've got some motivation now and after a quick brainstorming session, I post some new family photoshoot availabilities on my website. I haven't had any more cancelations for weddings I had booked, so that's good news. After taking a few minutes to update my social media, I close up my laptop and take myself to the shower.

It's Sunday, and that means family dinner at Alex and Connor's place. I know Johnny said he'd text me when he finishes his appointment, but I think that was just for show because my mom was here. Either way, I'm pretty sure I'll see him, so I take a little extra time with my hair and makeup today.

After my shower, I choose ripped-up denim shorts and a tank to wear. It's warm out today and I really want to get some use out of Alex's pool, so I get a bag and pack a bikini that I've never been brave enough to wear in public. It's not that revealing, but I've always hated having people look at me. I'm always afraid someone from my old high school will recognize me and call me Freddy and I'll freak out. But I should be safe enough at Alex and Connor's place. Plus, Johnny made me feel so beautiful last night, and this morning, that I have just enough extra confidence to try it.

I pull out my phone to text Alex about my swimming plans and I see that I have a message from Johnny.

Johnny- I'm all done now. Did your mom stay long?

I look at the time. It's only been a few hours since Johnny left and mom left right after he did.

Becca- No. She pretty much followed you out the door.

Johnny- Can I come by? Are you going to dinner at Connor and Alex's?

Becca- Yes, and yes. I want to go over early to swim, though.

Johnny- Perfect. I'll pick you up and we can go over now. I thought I'd help with cooking tonight. Alex is getting frustrated that Connor doesn't know his way around the kitchen.

Becca- See you soon.

An extra surge of bravery hits me and I unpack my bikini, taking it to my room and putting it on underneath my clothes. I'm going in that pool today if it kills me. Okay, maybe that's a little extreme, but I am going to get in the water. Alex is my best friend, and that means Connor and the rest of them are going to be in my life, too. I'm sure they have better things to do than stare at me.

At least, I hope they do.

I run around packing up the essentials for an afternoon of fun in the sun, namely sunblock. My skin is so fair that looking out the window can give me a sunburn if I'm not careful, so I always make sure to have SPF forty or higher with me. I'm busy slathering myself in cream when there's a knock at the door.

"It's me," Johnny calls through the door and I panic while trying to pull my shirt back on, somehow getting it wrapped around me too tightly, and all twisted up.

I'm stuck half in and half out of my tank when I let him in.

"This is an interesting look," he says with a laugh. "I like it."

"Yeah, yeah," I mutter, spinning in a circle like a dog chasing its tail. "Don't just stand there and laugh at me, help me."

He steps toward me, but I'm still spinning in a circle, one arm tightly strapped to my body and the other stuck at my waist, both hands flapping uselessly as I try to get myself free.

"Hold still if you want me to help," he says, still laughing. He grabs the hand near my waist, stopping my futile spins. "One sec."

Once I've stopped spinning around, Johnny makes quick work of fixing my problem.

"There. You're free."

"Thank you," I say, straightening my shirt. "I was putting my sunblock on when you knocked and I somehow got myself all tangled up when I tried to put my shirt on too quickly."

"Aww, babe. You know you don't need to get all dressed up for me. I think you look amazing in whatever you wear."

Hearing him call me babe reminds me of our little arrangement, sending a flutter of excitement through my belly. We've already set up some ground rules, like not letting feelings get involved, making sure our friendship remains intact, and not having sex.

So what if we've already broken a couple of rules? As long as I hold firm on not letting my feelings get involved, I should make it out of this situation unscathed.

At least, I hope I do.

Increased Affection

Johnny

BECCA WALKED INTO THE kitchen and, with barely a hello to anyone, she grabbed Alex and pulled her straight out the back door.

I shake my head and laugh as the door closes behind them.

"What was that all about?" Connor asks.

"She has her heart set on getting into the pool," I say, helping myself to a beer from the fridge. Becca and I should have stopped to pick up something a little tastier than this, but a couple of mass-produced domestic beers won't hurt me. "She doesn't like to show too much skin in public, so she's pretty excited you have a private pool."

Connor raises an eyebrow at me. "Oh? You know all about Becca now?"

"I wouldn't say that," I dodge the question with a half-truth. "But we have been hanging out a lot. Just as friends, though."

"Mm-hmm, okay," he says in his sassiest voice.

"Fuck off," I laugh.

"Yeah, yeah," he says. "Let's get out there. We don't need to be in here right now."

I look around, noticing for the first time that we're the only people in the house. "What about dinner? I thought I was cooking?"

"Not necessary, man. Alex got her cast off. But we're ordering pizza from Tino's tonight, anyway. I need to know if he still thinks I'm a sketchy fuck."

I snort out a laugh. "I think you're shit out of luck on that front, C. You wandered around their neighborhood, asking strangers about Alex when you were still trying to track her down after the last show. You will forever be a sketchy fuck to that guy. Just be happy he's still willing to make our pizzas."

We walk out onto the deck that leads down to the pool.

"Yeah, I haven't tested that theory yet. I never give them my name when we order."

I shake my head and laugh. "You're an idiot. You know that, right?"

Connor releases a breath and rubs his hand down his face. "Yeah, man. I know."

We stop at the railing and look out at the pool. It looks like it's a full-on party already. The lounge chairs are full, and there are people splashing in the pool. I can see Becca's head sticking up out of the water, a huge grin on her face as she throws a ball to Alex on the other side of the pool.

"Hey, I forgot to ask you, how did the tattoo go today?"

"Great," I say. "Lana is an awesome client. That woman's pain tolerance is next level. We have two or three more appointments to go, and then she'll be done."

"That's great, man. You do good work."

"You should check out the piece I did on Becca's leg a while back. It's the horror villain collage on her left leg."

The look of shock on Connor's face is priceless. "She let you touch her? Alex says she hates to be touched and there are very few people she even allows to be close to her. You think she'll change her one-night rule for you?"

I know she's changed her one-night rule for me, but whether it's only for the duration of our fake relationship remains to be seen. I'm going to enjoy every minute either way. My plan is to boyfriend her so good that she begs me to never stop.

"Well, I guess I'm one of those few people now. It might be because I let her tattoo me first. Allowing someone to stab you repeatedly with a needle usually involves reciprocal trust of some sort." I laugh at Connor's face when I say Becca tattooed me. It's surprise and disgust and disbelief had a baby and the result is his facial expression.

"You let her tattoo you? Where? How bad is it? Did she do more damage than necessary? Is it horrible? I need to see this."

I pull down the side of my trunks and show him the little camera.

"Hey, that's not bad. She has a steady hand."

"I know. I was surprised. She wouldn't tell me what she was doing, and she tattooed it freehand. I was expecting maybe an X or something like that."

Connor steps toward the stairs down to the main level, taking us toward the pool where everyone else is. The pool itself is about halfway between the main house and the pool house, with a large concrete deck surrounding it. If it were shaped like a rectangle, you could almost mistake it for a community pool. Its oblong shape, with a small offset section for a hot tub, coupled with the intricate landscaping surrounding it, makes it easy to tell it's a recreational pool belonging to someone with a lot of money.

I still don't know why Connor has this pool. He rarely uses it. I suppose it's one of those things that he thought he should have once he 'made it'.

And I live in a loft with my brother. Go figure.

"Hey, you guys coming in?" Becca looks up at me from the side of the pool, her head barely above the water.

I kick off my shoes and reach back, pulling my shirt over my head. "You don't need to ask me twice," I say, running to the edge of the pool, jumping over Becca's head, and splashing everyone in the vicinity with my flawlessly executed cannonball.

"Hey!" Becca laughs. "No splashing."

"What?! No splashing? That's a terrible rule. What is a pool for, if not for splashing?" I push a small wave of water toward her. It's barely even worthy of being called a splash.

"A pool is for this," she says, before ducking down and launching herself up out of the water, coming down on me at an angle and pushing my head under the surface.

For an only child, she's not so bad at this playing in the pool thing. Growing up, every trip to the pool for me was a fight for my life. With five girls versus two boys, Travis and I rarely came out on top of those interactions. The only reason we finally started winning was because, as they got older, our sisters started being more interested in laying on beach towels and getting tans than in playing in the pool with their siblings. One by one, the odds grew in our favor until one day it was just to two of us left to fight each other.

It looks like Becca has no interest in tanning, though, and I'm currently having my ass handed to me. I've never loved nearly drowning more. She's not the strongest swimmer, but what she lacks in skill she makes up for with enthusiasm.

"Okay, time out. Hold on," I splutter, wiping water from my eyes. "Why are you so vicious?" I laugh as she splashes me again.

"I'm not vicious. You just need to know who's in charge around here. Plus, it's been so long since I've been in a pool that I can't help myself. I love the water."

"Hmm," I say, swimming toward her. "Maybe you're part mermaid. I'll check." I drop under the water directly in front of her and look at her legs. God, she looks good in this bikini. It's black, with little boxer bottoms and a short top that's not quite a string top, but almost. Sexy and functional. Made for fighting in the water, really. I pop up out of the water, splashing Becca as I do. "Nope, you still have human legs. I don't think you're part mermaid."

I swim to the side of the pool and hoist myself out of the water. Becca swims up behind me and hoists herself up as well, following me to one of the lounge chairs set up under a big pergola with a sunshade. She picks up the sunscreen that she packed and hesitates before taking a deep breath and holding it out to me.

"Umm, can you do my back? I forgot to bring the applicator I normally use." She looks down, still holding the sunscreen out.

Holy shit. This is a big deal. She's asking me to touch her when we're not naked. Whoa. "Are you sure you want me to do it? I can get Alex for you if it makes you more comfortable." I take the sunscreen from her hand and sit on a chair beside her.

She looks at me, eyes glistening with unshed tears. "I haven't told her about my accident. She still doesn't know what the tattoos cover. I'm not ready yet."

Shit, that's right. She had said something about not having told anyone but me. I don't understand why an accident would be so hard to tell someone about, especially your best friend. It must be a heavy burden to carry all alone.

"Well then, I would love to help you. Let me slide in behind you and I'll get you taken care of, okay?" I motion for her to move forward on the lounge chair, which gives me room to sit right behind her.

It was only this morning that I woke up with her in my arms, but what I wouldn't give to have her lean against me right now so I could wrap my arms around her again. But we've broken enough of our rules already. We can't just keep breaking them, or one of us is going to get hurt. And I think keeping our fake relationship secret from our friends is a good idea. It will be easier to go back to normal after this is all over if no one else knows about it.

"Let me know if you get too uncomfortable," I say. I squeeze a generous amount of sunscreen into my hands and rub them together to warm it up. There's nothing worse than the shock of cold sunscreen on sun-warmed skin. "You ready?"

Becca takes a deep, shuddering breath. "Yes," she says. "Go ahead."

I work the sunscreen over her back first, slowly rubbing it in, ensuring she's fully covered. The texture of her skin under the tattoos is bumpy, and if I didn't know she'd been burned as a child, I'd probably assume the scarring was from bad tattooing. But I don't know if I would think that, because the tattooing is clearly good work.

I finally get a good look at her back tattoos. She has large cabbage roses stretching from her left shoulder to her right, and then all the way down her side, over her hip, extending down the back and outer edge of her right thigh. The pinks and greens are so vibrant, the tattoo looks almost fresh. Whoever did this does beautiful work.

"Do you want me to get your arms and shoulders too?" I know this is one of her least favorite spots to be touched, so I won't be offended if she doesn't want me to. "Or would you prefer to do that yourself?"

"You can... Can you do it? Please?"

"I would love to." I attempt to slow my breathing so she can't tell how excited I am that she's letting me do this. The last thing she needs is me breathing heavily all over her back like a creep.

I dispense more sunscreen into my hands, warming it again before I rub it on her arms. While I'm working on her right arm, I look and see Alex and Connor both staring at us, mouths hanging open, eyes wide. I'm sure Alex is wondering how I can touch Becca like this without her freaking out about it. I'm a little curious myself. But mostly I'm thrilled that she trusts me. It's a delicate balance.

I know we've had sex, and slept together, but allowing me to touch her like this, without the distraction of nudity and impending orgasms, shows how much trust she has in me. Now if I can just translate the trust she has in me touching her body, to trusting me with her heart, this fake relationship might not have to be so fake after all.

31

Pool Party

Becca

"WELL, WELL, WELL," ALEX says. "What's going on over here?"

I'm sitting in a lounge chair with Johnny behind me, rubbing lotion on my arms, when Alex and Connor walk over to join us. I'm sure Alex is in a state of shock over this because she's never seen me allow anyone to touch me this much, but she's fixed a smile firmly on her face. She's the one who bought me the lotion applicator I normally use after she witnessed my old application method of using a long strip of plastic wrap covered in lotion and rubbing it over my back like one would normally use a towel to dry off.

"Nothing," I say, gathering the courage to look at her. "I forgot my applicator and since I trusted Johnny enough to tattoo me, I figured he might be my best shot at getting sunscreen on without me freaking out about being touched."

"Oh, yeah. That makes sense, I gue—Wait! Johnny tattooed you? Did I know about this? Where I have been?"

Connor coughs meaningfully while pretending to look off into the distance, and Johnny and I burst into laughter.

"Oh," Alex says, her cheeks flaming. "Never mind."

"Connor, come grab a drink with me," Johnny says, sliding out from behind me. "It sounds like Alex and Becca have some catching up to do."

Connor nods before giving Alex a kiss bordering on inappropriate for public consumption. I was just about to yell at them to get a room before they separated, and Connor and Johnny left in search of drinks.

"Alright, spill," Alex says the second the guys are out of earshot. "And let me have a look at the tattoo while you're at it."

Alex waits for me to stretch out my left leg for her inspection. I love that even though she just watched Johnny rub lotion all over me, she doesn't assume everything is just fine for her to grab and touch me without express permission. She's hugged me hundreds of times, but she's always waited for my okay before she does.

"Oh, wow. Becca, that's fantastic." She gets closer to my leg to look at Johnny's work. "Johnny did this? He bakes the best cookies *and* does amazing tattoos?" She shakes her head in disbelief. "Didn't he think he should maybe leave some talent for the rest of us?"

"It really is great, isn't it? When he showed me the different designs he'd drawn up for me, I knew right away that it had to be this one. He said he thought of it when he saw my Freddy tattoo for the first time."

"When did he see your Freddy tattoo? You mean the one on your right thigh, right? When could he possibly have had the opportunity to see it? Hmmm?" Alex smirks at me, and with a waggle of her eyebrows adds, "I didn't realize you were seeing so *much* of each other that your Freddy tattoo would be on display."

I cover my face with my hands. "Ugh, I wasn't going to tell you."

"Well, now you have to tell me. I can't believe you're keeping secrets from me." Alex laughs. "Now tell me why you guys came here together today."

I huff out a breath. "Fine. But I don't want any shit from you about this, okay?"

Alex marks an X over her heart with her finger. "Promise."

"Remember the day you moved in here? When you found out you were working for Connor and you called and begged me to come for dinner?"

"Yeah," she says, confused. "You finally agreed to come when I said I was making lasagna. You love my lasagna. No one can turn down fresh noodles."

"Right. That's right. And I do love your lasagna. So much. But that's not really why I came that night."

I hear her sharp intake of breath. "You didn't come for my lasagna? I think I'm offended," she says in mock outrage. "I thought I knew you."

"Haha, very funny. No need to be so dramatic." I look around to see if anyone is close enough to hear me. "The night of the show, Johnny looked at me from the stage and I felt something. I wanted to see if we could make anything of it. So I invited him over after that first dinner."

Alex's eyes widen, and she shakes her finger at me. "You slept with him! I knew it. You gave him your one night, and *that's* how he saw Freddy."

"No, that's not what happened. He wanted more than one night, so we decided to just be friends. But I was wearing my pajama shorts when he came by, so he saw Freddy. He said he came up with the idea for this new tattoo as soon as he saw it."

"That's still pretty amazing. But it doesn't quite explain why you're so comfortable with him touching you."

"I think maybe it's time I tell you why I dislike being touched in the first place. So you know where I'm coming from."

After making room for Alex to sit down beside me, I get into the story. I spend the next few minutes filling Alex in on the details of my accident, my scars, what Milo did to me, and how I came to get my first tattoo. Even though I tell her all of that, I still don't say anything about my mom blaming me for my dad leaving, or for how disgusted she's been with me since the accident. That's something I keep locked away. If I think about it too much, it gets overwhelming.

As a proper best friend should, she becomes immediately outraged on my behalf.

"That dirty fucker. How dare he do that to you? Why didn't you tell me this when we were in school? I would have destroyed him. I would have brought him to Pops' gym and had the fighters there give him some 'training'." She's pacing the length of my lounge chair now, indignation rolling off her in waves. "We need to find that prick. Did he stay here after school? I know! I'm going to add him on Facebook. I'll befriend him, make him trust me, and then BAM! I'll meet him in a parking lot with my baseball bat."

I can't help but laugh, the chuckles bubbling out of me as she continues to rant.

"And then I'll take some unflattering pictures of him and post them online. Do you know where we can get a sheep? Not to keep or anything, just to take pictures with."

She spins in a circle, finally spotting Connor on the other side of the pool. "Connor," she yells. "Where's my phone? I need to add some asshole on Facebook."

Connor comes over to our side of the pool and produces Alex's phone from the pocket of his shorts. "Why are you adding assholes on Facebook?"

"Becca needs revenge," she says, pulling up the app on starting her search. "Wait. What's his last name again?"

"Yeah," I drawl. "I don't think I should tell you that. We need to try to keep you out of jail."

She flips me off and continues searching. "Never mind, I'll figure it out." She starts pacing again, mumbling to herself. "Stevens? No. Ericson? No, not even close."

"What's happening now?" Johnny comes back and holds out a beer to me. "It's not good, but it's cold."

"Thanks," I say, twisting the top off and taking a long drink. "I told Alex about Freddy and she's worked herself into a frenzy."

"Fun." Johnny sits beside me on the lounge chair, his still shirtless body giving off heat from when he was standing in the sun. I want to wrap my arms around him and soak it in. "Who doesn't love a good frenzy?"

"She's trying to track down Milo so she can meet him in a parking lot with her baseball bat." I don't think she remembers that the baseball bat in question is actually mine, not that she'd let that stop her. She'd buy a dozen new ones and test them all out. On Milo.

"Who's Freddy?" Connor asks. He's taking Alex's freak-out in stride. She's been trying to teach him to cook these last couple of months and she tends to get frustrated easily when people don't know what they're doing in the kitchen, so he's used to this. "I thought she was looking for some guy named Milo?"

"Freddy is my tattoo," I say, guzzling back the rest of my beer. Johnny's right, it is not good. Not at all. "Milo was the idiot who gave me the nickname when we were in high school. He tricked me into taking off my shirt so he could take a picture to show everyone in school what was under the clothes I wore. What he got was a picture of scars from a childhood injury. He got the entire school to start calling me Freddy Krueger after that."

Huh. That was a lot easier to tell than when I first told Johnny, or even when I just told Alex a few minutes ago. Weird.

"Freddy was the tattoo Becca got shortly after that incident, as her own way of saying fuck you to Milo and taking control back. She was fourteen when she got that, man. Fourteen!"

"And what did you say this guy's last name is?" Connor asks, anger flashing across his face.

"I really don't think it's a good idea, guys. No one needs to get involved. It was so long ago, I barely even remember it."

Alex hears me say that and shoots me a look that says she knows I'm lying. Fuck. I forgot she was still listening.

"Besides," I say, pointing to the new tattoo. "Johnny gave me this exceptional horror villain piece and I think it's really helping to take Freddy's power away. I just told you about the

Milo thing, Connor, and it flowed out so easily. I've been telling therapists about that for years and have never had such an easy time with it. It's getting easier and easier ever since Johnny did this for me."

Without thinking, I reach out and grab Johnny's hand. His body stiffens slightly, and he looks down to where his hand is in mine before looking up at me. He slides closer and brings his other hand up to cup my cheek, and I snuggle into the warmth of his palm. His resolve broken, Johnny pulls me toward him and seals his lip to mine. He kisses me softly, once, twice, and then pulls away slightly, before kissing me once more and dropping his hand.

I lean toward him, chasing the warmth of his lips before I open my eyes and realize we have an audience. Connor and Alex stand there staring at us, mouths open, eyebrows raised.

Fuck.

That's another rule broken.

32

Complications

Johnny

"Well, that went as well as could be expected, I suppose," Becca says when we get back into my car to leave Connor's place after the pool party.

"Yeah, sure," I say. "Except now we're not only in a fake relationship for your mom's benefit, we're also in one for our friends' benefit."

She blows out a frustrated breath. It's my fault we're in this mess to begin with. When she grabbed my hand, my mind went blank, and I kissed her without thinking. Although, to be fair, she kissed me back.

"It's fine," she says, finally. "We can deal with it. We'll just carry on for a while and then, once my mom is convinced I can find someone on my own, we'll stage a breakup for our friends. Easy."

Yeah, easy for her, maybe. I actually want this fake relationship to become an actual relationship. In fact, I'm counting on it.

Of course, having our friends think we're dating might make that part easier for me. We'll have to act like we're in a relationship more frequently than we would have had to before. I'm sure I can win her over with my excellent boyfriend skills by then.

"You're right. But I'm still sorry. I don't know what came over me. At least Travis wasn't there, or I'd have to lie in front of my parents, too. I just can't lie to Mom like that. She always knows." I throw Becca a quick smile. "It's her superpower."

"I could see that about her. Her eyes look like they can see through anything." Becca shudders.

"Cold?"

She laughs. "No. Just thinking about all the shit I got up to as a teenager. If I'd had a mom like yours, I'd have spent a lot of time in trouble, I think."

"She did have a gift in that regard. Just ask my sisters." I see her give me a funny look out of the corner of my eye. "What?"

"Just your sisters? Not you?"

I laugh. "I'll have you know I was almost never in trouble. I pulled a lot of pranks when I was young, but I never did anything outright dangerous. My mom actually taught me how to bake to help me redirect my energy, mostly so my sisters wouldn't kill me for all the pranks. I spent a lot more time in the kitchen than I spent out getting into trouble."

"Huh. That's not at all what I expected."

"Because of the tattoos, right? A lot of people think that. For me, it really is all about the art. I know some people think anyone who is as covered in tattoos as I am must be an ex-con or something, but I've always been pretty nice. I just don't look it." I waggle my eyebrows at her, making her laugh.

"That makes sense, I suppose. So many people make assumptions about me too. That's why I wear a suit and keep the tattoos as covered as possible when I shoot a wedding. Unless the bride has as many tattoos, or more, than I do, anyway. Then they don't care as much, but I still wear the suit, anyway. No one wants to see a bunch of scars on the happiest day of their lives."

I pull up in front of Becca's building and throw the car into park. "Your scars are hardly noticeable, you know. The tattoos do a great job of disguising them. And if I'm being completely honest, I can hardly even feel them when I touch you. Your skin is a little smoother in some spots, raised a little in others, and normal in others."

She looks at me like I'm crazy. "Yeah, okay."

I take her hands in mine. "I'm serious, Becca. I bet if we asked everyone who was at Connor's today if they noticed anything different about you, they wouldn't be able to point anything out. You can only see your scars when you're looking for them, up close. Everyone else wouldn't even notice."

She nods but says nothing.

"Okay," I say.

"So, do you want to come in?" Becca asks, looking down at her lap.

"More than anything in the world," I say, undoing my seat belt and jumping out of the car at lightning speed. I'm around the car and opening Becca's door before she even has her seat belt off. "For the record, the answer to that question will always be yes."

Becca steps out of the car and pulls her bag out behind her. It was early evening by the time we left Connor's place, and the cooler air prompted her to put on her threadbare old sweater. It's long enough, and her shorts are short enough, making it look as though she's only wearing the sweater. It's so fucking hot.

"Is that sweater even warm?" I ask, taking her bag from her. "It looks pretty worn out."

She holds her arm out and inspects the sleeve. "It's not that warm, actually. But it's more like a security blanket than anything else. I used to wear it when I felt like I needed to cover up and I guess I just got used to having it for protection. It's a comfort thing."

"So if I went and bought you a new one, you wouldn't wear it?"

She thinks for a second. "Probably not, but if I stole one of yours while you're my fake boyfriend, I'd wear that." She gives me a grin and proceeds to the door to the apartment building.

"Motherfucker!" she yells. "Again? Where are they getting all these rocks?"

I look around her and see that someone has once again propped the door open with a rock. I bend down and pick it up.

"Let's add it to the others," I say. "That's all we can do for now. Have you had stronger locks put on your door yet?"

"I talked to the building manager and apparently I will lose my deposit if I do that. I'll do it anyway, but I just haven't gotten around to it yet. I've been pretty busy with trying to rebrand my business, and deal with my mom's bullshit."

Jealousy flares in my chest at thinking of Becca out on dates with losers every weekend. The sooner we can convince her mom we're together, the better. Now that we have to keep up appearances with our friends too, I don't have to worry as much about dragging this out.

Becca unlocks her door and enters, and I follow along behind her. I take a detour to the bookshelves and add the newest door rock to the collection. There are a few there now, because I stop and grab them every time I come over.

"Here you go," Becca says, handing me a beer. This one is a double IPA; nice and light for the end of the day. "Something to wash the taste of that crap we had at Alex's out of your mouth."

"Thanks." I tap my bottle to Becca's in a toast — "To excellent beer and even better company." — then take a long drink.

Becca takes a long drink of her beer, then sets it on the kitchen table. "I think maybe we need to rewrite the rules," she says. "We've already broken a few, so a rewrite is probably necessary."

"Good plan. We haven't done a very good job of following them, have we? Maybe we should just throw them away altogether and see what happens?" I force a laugh to make it sound like I'm joking.

She gives me a look, then shakes her head. "No, it's better with rules. This way, no one gets hurt."

I know I'm getting hurt at the end of this, but I'm willing to risk it if it gives me a solid chance with Becca.

"Sounds good to me. Bring on the rules."

Revised Rules for Successful Fake Relationship

RULES FOR A SUCCESSFUL FAKE RELATIONSHIP – RE-VISED

- DON'T FALL IN LOVE.

- ~~DON'T LET OUR FRIENDS KNOW.~~

- ~~ONLY SHOW AFFECTION IN FRONT OF BECCA'S MOM.~~

- ~~NO SEX.~~

- NO RELATIONSHIPS WITH OTHER PEOPLE WHILE WE'RE DATING.

- DON'T DO ANYTHING THAT WILL JEOPARDIZE THE FRIENDSHIP.

- SERIOUSLY, DON'T CATCH FEELINGS.

Old Ladies Say the Darndest Things

Becca

I'M STANDING BY THE drinks table watching Denise and Ryder's friends and family dance on the small dance floor that we all pitched in to construct earlier today, when Ryder's Gran, a hilarious little spitfire named Delores, sidles up beside me.

"Well, girlie. How come you're not out there dancing with that handsome young fellow who's been staring at you all night?" She tips her chin in Johnny's direction. "He's doing downright indecent things to you with his eyes right now, you know."

I feel my cheeks heat and I'm thankful for the darkness. When we put up the lights earlier, we focused on getting them around the dance floor and the altar, with just one string decorating the drinks table. It makes it a little trickier to pour drinks, but I'm glad dim light right now.

Gran adjusts her shiny golden fanny pack so it rests on the hip of her matching shiny golden tracksuit. She and her best friend Gladys love wearing tracksuits. Gladys wore a shiny silver one tonight when she performed Denise and Ryder's wedding ceremony. She also had a matching fanny pack. Usually, their tracksuits are more brightly colored, so I'm guessing these are their formal tracksuits. It is a wedding, after all.

"Oh, yeah," I say, looking for something to tell her that doesn't make me sound like a lunatic. "It's... complicated? And I'm kind of working." I hold up my camera for her to see. *Brilliant, Becca. I'm sure that'll work.* I roll my eyes at myself.

"You've taken plenty of pictures. I'm sure you could spare a few minutes for a dance. You kids and your 'it's complicated' nonsense. You're interested, he's interested, it's not rocket science. Spend time together, play with each other's genitals a little bit, and see where it goes from there."

I choke on my drink and splutter out a laugh. No matter how often I hear it, I still can't believe how Gran talks sometimes. And Gladys is even worse.

"There, there, dear. Get it out," Gran says while she gently pats my back. "You're okay."

Ryder and Johnny walk up at the same time, coming from opposite directions, both wearing amused smiles.

"What's going on here? Gran, are you corrupting Becca?" Ryder wraps his Gran up in a big hug, no doubt happy she's still here.

I still can't believe she orchestrated this whole wedding on the same day Denise's crazy ex-boyfriend tried to take her hostage. He didn't plan on the little old lady having bigger balls than he did, though, and now he'll be spending several years in prison.

"How dare you, young man," Gran says with feigned outrage. "Of course I am. It's my job as an old lady to corrupt the younger generation, and I take that responsibility very seriously. Just wait until that baby Denise is having is old enough for me to corrupt. We'll have some real fun then."

"It's fine. Don't worry about it." I tell them, hoping they drop it. It's bad enough Gran told me I should be playing with Johnny's genitals. I really don't want her announcing it to anyone else.

"What did you say, Gran?" Johnny asks her.

"I just said that love shouldn't be complicated. You spend time together, you play with each other's genitals, and you see where it goes. Nothing could be less complicated than that."

A laugh explodes from Ryder. "Oh Gran," he says, shaking his head, "never change."

He's still shaking his head and chuckling a few seconds later when he walks away.

"Well, you two mind what I said, alright? I need to be moving along. I see Gladys calling me over and she has that poor Aiden backed into a corner. Look at his little red face." She grins and begins backing away while making an obscene gesture by repeatedly pushing her finger into a hole she's made with the fingers of her other hand. "Don't forget about playing with each other's genitals. That part's the most fun."

I choke on a laugh and hear Johnny's strangled laugh in response. We look at each other and let the laughter free.

"Gran is... interesting, isn't she?" Johnny asks. "She's gotten a lot stranger since she moved into the Peaceful Pines retirement home and met Gladys. Did I ever tell you about Hunter and the firecracker incident? At the end of it, he didn't have a single hair left on his body."

"Did I hear someone say my name?" An attractive man walks up to us, smiling ear to ear. He looks like Ryder, just a little shorter, with lighter hair and more tattoos. "Johnny, introduce me to your beautiful friend."

A low growl escapes Johnny. Aww, he's jealous. It's a cute look for him. He paints on a fake smile and introduces me. "Hunter, this is Becca. Becca, this is Hunter. Hunter owns the shop that I brought you to for your tattoo. Becca is an incredibly talented photographer."

"I thought your purse looked incredibly realistic," Hunter jokes, gesturing to my camera.

I laugh. Johnny scowls. Hunter looks confused.

"Oh, wait," Hunter says, recognition lighting his eyes. "You're the one Johnny did the horror tattoo on?"

"That's me."

"He told me you got a giant Freddy Krueger tattoo as your first when you were only fourteen. That's crazy. Would you mind showing it to me?"

I shrug my shoulders. "Why not?" My eyes drift to Johnny. "Can you hold my camera for a sec?"

He nods and I slip the strap off my shoulder, handing it to him. I motion for Hunter to follow me to the dance floor, so we have more light. Once there, I slide my dress up over my right thigh, showing him the piece that Uncle Silas gifted me with so many years ago.

"Wow, that's bigger than I was thinking. And it looks so fresh for being ten years old."

"What?" I say in surprise, dropping the hem of my dress back in place. "It's more like twenty years old, a little older even."

"Really? Are you sure? Did you know that, Johnny?" Hunter looks at Johnny, who's standing right next to me again. "That tattoo is twenty years old?"

Johnny smiles. "Yeah, I knew that." He puts his arm around me. Even though this relationship is fake and temporary, I have to say this feels nice.

"I would not have guessed that you're in your thirties," Hunter says to me.

I laugh. "I get that a lot. One good thing that came from my accident is that I'm *very* diligent with sunscreen."

"Accident?"

I look at Johnny, surprised. "You told him about Freddy, but not the accident?"

"I told him about the tattoo. Not why you got it, and not about the accident. I was bragging about how you're such a bad bitch that you got a huge horror icon tattooed on you at fourteen years old. The rest of it had nothing to do with it. Plus, that's not my story to tell."

Hunter raises his eyebrows, looking back and forth between me and Johnny.

"Here's the short version. When I was four years old, I accidentally pulled a pot of hot soup off of the stove and onto myself. I burned the skin on almost half of my body. In high school, some asshole tricked me into taking my shirt off and got all the other kids in the school to call me Freddy Krueger because of my scars. My uncle helped me out with all of my tattoos, starting with Freddy, who I chose as a "fuck you" to the guy who started the whole thing."

Hunter stands there stunned for a minute, then he looks at Johnny. "You're right, man. She is a bad bitch." He turns back to me, inclines his head, and says, "You are a bad bitch, Becca."

I snort out a laugh. It was so easy to tell Hunter about the accident and Freddy. I wish I'd known before how good it would feel to tell people about it. I would have started sharing a long time ago.

Ryder's voice cuts through the noise of the crowd. He thanks everyone for coming, then says goodnight before taking Denise into the house.

"I guess that's it? You guys want to go out and do something?" Hunter asks.

I shake my head no. "I'm exhausted. I started my day too early yesterday. I went to the spa, where I had to witness Ryder having a full body wax. Full. Body." Johnny and Hunter both wince. "And then there was the engagement party for Alex and Connor. Then today we threw a surprise baby shower for Denise, which involved a lot of running around. And then, of course, what happened with Denise's ex and your Gran. Then we came and built this dance floor and set up for this wedding. I have a date with my comfiest pajamas and my bed."

"I'm out too. I also have a date with her comfiest pajamas and bed. I'll talk to you soon, Hunter."

Hunter chuckles and shakes his head. "Guess I'll have to see what Gran and Gladys are up to if I want to have any fun tonight. I was kind of hoping to keep it more low key than what they usually get up to, though." He waves and he walks away. "Keep your phone on. I'm calling you if I need bail money."

"Just steer clear of explosives this time and you'll be fine."

Hunter flips Johnny the middle finger but doesn't turn around again.

"So, are you completely exhausted, or do you want to stop and grab something to eat before you go home?" Johnny asks. "I don't know about you, but I could really go for some pancakes."

My mouth waters at the thought of a tall stack of fluffy pancakes, and suddenly I'm not so tired.

"Fine, pancakes first. But then I'm going to bed and sleeping for at least two days." I grab Johnny's hand and lace our fingers together. "Let's go get some pancakes, *boyfriend.*"

35

Pancakes and Pee

Johnny

I'M SO GLAD MY pancakes ploy worked. I was wracking my brain looking for some way to spend more time with Becca tonight, and thank god she found pancakes interesting enough to put off going to bed.

I can understand why she's exhausted. She's been going pretty much nonstop since early yesterday morning. I can't see spending time at the spa with Ryder as being too relaxing. He's so off the wall that it can be tiring to spend time with him on a normal day, never mind when he's having the hair ripped off his entire body.

It would have been hilarious to hear him getting waxed, though.

"Back," Becca says, getting into my car. She insisted on stopping at her place first to change into more comfortable clothes. "Take me to the pancakes."

"You got it," I say with a laugh.

She's wearing the same baggy joggers she wore that day in the tattoo shop and even though we've done plenty more since my dick still enjoys the memory of that first encounter. I reach down and adjust myself discreetly. Becca notices anyway and raises an eyebrow at me.

"Really? This does it for you?" She grabs some of the excess material from her legs and pulls it upward, reaching at least a foot above where her thigh stops. "You, me, and Hunter could fit in here together," she says with a wink.

"Not funny," I say, the jealousy I was feeling earlier burning another hole in my chest. Hunter is a good-looking guy who owns his own business. How could I not be jealous? Not to mention he operates in much the same way as Becca, with her one-night rule. He loves women. Lots of them.

"You have nothing to worry about, Johnny. That's a rule that I won't break. It's just you and me until this fake relationship has served its purpose. *No relationships with other people while we're dating.*" She turns to look out the window and starts humming along to the radio.

I exhale a relieved breath. I want nothing to interfere with this fake relationship until we've seen it through. I need all the time I can get if I'm going to convince Becca I'm worth taking a chance on.

The parking lot of Maggie's is nearly empty when we pull in. I pull into a spot close to the door and shut the car off. I reach out and grab Becca's hand before she opens her door.

"I'm sorry, Becca. I shouldn't have acted like a jealous ass. Hunter just gets to me sometimes."

"Thanks," she says, patting her other hand on top of mine. "It's okay. You looked kind of adorable, all jealous like that at the wedding. No one has ever wanted me all to themselves before. I can see how a woman could get used to that."

She opens her door and gets out before me, leaving me scrambling to catch up. None of our friends are around, but I weave our fingers together anyway, and we walk into Maggie's holding hands. Becca leads us to a booth about halfway down the train car, and slides into the seat facing the back, leaving me the seat facing the door.

"Evening folks, get you something to drink to start off with?"

"Ivy!" Becca squeals. "You must work every shift here, hey?"

"Oh, hi," Ivy says, a grin splitting her face. "Yeah, they want us available for all shifts, and that's what they schedule us for.

Keeps us from getting second jobs so we can actually afford our rent." Her smiles drops. "Shit, sorry. I shouldn't have said that. Coffee? Iced Tea?"

Becca barks out a laugh, and I chuckle.

"Don't worry about it. Believe me, I know what it's like to struggle to make rent. I'm a freelance photographer. Some months are leaner than others. It sucks that you need to be available all the time, though. Have you thought about working in a bar instead? It's all evening hours and the tips are great."

"Been there, not going back. I'm trying to get out of that scene. Working in it makes it that much harder. It's hard to get into too much trouble serving coffee and milkshakes, you know? I have a line on another job, though. So maybe I won't be here much longer."

"Ha! You have a point. And good for you. I hope it works out."

"Thanks. Me too. So, what can I get you?"

As much as Ivy seems to be enjoying the conversation, it's clear that she has work she needs to do.

"I would love you forever if you could bring me the tallest stack of pancakes you have, and a glass of chocolate milk. Please."

"I'll have the exact same," I say. "But can I also get a side of bacon with that, please?"

"Coming right up."

Ivy turns to leave, and Becca looks back at me.

"So, when should we have you meet my mom for real?"

Shit, I was hoping to have more time before she started asking about this. I should have guessed she'd want to get it over with soon, though. She doesn't do relationships, after all. One night only.

"Soon I guess. What do you think?" *That's it, Johnny. Stall.*

"Ugh, not too soon. She takes a lot of getting used to, and I've seen her recently. I need to gather my wits before going back into the lair of the beast. She was not pleased when she saw you were at my place that day." She laughs, but it sounds forced. I wonder what's up with that?

"It's up to you. I'm here to help. I enjoy spending time with you, so it's not like it's a hardship to pretend to be your boyfriend."

"Plus, the benefits aren't too bad either, hey?" She shoots me an exaggerated wink.

I burst into laughter at the look on her face.

"I was talking about the cookies, perv. Get your mind out of the gutter." She bursts into laughter, too, and together we're so loud that the other patrons of the restaurant start to turn and look.

"Haaa," Becca wheezes out a last laugh, wiping under her eyes with her fingers. "Shit. I knew I should have taken off my makeup before we came here. I must look like a deranged raccoon."

She looks great, as always, but there is a little makeup smudged under her eyes and I tell her as much.

"Ugh, I'll be right back." She gets up and heads to the back of the dining area where the restrooms are located. "Don't drink my chocolate milk," she yells before going through the door.

Just then, a group of three guys enters the restaurant and heads to the booth just past ours. The last guy in the group does a double take and has the audacity to sit in Becca's spot across from me.

"Umm, can I help you?" I ask, eyebrows drawn in confusion. What the fuck does this guy want?

"Hey, hi," the guy says. "Wow. Sorry. Are you Johnny Donovan? From Sleeping Dogs?"

Shit, just a fan. I don't know what I was thinking. Of course, that's all it is. Being with Becca, everything just feels so normal that I forget sometimes people know who I am. I'm finding that I really enjoy feeling normal again.

"Hey, man. Nice to meet you." I offer my hand for him to shake.

"This is unbelievable. I can't believe I'm meeting you at a diner in the middle of the night, of all places. What are you doing here? No wild parties tonight? Run out of bitches to fuck?"

What an asshole.

"No. I'm here with my girl," I say through gritted teeth. "We wanted pancakes before heading home after our friends' wedding."

"Ha. Girl of the week, am I right?" He holds a hand out for a high five, which I ignore completely.

"So you want an autograph or something, guy? My girl's going to be back any second and…" I leave it hanging, hoping he'll get the hint and fuck off and go sit with his buddies. He doesn't, though. He just sits there looking at me. "Do you need something?"

"Oh, no. Sorry, man. It's just so crazy that you're here."

"You know we're all from here, right? You were bound to see one of us around somewhere, at some point."

"Yeah, yeah. I know tha—"

"Milo?" Becca's shaky voice sounds from behind me, and I turn to see who she's talking to.

That's not right. She's looking at me?

Oh, fuck. She's not looking at me.

I turn around, my rage a fire slowly burning in my stomach. "You're Milo?" I say through gritted teeth.

His eyes are wide and he's staring at Becca. Then he looks back at me. Then back at Becca.

"Freddy?"

"Alright, dumb fuck. You're doone." I slide out of the booth and slam my hands down on the table in front of him. "You need to get out of here before I do something that gets me thrown in jail."

His mouth is still open wide, and his head is swiveling between me and Becca.

"You're with her?" A look of disgust crosses his face. "But… why?"

"What's going on here?" Devon walks into the restaurant with Denise's pixie-like friend, Xena stumbling along in front of him. She must've enjoyed a few drinks at the wedding after we left. It appears that she also went home to put on her extra comfy clothes. Her joggers look like they could fit Devon, and he's a giant. "Do you need your security guy to deal with this?"

Milo turns around and looks up, and then up a little more until finally, he sees Devon's vicious grin shining down on him.

"Who's this loser?" Xena asks Becca. She passed by me and walked right up to Becca and grabbed her hand, realizing right away that she needed some support. "He looks like a penis-head."

Becca snorts out a laugh. "You could say that. He's just some asshole that took a picture of me topless when we were in high school. And then he showed everyone and convinced them to call me Freddy Krueger because of my scars."

"Oh shit! Is that why you have that badass tattoo of Freddy on your leg?"

"Yeah. It was my first tattoo, given to me by the dickhead's uncle."

Devon reaches down and grabs Milo's shirt, pulling him out of the booth. "I think you've had enough fun for one lifetime. What do you think?"

Milo looks terrified, and rightfully so. Devon is six and a half feet tall and has to be closing in on three hundred pounds. He's a scary-looking dude. I'd run if I met up with him in a dark alley, that's for sure.

"Come on, Fred—I mean, Becca. It was just a joke. People didn't even call you that for very long."

"People stopped calling me that when your uncle covered all of my scars with tattoos. If he hadn't done that for me, I'm sure people would *still* be calling me that. Just like you are."

Becca steps forward and pokes Milo in the chest. He sways a little since Devon is still holding him up by his shirt, reminding me of a heavy bag at a boxing gym.

"Ew, gross. I'm sorry, sir. You can't stay here like that." Ivy has two plates of pancakes balanced in one hand, on her way to our table, but she's stopped to address Milo. "That's a biohazard. I'm going to have to ask you to leave."

I look and see what she's pointing at. There is a rapidly darkening patch on the front of his pants.

He's pissed himself.

I stifle a laugh. "You heard the lady. Devon, can you deposit him outside?"

"You got it, man. Becca. Anything you want to say to him before I throw him out?"

Becca looks him up and down, her lips settling into a smirk. "Nah. He's not worth it. Get rid of him," she says with a flick of her wrist.

Devon turns, dragging Milo to the door. "You better not get piss on me," he growls at Milo. "or you're going to have a lot more to worry about than wet pants."

"Great. Glad that's settled." Xena claps her hands together. "Mind if we join you?"

"I would love that," Becca says, sliding into her seat. "Ivy? Can you bring our friends four orders of pancakes, four orders of bacon, and two chocolate milks, please? Devon's probably worked up quite that appetite carrying that pissed-soaked loser out of here."

I shake my head and huff out a laugh. Looks like Becca doesn't give a shit about Milo anymore. That's amazing.

I'm just sorry I didn't break his legs.

36

Meet My Mother

I PICK AT A loose string hanging from the hem of my skirt as Johnny turns onto my mother's street. I don't know why I ever agreed to this. I've put it off for the last couple of months, not wanting to come down from the high that finally exorcising Milo Mathews from my brain had left me with. I relive that night at the diner every night in my dreams, and every night, when I tell Devon that Milo's not worth saying anything more to, it feels just as good as it did that first time.

Freddy peeks out from beneath my sheer tights, and instead of anger at Milo, I just feel grateful that Uncle Silas gave me such a cool ass tattoo. I don't know if I would have gotten tattooed if I hadn't been scarred as a child, but my life is what it is, and I love the tattoos on my skin.

I'm also incredibly thankful to Johnny for the tattoo he gave me. That piece of swirling horror villain artwork has been a catalyst in my life. And so has Johnny, himself. Together, they've helped me put Milo in the past and leave him there.

But now, on the way to my mother's house, I feel like I'm moving backward in time. Back to when Milo, and what he did, had such an effect on me.

My mother has a way of making me feel guilty for things that aren't my fault. For things that happened so long ago, there's no way for me to do anything about them. I know it's not right that she blames me for the accident when I was four years old,

I know that. But if it wasn't my fault, whose fault was it? I was the one who pulled that pot down on me, so technically, it *was* my fault.

"I can hear the gears in your head turning from here," Johnny says with a soft smile. "Everything okay?"

And then there's Johnny. I haven't told him the extent of my mother's behavior toward me. She's usually better when there's company, but who can say what she'll do in front of Johnny tonight? She's already mad that I skipped out on the last date she made for me, and she blames Johnny.

She's been leaving messages, all of them with a similar theme. *'Johnny is too good for you.' 'He deserves better.' 'You're not attractive enough to be with him.' 'Don't mistake his pity for genuine affection, Rebecca.' 'Why would you want to burden him for the rest of his life?' 'He needs someone who is more attractive, more like him.'* I haven't answered a call from her in weeks, except the last one, when we planned this dinner.

"Hey," Johnny reaches over and grabs my hand. He's pulled over and parked at the curb a few houses down from my mother's place. "We don't have to do this, you know. We can cancel and do it another time."

Johnny doesn't know about the messages my mother has left me. He has no idea what he's in for. This has been coming since the day they met at my apartment. It was inevitable.

And it brings us one step closer to the end of our fake relationship.

Am I ready for that?

"No, it's fine," I finally say. "We need to get this over with. But can you promise me something?"

"Of course," he says without hesitation. "Whatever you need."

"Just... whatever my mother says, please don't let it change your mind about me."

Johnny looks at me curiously. He turns my face toward him. "Nothing she could say would change my opinion of you, Becca. Nothing." He leans forward and places a gentle kiss on my lips, lingering just a moment.

The way he looks at me, I can almost believe he could feel something real for me. Could he love me enough that my hideous scars wouldn't matter? Could anyone?

According to my mother, the answer is no. She wants me to settle for a loveless relationship with a loser of her choosing.

I may not be able to keep a man like Johnny, but I refuse to settle for anyone my mother chooses. I'd rather be alone. Just like she always told me I would be.

I take a deep breath and release it slowly. "Alright. Let's get this over with."

We untangle our hands and get out of the car. Johnny joins me on the sidewalk and pulls me into a hug.

"Everything will be fine," he says, kissing me on the forehead. "Now, let's go convince your mom we're madly in love."

If only it were that easy.

"I WAS WONDERING HOW long it would take you two to get out of the car," mom says, giving me a once over, her look of disgust telling me the skirt I've worn is not to her liking. She turns around abruptly to lead us from the front door and further into the house. "I was sure the neighbors would call the police."

"Your neighbors know what I look like. I think they would know not to call the police."

Mother leads us into the living room, where she offers wine. Johnny and I each take a glass, even though I know for a fact we'd both rather have a beer. Maybe we can go see his dad after this and explore that beer cave a little more. I'm sure Dennis has found some great new brews since I was last over there.

"Yes, well. From a distance, the two of you look... well, you know."

"Like a brilliant photographer and an award-winning musical artist?" Johnny says, his grin dazzling and his voice dripping with sweetness. "That's kind of you, Mrs. Morris, but I don't get recognized as often as one would think."

Johnny has mentioned before that he and the guys love Westborough because despite the city knowing that Sleeping Dogs originated here, they all get left alone more often than not. He said that Westborough fans are the most respectful they've met anywhere.

The stalker who tried to sexually assault Connor, and Milo excluded, of course.

"Oh? Why would anyone recognize you?"

"Really, mother?" I say. "Didn't I tell you that Johnny is in a band?" I think I did, anyway. I usually try to block out our conversations after they happen, though, so I could be wrong.

"Oh, is that right?" She gives me a look that tells me she's even more convinced now that Johnny needs someone better. "And you're famous enough to be recognized?"

"Some would say so," Johnny says, humble as ever. "But the citizens of Westborough have an unspoken agreement with the band. They maintain a polite distance and we put on lots of events here and volunteer our time for many good causes."

"Interesting." Mom takes a sip of wine. "And do you do televised awards shows and make lots of public appearances?"

Johnny tastes his wine and I can tell by the way he squints ever so slightly that he won't be having a second glass. It's not very tasty, but my mother likes to show off and thinks that drinking wine makes her look cultured.

"Yes, unfortunately, that is part of the job. It was fun when we first started out, but I know I'm not the only one in the band who is getting a little tired of the whole thing. We owe the label one more album and then we're hoping to take a small break."

"Hmmm," mom sets her wine down and stands. "Excuse us for a moment, would you, Johnny? Rebecca, can you help me in the kitchen?"

She turns and leaves the room without waiting for me. I can already tell what she's going to say to me. She already believed Johnny deserved better than me. Now that she knows he's a famous musician, she's going to insist that he deserves someone much more attractive.

"I'm sorry," I whisper to Johnny. "I'll be right back."

He nods and leans back against the couch, already lost in thought. I wonder what he thinks of how the evening is going so far? Does he see the looks my mother gives me when he talks about what he does for a living? Did he notice when she asked about award shows and public appearances that she widened her eyes at me?

I take a breath and brace myself before walking into the kitchen. This is going to be bad. Worse than the things she normally says to me, I can feel it.

"What can I help with?"

"I've already done it. I wanted to speak to you privately for a moment." She leans against the counter and crosses her arms over her chest. "I'm disappointed in you, Rebecca. For several reasons, not the least of which is letting yourself take up that poor man's time. What could ever make you think you are up to being the significant other of a celebrity? Can you imagine what a scandal it would be if he were to be seen with *you* in public?"

Ouch. Thanks, Mom. Love you too.

"I appreciate your concern, but that is between me and Johnny. I know where you stand on the matter."

"You'll regret not listening to me when the tabloids rip you apart. How could you do that to him? A man like that deserves to be proud of the woman on his arm, not ashamed of the way she looks."

I snort a laugh. And then another. Before long, I'm laughing hysterically, bent over and holding my stomach.

"Rebecca, you're being ridiculous. It's quite selfish of you to think that his feelings for you are anything more than pity."

"Everything alight in here?" Johnny asks, coming into the kitchen. "You okay, babe?" He asks me.

The look of concern on his face sets me off into another furious fit of giggles, and the only response I can muster is to shake my head no. Tears are streaming down my face, and the giggles are morphing into choking sobs. I need to get out of here. I need to get away from my mother.

"Thank you for the invitation, Rebecca, but I think I need to get Becca home. She's suddenly not feeling well." Johnny takes my arm and turns me away from my mother. "Becca will call you to reschedule. We'll have you over at our place next time. I would hate for you to have to go to this trouble all over again."

He doesn't wait for my mother's reply, but I can hear her huff a breath, the sound she makes when she's offended. She honestly expected me to listen to her talk about me like that and just take it. Of course, I've been doing that my whole life, so she had good reason to believe I would just go on and keep doing it. She didn't count on Johnny stepping in, though. Once again, I find myself grateful for his presence in my life.

We're out the door and down the steps and before I know it, Johnny is opening the car door and helping me inside. He gets into the driver's side, starts the car, and drives us to a local green space. A garden with a small walking path is visible from our parking space.

"Let's walk," Johnny says.

He comes around and opens my door, taking my hand to help me out. He laces our fingers together and brings the back of my hand to his lips, kissing me gently.

We start out on the walking path, meandering slowly, just breathing in the crisp air. I'm sure I'll be too cold soon, with only sheer tights and the skirt covering my bottom half, but right now, this is exactly what I need. Fresh air, a little movement, and Johnny beside me.

"So... your mother is interesting."

I choke out a bitter laugh. "That's one way to put it. I usually prefer to call her a bitch."

Johnny laughs. "Yeah, I didn't think it would be polite of me to say. We were only there for fifteen minutes after all."

"Well, that's fourteen minutes more than most people need to decide she's a bitch. You are a wonderful person, Johnny Donovan."

He stops and pulls me into his arms. A kiss lights on the top of my head. "I was trying to be nice, for your sake. But if I hadn't pulled you out of there, I would have had some choice words to say to your mother. Bitch was the least offensive of the lot."

I giggle into his chest. "How about I take you out for dinner and you tell me all of them?"

He leans back, and I look up into his eyes. "That sounds perfect." He cups my face and kisses me.

And it's perfect.

And that's when it hits me.

I love this man.

Fuck.

37

Change is Coming

Johnny

"BECCA, MY GIRL. COME and try this new cream ale I've found." Dad takes Becca's hand as soon as we get in the house and pulls her away toward his beer cave. He's been more excited lately to show her his new beers than he's been to show me. It makes my heart swell.

I can't help but notice the smile on Becca's face, and how different she looks compared to several weeks ago when we tried to have dinner with her mother. She was just so tense with her mother, but here, with my family, she's so relaxed. Every time I bring her here, it becomes more obvious that she is meant to be here with me. I only hope she realizes that before our fake relationship ends.

I've brought her here once or twice a week since our fake relationship started. In that time she's completely won my dad over, dazzled my mother, met all my sisters and their husbands and boyfriends, and met all of my nieces and nephews. Everyone loves her.

I love her.

I love her, but if I were to tell her, it would just scare her away, so I keep it to myself.

"Johnny? Where'd you go just then?" Mom asks. "You were gathering so much wool I was beginning to wonder if you were taking up knitting."

She gestures for me to follow her into the kitchen. Tonight's dinner is simple; a hearty stew with fresh-baked dinner rolls, and it's already bubbling away on the stove, so Mom doesn't need any help. That can only mean one thing. She wants to talk.

"Sit." She points to a chair at the kitchen table. "Now, tell me what's going on with that lovely young lady you keep bringing around. You two seem to spend an awful lot of time together for people who are just friends."

She's not wrong. Ever since we started this fake relationship, we've spent as much time together as we would if it had been real. I usually spend the night at her place after a day in the studio. Her bookshelves are becoming overloaded with all the rocks I bring her from her front door. The guys give me shit when I run out of Connor's studio every day grinning like a fool because I can't wait to see Becca.

I drop my head into my hands on the table. "I don't want to talk about it," I tell Mom, knowing she won't let me get away with not talking.

"Oh, my boy," she says, ruffling up my hair, making my curls fluff up. "It can't be all bad. She's a smart, beautiful, talented woman, and you're spending all your time with her. That sounds like a pretty good deal to me."

I slouch back into my chair, giving a quick look around to make sure we're alone. "I offered to help her with her mother. She kept setting Becca up on dates with horrible guys, so I said I would pretend to be her boyfriend to get her mom to back off."

"And you hoped it would turn out like one of the romance novels you like to read. That the two of you would fall in love and you'd live happily ever after?" Her eyebrows are raised in question. "Did you really expect that to work?"

I huff out a breath. "Not in so many words. But yes, I did. I'm a great boyfriend. Women love me."

"I'm sure you are, son. And I'm sure most women do. But that woman has been through trauma. Has she talked much about her accident?" Becca told my family about her accident, and even about the Freddy story. Compared to when she first told me about them, her words flowed easily. She is so much stronger now. She used to talk about both things as though she were the one who should be ashamed and now she knows her accident was just that, an accident and the Freddy thing was just that dickhead Milo's doing.

"She told me a little. Just what happened and how old she was, mostly. Why?"

Mom gets up and starts pulling bowls and side plates down from the cupboard and passing them to me. "Has she told you what healing was like? What happened to her family after? An accident like that can do emotional damage to everyone around, besides the physical damage that was done to her."

I stand and start setting the table with the dishes Mom has passed me. "She said her dad left when she was little, but she didn't get into it. I didn't think to question it. Do you think he left before or after the accident?"

Could a man really leave his little girl after a terrible accident like that? Or had he left before?

What if Becca's mother drove him away, and he didn't leave on his own at all?

I grab the cutlery from the drawer and begin adding them to the place settings I've already laid out.

"I wouldn't know," Mom says, setting a trivet in the middle of the table. "But maybe you should ask Becca. She might re-member."

"Might remember what?" Becca says, coming back into the kitchen with Dad. She hands me a pint of the cream ale Dad must've been talking about.

"What song Ryder and Denise danced to at their wedding?" I blurt off the top of my head. "I can't remember."

"Oh, umm," Becca taps her finger against her lip. "I think it was that Etta James song, *At Last*? Does that sound right to you, babe?" She turns and looks at me, her eyes widening as she realizes what she's done. "I mean—"

"Sure does, *kitten*," I say with a laugh, turning her slip into a joke. Maybe I can make it look like an inside joke to the rest of my family, who have started pouring into the kitchen for dinner.

It seems to work because everyone busies themselves with finding seats and talking amongst themselves. They either didn't hear Becca call me babe or they didn't care enough to comment.

"Alright kids," Mom sets a giant pot of homemade stew on the trivet and turns to get the trays of dinner rolls. "Dish up and don't be shy. There's plenty more on the stove for when this pot is empty."

Becca and I slide down the side of the table and sit near the end, in the spot that has become 'ours'. It's a comfortable family-style dinner, with two of my sisters here with their kids, and Finley from across the street with her three kids.

I can hardly even eat because my brain is spinning with thoughts of Becca's mother. I overheard a little of what she was saying to Becca the day we went over for dinner, and I've been obsessed with it ever since. I tried to talk to Becca about it, but she just shrugged it off, saying that's how her mother is.

But if my mother ever said someone's feelings for me weren't real, that they were only pity, I'd be pissed. Moms are supposed to support you and lift you up, not tear you down.

"Hey, Johnny. How's the album coming?" My sister Jocelyn asks. "I haven't much of anything about it from you. Or Travis."

Finley glances at Jocelyn when she mentions Travis. I wonder where he is tonight, anyway.

"It's going fairly well. We're postponing the release a bit since Denise is pregnant. And we're working out whether she'll be on the next tour with us. Or whether Ryder will, for that matter." I take a minute to explain that Denise and Ryder got married and they'll be having a baby before the next tour starts. "Denise has been training a new assistant, so they have time to get the hang of things before the band gets too busy again."

"What about you, Becca? Will you be going on tour with Johnny when he leaves?"

The question takes Becca by surprise, and she chokes on a bite of bread. She gets her coughing under control and looks at me, wide-eyed, before answering my sister.

"Oh, well. I don't think so. I still have my business to run. And Johnny and I are just friends, so it might be a little weird to have me on tour."

Jocelyn looks between me and Becca, eyebrows raised. "Just friends? Okay, sure." She chuckles a little. "If I looked at my friends the way my brother looks at you, I'm sure my husband would have something to say about it."

"Alright, Jocelyn. Stop teasing your brother," Dad says. "Now, Becca and Johnny, tell me what you thought about that cream ale. Good, right?"

I look at Becca, checking to see if she's okay. She nods and pats my leg under the table to reassure me. We can talk more later, hopefully, when she lets me come home with her.

"It was great, thanks, Dad."

"Yes, thank you," Becca adds. "It's been great having people to talk to about beer. None of my other friends like it. Well, good beer anyway. My best friend Alex sometimes picks a winner, but that's because she picks based on whether she likes the packaging, not because she spends any time looking for a good beer."

Dad smiles. "Well, as I said before, you are welcome here anytime."

The conversation starts up again around the table, so I turn to Becca. "Are you okay?" I whisper. "I've told them all we're just friends. It appears that Jocelyn didn't get the memo."

"Yeah. It's fine."

"Are you sure you're okay?"

"Yes, Johnny. I'm fine. Drop it."

Something tells me she's not as fine as she says she is, though. I have a feeling that things are about to change.

38

The Truth Becca

Becca

JOHNNY HAS ASKED ME several times since we left his parents if I'm truly okay with what his sister said. And I am. Mostly.

I suppose I always knew this fake relationship scheme wasn't the best idea, but I really wanted it to work. And I was hoping it would help me get Johnny out of my system. Despite his assertion that he would end up bored with me within a few weeks, here we are, months later, and he seems to feel the same as he did at the start.

And I'm falling head over heels for him.

Fuck.

Soon enough, he'll get tired of me. Or he'll need to make a public appearance and he'll want to take some model or actress who will make him look good. Where will that leave me? Can I handle being kept a secret for the sake of his reputation? If that's even something he would consider. Or will he decide I'm not worth the trouble and just move on and forget all about me?

"Here we are," Johnny says, pulling up in front of my building.

I can tell he wants to come up. We've been spending nearly every night together, either at his place or mine, and it feels so natural. Waking up with him is always the best part of my day. Other than falling asleep in his arms after he brings me such intense pleasure I almost black out, that is.

But I need to put some distance between us or I'll never survive it when he walks away completely.

"I had fun with your family," I say, opening my door. "I'll call you soon?"

Watching his face fall when he realizes I'm brushing him off nearly changes my mind. But I stay strong. I need some time to get perspective. To stop living in a fantasy world where a guy like Johnny could really want someone like me for the long term.

"Yeah... yeah, that sounds good. Goodnight, Becca." He turns his head away from me and looks straight out the windshield. "See you around."

"Goodnight, Johnny," I choke out, my eyes already filling with tears. I jump out of the car quickly and slam the door just as Johnny pulls away.

Silent tears roll down my cheeks as I turn to enter my building.

"Are you fucking kidding me?" I yell to the sky. "Where are these fucking rocks even coming from?"

I bend and pick up the rock in the door.

"Fuck!" I scream. I throw the rock as hard as I can into the empty street. "That's it."

I throw my bag over by the door and storm down the sidewalk, picking up every rock I find and hurling it down the street as hard as I can. One after the other, big rocks, small rocks, it doesn't matter. I wind up and throw each one as far as I can, tears continuing to stream down my face the entire time, an indecipherable roar escaping me with each throw.

When I've walked as far in one direction as I'm willing to go, I turn back and scour the gutter for more rocks. Each one I find gets the same treatment as the others, until I collapse at my door, exhausted and sobbing.

That's where Alex's grandfather, Pops, finds me when he's leaving his gym.

"Alright, darling." He holds his hand out to help me up. "You've made enough racket out here for one night. Let's get you inside and you can tell me why you're screaming at the top of your lungs and throwing rocks all over the street."

I sniffle and wipe my eyes with one arm and give Pops the other. He may be old, but he's still strong, and he pulls me to my feet with almost no help from me. He stoops and picks up my bag, finds my keys, and lets us into the building.

"I'm okay, Pops. You don't need to come up."

I just need to cry for a few more hours and then I'll be ready to plan out the rest of my life. I need to figure out how I can survive knowing I can't have the one man I love more than anything. Not just that I can't have him, but that he'll likely end up with someone better than me in no time at all like I didn't even exist.

"Bullshit, kid. Women who are okay don't spend half an hour screaming and crying while throwing rocks into the street." He gives me his arm and together we walk up the stairs.

Pops lets us into my apartment and deposits me on the couch. I hear him rummaging around in the back of the apartment before he comes back with a cool washcloth.

"Wash your face, darling. You look like a rabid raccoon."

I make a noise that is somewhere between a sob and a laugh. "Thanks, Pops. You sure know how to make a lady feel good."

He barks out a laugh. "Is there a lady in here?" He swivels his head around and spins in a circle. "All I see is the crazy person who was throwing rocks and carrying on in the street, disturbing all the neighbors."

"Knock, knock. Is there room for one more?" Alex knocks on the already-open door of the apartment. "I brought whiskey."

"Oh, Pops. Really?" I shake my head in disappointment. "You told on me?"

"Hey, don't look at me. I didn't call her." Pops give Alex a hug. "Hey, Lexi Girl. What're you doing here?"

"Tino called me. Said he saw Becca screaming in the street in front of his pizza shop. Told me she was throwing things and scaring away his customers. I thought maybe I should come and see if she was alright." Alex steps away from Pops and sits next to me on the couch. "So? What's going on?"

I release a shuddering breath. "Nothing. I'm good. It was just a little overreaction to finding another rock holding the door open." I point over to the collection of rocks on my bookshelves and more tears well in my eyes.

It's not like the rocks were actual gifts or anything, but I thought it was sweet how Johnny would always bring me the rock from the door when he came over. Now that he won't be coming over anymore, I suppose it's good that I threw as many rocks as I could tonight.

"I'm going to leave you girls to it," Pops says, heading toward the door. "I have a feeling this has to do with a lot more than just rocks and I'm afraid I'm not the best advice giver in those situations. But you make sure you call me if someone needs a beating. Alex never did let me hurt any of her loser ex-boyfriends. Don't you deny me the pleasure, too. It's a grandfather's job to beat up shitty boyfriends. Alright, Becca?"

I chuckle. Pops was always a little put out that Alex wouldn't let him hurt her boyfriends. The man's been training fighters at his gym for years and is in better shape than most men half his age, so it wasn't because she was worried about him. It's because she prefers to take care of things herself. I'd like to think I'm the same way, but I've always avoided the boyfriend situation altogether. It's easier that way for me. But still, Pops means well.

"You got it, Pops. If anyone needs a beating, you're the first person I'll call."

"Good. You ladies behave." Pops blows us both kisses and then he's out the door.

Alex gets up and goes to the kitchen to get a couple of glasses for the whiskey. She grabs something from a drawer before coming back to join me on the couch. Onto the coffee table go the glasses, as well as an ashtray and a lighter. She opens the whiskey and pours us each a glass before pulling a pack of cigarettes from the pocket of her joggers.

"I figured it was a whiskey and angry smoking kind of night."

I take the pack from her, pull out a cigarette, and lean forward to grab the lighter. I light the smoke and inhale deeply. I rarely smoke, but Alex and I decided a long time ago that there's just something about furiously smoking when you're angry.

Alex passes me my drink and gulp back half of it before letting it rest against my knee. We sit there in silence while I alternate between drags of my smoke and sips of my drink until I've finished both. I'm stubbing the cigarette butt out in the ashtray when Alex starts in.

"Alright," she says, filling my glass again. "Time to talk. Why were you screaming and throwing rocks down the street tonight?"

I take my glass and sip my whiskey slowly this time. I'm glad she didn't bring me beer. For one thing, she sucks at choosing beer. And for another, it would remind me too much of Johnny and that's the last thing I need.

"I told you, I got pissed off when I found another rock propping the door to the building open. I may have overreacted a little."

"Why didn't you just bring the rock from the door in here with all the others you have?" She points to my shelf. "Why stop collecting and start throwing?"

Alex sips her whiskey, still on her first glass. She'll be the sensible one tonight.

We always take turns helping each other through our issues, usually using whiskey and cigarettes, but the helper always attempts to stay sober enough to get the drunk, upset one into bed. It's a nice little arrangement. Really, what more could want from a best friend?

"I didn't bring those in here. Johnny picks them up and brings them in every time he comes over."

"Like a penguin? That's so cute." Alex has a big grin on her face.

Cute? What am I missing?

"What? Why are we talking about penguins?"

"You know," she says with her eyebrows raised. "A male penguin will present the female with a pebble and if she accepts it, they bond and mate for life."

"What the hell?" Is that what he was doing? No. He can't have been. That's crazy. We're not penguins. "No. No, no, no. He brought them up so that they couldn't be used in the door again. Because he knows how angry it makes me when people leave the door propped open."

"Okay. Sure," she says, turning to look at me. "Now then, why don't you explain the part where you and Johnny have been inseparable for months and suddenly you're home alone and sobbing in the street?"

I burst into tears, sobs choking my voice, my words lost as I try to catch my breath.

Why does it hurt this much? I stopped it before I fell too hard for him. Didn't I?

Alex takes my drink from my hand and puts it on the table before pulling me into a hug. "It's okay, Becca. It's going to be fine." She whispers over and over that everything will be fine until eventually, I run out of tears.

My breath comes in huge, shuddering gasps. Alex passes me my drink and lights me a cigarette, putting it in the corner of my mouth for me. I lean forward and rest my elbows on my knees, and Alex rubs circles on my back.

Funny how I spent so many years afraid of being touched that I never knew how calming and reassuring the touch of a friend could be.

I stub out my cigarette in the ashtray, blow out the last of the cigarette smoke, and without looking at Alex I say, "I think it's time I told you everything about my scars."

Alex looks at me. Her eyebrows scrunched down and a slight frown on her lips. "I thought you already told me all about it at the pool party? You have scars from a burn you got when you were young, and that asshole Milo from high school made you even more self-conscious about it."

My heart is pounding so hard I can feel it in my ears. I can practically hear the blood flowing through my veins. But I need to get this out. And Alex is my best friend. If anyone will be on my side in this, it's going to be her. And if, for some reason, she's not on my side, well, I'll deal with that if it comes to pass. No sense borrowing trouble when I have enough trouble of my own.

"Yeah, that's part of it. But I didn't tell you the part about my mother. Or my dad."

39

Redemption

Johnny

OUT OF HABIT, I grab the rock from the door of Becca's building and run up the stairs. Every time I come over, I bring her the rock from the door. One day, all the rocks from her neighborhood will be in her apartment.

But the rock isn't what really matters right now.

It's been a week since I last saw Becca and I'm going a little crazy. She hasn't returned any of my calls or texts. She hasn't even answered the door when I've come to see her at her apartment. But I don't blame her. I was a bit of an ass the last time I saw her. Okay, maybe I was a complete ass. But that only lasted for a couple of hours, and then I was trying to find her to apologize.

I feel a bit like Connor when he first found Alex again, and it's only a matter of time before the people in this neighborhood notice that I've been hanging around and start calling me a sketchy fuck, too. I've been here every night in the last week, and every night I've brought the rock from the door.

Now there's a pile of rocks beside Becca's door, but still no sign of Becca. She's not home, she's not with Alex, and she doesn't have any photo shoots booked tonight. There's only one other place that I can think she might be.

I leave Becca's and drive over to her mother's house. I park my car and run up to her door, knocking loudly as soon as I'm close enough. The door swings open, and suddenly I'm standing face to face with Becca's mother, with my hand still raised to knock.

"Oh, hello, Rebecca," I say, lowering my hand. "Sorry to bother you, but I was wondering if maybe Becca was here? I've been looking all over for her and I'm having a hard time tracking her down."

She looks me up and down and raises an eyebrow. "My daughter is out this evening. On a date. With a more suitable man."

Fuck. No, this can't be happening.

"Do you know where she went?" Why would I bother asking this? She won't tell me. She thinks her daughter is out with a better man. "It's... it's, uh, very important I speak to her."

"Why would you bother? You're free to move on to someone more suitable for you now. Rebecca needs to be free to date a man more appropriate for someone like her."

Holy shit, this woman really doesn't think much of me, does she? I don't disagree that Becca is too good for me, but to hear her mother say it straight to my face like this. That hurts. I'm not *that* bad, am I?

This new guy she's out with must really be something special if he gets her mom's approval.

"I just really need to speak to her. Can you please tell me where she is? I won't disrupt her date. I just need to see her for a moment, and then I'll leave her alone."

She stands in the doorway, looking me over before she huffs out a huge breath. "She'll be at Club Redemption tonight. I believe they'd planned to go to dinner beforehand. But don't go putting ideas into her head and making promises you can't keep. She deserves to be with someone on her level."

"Yeah, okay. Thanks," I say, already halfway down the stairs.

I pull my phone from my pocket as I get in my car and immediately call Travis.

"Hey, what's up?"

"Hey, Trav. I need you to come with me to Club Redemption tonight. Becca is on a date with some guy her mom thinks is better for her than me, and I just need to see for myself." And hopefully, win Becca back, but I keep that part to myself.

"Oh, umm. Yeah, I can't come with you, but do you need a ride or something? I can hang out for about an hour."

"Why? What are you doing?"

I hear him laugh. *"I'm babysitting for Mom and Dad's neighbor tonight. You met Finley, right?"*

"Since when do you babysit?"

"Since she hired me as a handyman around the house and her kids' dad backed out at the last minute. I was at her place fixing the dishwasher and I offered."

I can't even begin to wrap my head around this development. Hired him as a handyman? And now he's babysitting?

"Okay, whatever. I'll come pick you up and you can drop me at the club. Where are you?"

"At Mom and Dad's."

"On my way."

I hang up and pull away from the curb.

Does Becca's mom really think I'm that bad for her daughter? Becca is the most amazing woman I've ever met, and I have no doubt she deserves the best. But I also know, no matter what her mother thinks, I'm the one to give it to her.

I can't just go walking into Club Redemption myself tonight. I wonder if Aiden will be up for coming out with me?

When I pull up in front of my parents' place, Travis is already waiting outside. Thank god for that, because I don't want to tell Mom what I'm planning to do tonight. Hell, with the way she and Dad fawn all over Becca when she's here, I wouldn't be surprised to learn that they think she could do better than me, too.

"Hey," Travis says when he gets into the passenger seat. "So, you want to tell me what's really going on with you and Becca?"

"You want to tell me why Mom and Dad's neighbor hired you as a handyman and has you babysitting her kids?"

He laughs. "It's kind of a long story. I don't think you have that kind of time tonight. Short version? She's cool, her ex is a deadbeat dad and an asshole, and her kids don't deserve to be treated that way."

Coming from such a big family has shaped the way both Travis and I view families in general. And if there's one thing I know Travis can't stand, it's a dad who won't take responsibility for his family, especially for his kids.

"I guess that's enough for now. But I expect to hear all about her hiring you soon, too. How does someone hire a famous musician to be a handyman?"

I glance at Travis out of the corner of my eye and see his cheeks redden.

"Uh, yeah. If you could maybe not mention the musician part next time you see her? I'd appreciate it."

"Wait. She doesn't know we're in a band?"

This is getting good. If I weren't so wrapped up in Becca right now, I'd be all over this story.

"She knows *you're* in a band." He shakes his head and laughs. "She wondered how come you look the way you do and the rest of us... don't."

Ah, yes. Of course. Old Johnny, not fitting in again. I suppose it would be easy enough to look at me and Travis and decide that I was the one in the band, not him. How we're both in the same band, yet look completely different, amazes people every day.

"Oh, right."

"So. Becca?" Travis asks, changing the subject.

The anxiety is already eating at me, so I may as well fill Travis in on the details. Before we make it to Aiden's place, he knows how I feel about Becca, how I think she feels about me, and how I know her mother feels about me.

"Okay, let me get this straight. You haven't even spoken to her since that night? And now you're going to interrupt her date with someone who is probably better for her than you?"

"I mean, when you put it that way, it sounds almost like you think I should bow out gracefully and let her move on with this new Mr. Perfect."

I pull into Aiden's driveway, parking next to his classic Volvo station wagon (which I keep trying to tell him is an old man's car, but he doesn't pay me any attention), and Travis and I step out of the vehicle.

"No, that's not what I'm saying. But you should take a minute to think about why her mother has such a strong opinion on the matter."

I nod my head. "I'll think about it. But Becca did tell me once that her mother was the worst person on earth. I'm not sure her opinion is trustworthy."

Travis gets into the driver's seat and I head up the stairs and into Aiden's house. Now I just need to convince Aiden to come with me to the club so I can get a look at this guy who Becca's mom seems to think is so much better than me.

I'll look and that's it.

Maybe.

Probably not.

"Hey man, I need a favor." I walk past Aiden and go directly to the kitchen. "I need you to come with me to a club tonight so I can see who Becca is on a date with."

Aiden turns his video game off and joins me in the kitchen. "And why would you want to do that?"

Why do I want to do this? Do I just want to torture myself by seeing Becca with someone else? Convince her to come with me instead?

"I don't know," I admit. "But I feel like I need to."

"Okay, give me a couple of minutes to get changed and we can go."

* * *

"This place is packed. What's your plan?" Aiden asks. "Even with how much she'll stand out in this crowd, it's going to be almost impossible to find her."

"She's right up there," I say, pointing to the second floor. I spotted her as soon as we walked in. Oddly enough, she was looking right at me.

"Dude, how did you know she was there?"

"I have no idea." I shrug. "I just knew." As soon as I walked in, my eyes were drawn to her.

I watch as some guy joins Becca at the table and she turns to face him. He looks like every other guy in here.

"OK, you've seen him. Ready to go?"

"I'll be right back," I say, waving Aiden off and heading for the stairs. "I need to get a closer look."

I climb up to the second with my eyes on Becca the entire time. Fuck, she's gorgeous. It's no wonder her mom is pushing for her to find someone better than me. She is way out of my league.

I take my time going up the stairs, waiting to see what Becca will do, but as I walk, I can tell people are starting to notice me. The music in here is too loud to hear conversations, but I can hear my name and Sleeping Dogs both mentioned as I walk by small groups of people on the wide staircase.

Shit. I didn't do anything to avoid being recognized and even though our fans are usually respectful, I can already see people getting their phones out, ready to snap my picture. This club isn't the kind of place that plays Sleeping Dogs music, so I didn't even consider that anyone would care about me here. Whatever I'm going to say to Becca, it'll have to be quick, because I'm about to be mobbed with requests for selfies from people who aren't even fans of our music. I guess Club Redemption hasn't heard of the silent agreement the rest of Westborough made to leave us alone.

I reach the top of the stairs and get to Becca's table in a few long strides.

"Holy shit," the guy she's with says when he sees me. "You're Johnny Donovan. Can I get a pic with you? Rebecca, take our picture."

I ignore him and reach for Becca, pulling her against me.

"Wha—"

I cut off her question with a kiss, and relief floods my body when she kisses me back.

"I'm so sorry," I tell her. "I have so much more groveling to do, but we need to get out of here. Did you drive?"

She nods, kisses me one more time, and laces her fingers with mine. "Let's go."

Fuck, I love this woman.

"Hey! What about my picture?" her date yells after us as we hurry down the stairs and out the door before anyone tries to stop us.

I guess I'm leaving Aiden here alone, but he'll figure it out. He probably went home as soon as I saw Becca, anyway. I'm sure he knew exactly what was going to happen before we left his house, even before I did.

40

I Missed You Becca

Becca

"Quick, this way." I pull Johnny through the crowd gathered at the entrance to Club Redemption and turn us in the direction of the parking lot. "My car's over here."

Thankfully, I insisted on driving my car here tonight, so when Johnny said we had to leave, I didn't hesitate to take the lead. When we get to my car, though, Johnny takes over. He pulls me against him, wrapping his arms around me, and burying his face in my neck.

"Fuck, I missed you this week. I'm so sorry I drove away like that," he says into my hair. "And then you didn't answer my calls or texts. Or the door when I came to your apartment. I was worried."

I hug him tightly, breathing in his scent. I didn't realize the smell of him was so familiar and comforting to me until it was gone. Seeing him every day, being near him every day, was something I missed more than I thought I would, than I thought I could.

"I wasn't at my apartment. I didn't mean for you to worry. I just needed some time away."

He leans back without letting me go. "When was the last time you were at the apartment?"

"Umm, the day after you drove away? Alex came over that night and did her best friend duty and got me drunk. It's kind of our thing." I grimace a little, thinking of Tino watching me freak out in the street before he called Alex to come check on me.

First, he protected Alex when Connor was creeping around the neighborhood looking for her, then he found someone to come check on me when I was losing my mind in the street. Neighborhood watch has nothing on Tino.

"Right. I remember when you helped her move out of Connor's place briefly and you drunk-texted me after you put Alex to bed." Johnny tips his head forward and whispers, "You have no idea how hard it was for me to leave you that night."

His breath causes a shiver to run down my body, the tingles blazing a trail from his lips to every part of me. Johnny leads me two steps backward and I feel the cold of metal against my back. He presses into me, his hips pinning me to the car, his hands reaching up and cupping my face.

Butterflies run riot in my belly and heat floods my core as Johnny lowers his lips to mine. What starts as a gentle kiss gradually becomes more demanding and I pull him closer to me, attempting to occupy the same space. My brain has one thought: *closer.* Johnny flutters his tongue against mine, alternating the quick movements with long, slow sweeps, and a whimper escapes me.

What is this man doing to me?

He groans, breaking off the kiss and lowering his hands. I can feel his erection pressing into my hip and I watch with lust in my gaze as he adjusts himself.

"We need to get out of here," he says, kissing me again. "Before I fuck you right here in this parking lot, standing up against your car."

The throbbing in my pants likes the idea of having him inside me *right now,* but the fear of being arrested for public indecency wins and I hold up my keys.

"I'm not sure I should be trusted to drive after that kiss. Will you do the honors?"

He smiles and pulls me toward him again, kissing me even more deeply than before, before suddenly breaking away and releasing a huge breath. He takes the keys from me and unlocks the doors, opening the passenger side to let me in. When he's in the driver's seat, I reach over and grab his shirt, pulling him toward me, and kissing him with everything I have.

"Drive fast," I whisper against his lips. "But don't kill us."

I let go of his shirt, and he falls back against the seat with a laugh. "Yes, ma'am."

He starts the car and gets us out of the parking lot. I can't stop touching him, even though he's driving, so I settle for playing with his hair. Running my fingers through his soft curls and gently stroking my fingers along the back of his neck. I don't even watch where he's driving. I'm too busy staring at his profile, memorizing the lines of his face.

This feels big. Like something important is happening.

What does this mean? Am I ready for it?

"You're staring," Johnny says, a grin on his face.

"You're hot," I shoot back. "What do you expect?"

He laughs, reaching back for the hand I'm still running through his hair. He laces his fingers through mine, bringing my hand to his lips for a kiss.

"I think we both know who the hot one is around here," he tells me with a smirk.

Yeah, we do.

Johnny drives us to his place and parks beside Travis' truck, where he normally parks his own car. We both get out and walk toward the elevator at the far end of the parking structure.

"Where's your car?"

"Travis has it. Get this. He's babysitting tonight."

"Yeah? Uncle Travis to the rescue?"

Johnny reaches out and pushes the call button for the elevator, then turns and pulls me into him, wrapping me up in his arms. His lips find their way to my neck, and he lays a trail of kisses up to my ear.

"Not for my sisters. He's watching Finley's kids. Do you remember the single mom across the street from my parents? You met her the day I was an idiot."

The elevator doors open and Johnny pulls me inside, pressing me against the wall as soon as he's keyed in the entry code for the loft he shares with Travis. His hands rest just above the hem of my jeans, teasing the bare skin there with his calloused fingers.

"I remember her," my voice tremulous from his teasing.

Johnny caresses my jaw with his lips, trailing breathy kisses until his lips meet my own. He pokes his tongue out, just barely skimming my lower lip, pulling away every time I try to deepen the kiss, teasing me. The elevator jolts to a stop just as I'm about to smash my lips into his, and he turns to unlock the gate to the loft.

Damn it. Why is he so intent on teasing me right now?

He throws the gate open and reaches back, grabbing my hand. I follow him off the elevator and wait while he locks the gate back up. When he turns back to me, the first thing I notice is how dark his eyes are. Then I notice his careful steps toward me.

"Becca," he practically growls my name. "I hope you don't have any other plans tonight, because I'm not letting you out of my bed until you know exactly how I feel about you."

He closes the distance between us, wraps a hand around the back of my neck, and drags me into his body. He shoves his hands into my hair and tilts my head, closing his mouth over mine. His tongue parts my lips and he kisses me so deeply my head spins. We kiss while we walk to his bedroom, bumping into furniture, nearly tripping at least a dozen times. I push my hands up under his shirt, forcing it up and over his head, discarding it somewhere in the hallway. He does the same with mine before I undo his jeans and shove them down until he kicks them off. We continue to undress each other, discarding clothes all down the hallway and into his bedroom, until we're both naked and panting.

Johnny backs me up against the bed, laying me down and crawling on top of me. He reaches over and turns on a lamp, settling in on his side next to me.

"I need to see you," he says, tracing the lines of the tattoo on my chest with his fingers. "Will you let me touch you?"

He's already touching me, but I know that's not what he's asking. He's asking if it's okay for him to touch my scars. He's done it before, like when he rubbed sunscreen on me at Alex's pool party, but he's never touched with the intent of exploring.

"Yes," I whisper, my heart skittering with the decision. I've never let anyone touch me like this before.

Johnny's fingers trace patterns down my right arm, following the artwork, not the scars. I know he can feel them, though, and it's making me tense up.

"Thank you," he says, cupping my cheek and turning me to face him.

Our lips meet in a soft kiss. Then another. And another.

I push Johnny onto his back and climb on top, straddling his legs. I trace the lines of his abs with my fingers, then my mouth, while sliding myself back down his legs. His eyes darken as he watches me enjoy his body. And boy do I ever enjoy it. I trace the line of the sexy V made by his Adonis belt with my tongue and when I reach the base of his dick, Johnny groans in response. His hands tangle in my hair, tightening on the strands when I swirl my tongue around the head of his cock.

"Fuck," he moans.

I pull him into my mouth, being extra mindful of his piercings. I lick and suck, and lick and suck some more until he's writhing beneath me.

"Becca," he says, attempting to pull me up. "I'm going to come if you don't stop," he warns like that isn't exactly what I'm hoping for.

I grasp for his hands and guide him to fist my hair, pushing down slightly when he's holding on tightly. The answering moan and thrust of his hips tell me he's enjoying this as much as I am.

Johnny holds my hair and pumps up into my mouth twice before releasing into me. I swallow every salty drop, taking what he gives me, moaning and humming my pleasure, while he groans and then stills.

I sit back, wiping my mouth with the back of my hand, a self-satisfied grin on my face. Johnny lays with his eyes closed, panting. When he finally looks at me, I see his eyes are even darker than they were before. He bolts upright, grabbing me and pulling me into a deep kiss.

"That was fucking amazing, babe," he says, resting his forehead against mine. "But now it's my turn."

I'm expecting him to flip me over and lay me on my back to reciprocate, but instead, he lays back and pulls me up his body, settling my knees on either side of his head with his arms wrapped around my legs. I look down to see his face smiling up at me.

"Take a seat, babe," he says with a grin.

"Oh my god, no." I gasp. "I'll suffocate you."

"Then I'll die a happy man," he says, grabbing my hips and pulling me down to sit on his face. "Now sit."

His tongue pokes out and starts working magic on my clit. He's focused on making me come, but when I look down, he's still looking right at me. He groans against me when I make eye contact and I involuntarily rock against him. He groans more and encourages me to keep going, using his hands to guide me to rub myself over his face.

My body starts tensing, my orgasm building, and I close my eyes. I feel a smack on my ass and my eyes fly open. Johnny stares into my eyes, widening his momentarily as if to say *look at me*.

I stare into his eyes as he uses his tongue to drive me over the edge. I shatter into pieces, my body trying to fly apart, held together only by Johnny's eyes. As my orgasm subsides, Johnny lifts me off of him, placing me next to him on the bed.

I close my eyes and try to catch my breath. The crinkle of a condom wrapper gets my attention again. I watch as Johnny rolls the condom down over himself, as he covers each of those barbells one by one, and heat coils low in my belly. He settles himself between my legs, reaching down and pulling my right leg up by the back of my knee, before sliding into me with one long thrust.

I'm not sure who moans louder, me or him.

"You feel so fucking good," he says, rolling his hips and pumping into me slowly. "And the way you came all over my face like that? Fucking. Amazing."

He looks into my eyes again before kissing me, thrusting his tongue in my mouth, claiming me. Another orgasm builds in me on top of the pulsing from the last.

"But what really blows me away is how you swallowed me down," he whispers in my ear. "You made me come with your mouth, and then swallowed every drop. Fuck. That was so fucking hot."

The way his body is rubbing against my clit combined with the things he's saying is just too much, and suddenly my orgasm rips through me. A scream escapes my throat, and my body spasms, the climax taking me hostage. In the distance, I hear Johnny yell in response as he drives into me, settling himself in as deep as he can, while my pussy continues to pulse and his cock pulses right back in response.

Orgasms fully in sync, the pleasure seems endless, shocks of electricity fly through my body, tingles run up and down my spine, and nothing, nothing, has ever felt better.

Finally, he collapses on top of me, kissing my neck lazily. I wrap my arms around him, not ready to let go. He rolls to the side, pulling me tightly against him, and I listen to the sounds of our heartbeats as they gradually slow to a normal pace.

Johnny tilts my face and kisses my lips softly, then disentangles our legs and arms and rolls away.

"I'll just take care of this and be right back." He gestures down and I realize he's talking about the condom.

While he's gone, I make myself comfortable by snuggling down into the blankets and fluffing up pillows. He comes back with a warm washcloth and cleans me up before climbing into the bed with me again. He pulls me into his chest and wraps his arms around me. I lean forward and kiss him, slowly tracing his lips with my tongue, until he moans and deepens the kiss.

"Shh, baby," he whispers against my lips. "Close your eyes and rest. I'm not as young as I used to be. I'll need a few more minutes before I can go again."

I chuckle. "I'm not ready either. You wore me out. I just love kissing you," I say, placing another kiss on his lips.

"Hmm." He kisses me again. "I love kissing you, too. And touching you. And holding you. And just being near you." He wraps me up tightly against his chest and kisses the top of my head. "Now go to sleep so I can fuck you properly in, oh, about an hour."

"Wait, are you saying what we just did wasn't a proper fucking?" I lean back, pretending to be outraged. "That's it, then. I want a refund."

"Oh my god," he says with a slight chuckle, eyes remaining closed. "Your mom was right. We are definitely on different levels."

41

She's Gone

Johnny

"WAIT, ARE YOU SAYING what we just did wasn't a proper fucking?" I feel her push away a little. "That's it, then. I want a refund," she says with a laugh.

"Oh my god," I say, trying to stay awake to keep talking to Becca. "Your mom was right. We are definitely on different levels." I tuck her in against my chest again and before I know it, I'm asleep.

When I wake up, it's mid-morning, and Becca is gone.

No note, no text, no phone call. Nothing.

I thought the night ended perfectly, but now I'm thinking I must've done something wrong. She was joking with me right before I fell asleep, though.

I need to figure what is going on, and what I need to do to fix it. Yet, again, she isn't answering my calls or texts. And I can't even do anything about it today. At least not right now.

The guys and I all promised to be in the studio today to work on the album. With everything that's been going on with Alex and Connor, and Ryder and Denise, we've fallen behind schedule. I mean, we've postponed the tour already, but finishing the album before Denise's baby arrives would be nice. So instead of finding Becca, I have to go and make music.

Great.

I jump in the shower and clean off the scent of sex. I'd much prefer to continue to smell like Becca, but the guys would probably give me shit when I showed up at the studio smelling like sex.

I'm walking out of my room, pulling my shirt over my head, when I see Travis sitting at the island eating a bowl of cereal.

"Hey," he says with a mouthful. "You get drunk last night, or did you come back with a lady friend?"

"What?"

"You left a trail of clothes from the elevator to your room."

I look back and see that he's right. "Becca came back with me," I say, running around and picking u p all of my stuff. Images of us frantically ripping each other's clothes off run through my head. "She left after I fell asleep, and I don't know why." I walk back and throw my clothes into my bedroom.

"She left?"

"Yup. Ran off like a thief in the night. But the only thing she stole was my heart." And I'll be damned if *that* isn't the saddest, sappiest thing I've ever said.

"So... the sex was that bad, huh?" He laughs.

"No, asshole." I grab a cup of coffee from the pot that Travis made. "Best I ever had, and she seemed to enjoy herself too."

He gets up and brings his bowl to the dishwasher. "I think you're doing something wrong if you can only say she 'seemed to enjoy herself'."

I grab a dishtowel from the counter and throw it at him. "Fuck off, man. I said it that way because I'm not giving you the details. I *know* she enjoyed herself. What I don't know is why she left."

Travis grabs his keys, and we make our way to the elevator. On our way down, he asks if I've called Becca yet.

"Of course, I have. I've left so many messages already I'm probably going to steal the record from her mother." Okay, no. Twenty-seven messages are way too many. I'll stop myself long before then. Probably.

"Well, then you'll just need to wait. Maybe she's not 'the one' after all."

I suppose that is always a possibility, but my heart doesn't agree. It's decided on Becca, and all I can do is follow along and do what it says. I need to find her and make this right.

Now, if only I knew what it was I did wrong in the first place.
* * *
After spending most of the day working in the studio, the guys and I are packing up, talking about my Becca problem.

"You know what this is? It's karma." Ryder gestures toward me with the licorice he's eating. Denise has been craving it non-stop, thanks to her pregnancy, and Ryder can't get enough of it now either. "You were a love 'em and leave 'em wanting more type for so long that this is karma getting back at you."

"Haha. Fuck off, Ryder. We can't all magically fall in love with someone who's already in love with us. Some of us need to work for it." Things would be a lot easier if Becca were in love with me.

"If you have to work too hard, maybe it's not meant to be?" Aiden asks. "There comes a point where you will need to just leave her alone, you know."

"Yes, thank you, Aiden. I am aware of that. And if Alex hadn't confirmed that Becca is actually interested, I wouldn't be pursuing her. But she's interested, so I will keep trying. At least as long as she wants me too, anyway."

"just don't ghost her like you do all the others," Aiden says. "You give them a few weeks, make them fall in love with you, and then you disappear."

"I do not do that," I say. "I always give it a fair chance. I just refuse to stick around after I realize the chick isn't the one. How fair would it be of me to waste their time and mine?"

"Give him a break," Travis says. "He's a romantic at heart. Johnny wants to feel Cupid's arrow when it shoots him through the chest."

I open my mouth to protest, but he's not wrong. The thing is, I've already felt that with Becca. Because she is the one.

I already spoke to Alex, and she confirmed Becca is still interested, as far as she knows, but she hasn't talked to her yet today.

If she doesn't get back to me today, at least I know she'll be here tomorrow for Alex's Sunday dinner. This weekly tradition of having dinner together is one of my favorite things that Alex has brought to our little group. Not only is Connor happily in love now, but we're all spending time together as a family, not just making music and going our separate ways.

* * *

I spend a long, sleepless night thinking every noise is a notification on my phone from Becca finally getting back to me. Spoiler: they're not. Not once. I haven't heard a word from her since we fell asleep together at my place.

This morning was a nightmare. I looked at the clock every five minutes, waiting for it to be late enough to go over to Connor's place. In the past, I would have just gone over, but now that he has Alex, I can't allow myself to intrude on their private time. Especially since we'll all be there for dinner, anyway.

I plan to take a little extra care dressing today. If I'm going to see Becca, then I want her to look at me and like what she sees. I assume she already does, but dressing better can't hurt. Luckily, I have a pretty good idea of what Becca likes, and I just so happen to have a closet full of it.

I pull out ripped jeans, a faded black vintage Ramones t-shirt, Black Doc Martens, and the dark gray survival-style jacket I won off a roadie in a game of poker during our first tour. After a quick shower, I get dressed and put a little product in my hair, just to keep the curls from getting too fuzzy, and I'm ready to go.

Here's goes nothing.

42

Leaving Tonight

Becca

"Thank you, all of you, really, for your concern, but whatever you think is or is not happening between me and Aiden is really none of your business. I'm a grown-ass woman. I can handle my own love life, thank you very much," Rhea says, defending herself from the grand inquisition being directed at her by all the women gathered around in Alex's kitchen.

Everyone is silent for a beat before we all burst into laughter in unison.

"Oh, honey, you're one of us now. Your love life is everyone's business, I'm afraid. It's probably even scheduled on Ivy's calendar to check in on you two sometime," I say and Ivy nods in agreement like she does have it booked already.

In the last few weeks, Denise hired Ivy, the server from the diner, to be her new assistant, and it sounds like she's doing a fabulous job. I'm glad. I really enjoyed talking to her at the diner. She'll be fun to have around.

Alex jumps in. "Just wait. As soon as we're done with you, we'll be talking to Becca about Johnny." She winks at me while everyone laughs some more.

"That *is* on today's agenda," Ivy jokes. "I've got you penciled in for six o'clock."

"Look, that really is none of your business. I'm serious," I say firmly, pointing a warning finger at everyone around the table. "Stay out of it." Maybe I don't like Ivy as much as I thought.

The laughter gets louder, and I can feel my anger growing. If only they knew what he said to me after sex the other night. How could he agree with my mother? Okay, I can see how he could. I'm not on his level. But how could he think saying it to me at all, let alone at that exact moment, was a good idea?

"Oh, so you're the baking muse Aiden was talking about? The reason that Johnny has crazy baking marathons?" Rhea asks me.

A muse? Me?

Yeah, right. I snort a laugh.

"What do you mean, *baking marathons*? Johnny bakes?" Alex has calmed herself down enough to join in the conversation. "He's never baked for me." She sticks her lip out in a pout.

"Oh, I mean, that's just what Aiden told me. Maybe I misheard?" Rhea backpedals.

"No, Rhea's right. He bakes when he's stressed. I keep telling him I don't want a relationship and he's upset about it. So he bakes and brings most of it to Aiden for the shelter." I was almost ready to give in to him too before he told me he agreed with my mother. I would have had my first actual boyfriend. At thirty-five years old.

"What do you mean, he brings it to Aiden for the shelter?" Rhea looks even more confused than she sounds. For all that we're giving her shit about Aiden, it doesn't seem like she knows him all that well yet.

"I volunteer at a local domestic violence shelter. I bring Johnny's baked goods for the moms and kids that are using our services there. A home-baked treat goes a long way when I'm making friends with the new kids. I usually play with them while their moms talk to the director in private." Aiden walks into the kitchen, followed by the rest of the guys in the band.

"And I do the baking." Johnny looks amazing and now I'm even more pissed off. Why didn't I think to dress up and make him sorry for what he's missing out on? "I'm Johnny. It's nice to meet you." He turns to look at Aiden. "You're right, man, she is hot."

The rest of the conversation flies right by me as I sit and seethe. Rhea is a beautiful woman. And she's not covered in scars. She'd be a much more appropriate partner for Johnny. No wonder he thinks she's hot. I cross my arms tightly over my chest and I sit there, replaying the other night over and over in my head.

Laying there with Johnny, satisfied, tired, and so happy for the first time. And then he says it. My mother is right. We're not on the same level. Why would he come out and tell me I'm not good enough for him?

It was good, right? He said so. I know *I've* never come so hard in my life. Nor so often. The problem with one night is your partner rarely cares about your needs. Johnny seemed to care. Like getting me off was his only concern. Like he wanted it more than he wanted his own release.

So why tell me I'm not good enough for him?

I'm jolted out of my thoughts when I look up and everyone is already leaving the room. Soon it's just me and Gran.

"Well, my dear. Looks like things between you and Johnny are still complicated. Didn't you take my advice to play with each other's genitals?"

I choke on my spit, not sure whether I'm trying to laugh or protest.

"It's okay if you haven't yet. I just figured you kids moved faster these days."

"That's not it, Gran. We, uh, we tried. But he's decided I'm not good enough for him and I refuse to hang around and keep his bed warm while he waits for someone better."

Gran sits up straighter and looks me in the eye. "He said that to you? That little fucker. Go get me a wooden spoon. I'm going to teach that boy a lesson his momma should have taught him long ago. JOH—"

"Shhhh," I whisper, putting my hand over her mouth. "No, Gran. No. Thank you, but that's unnecessary. His mom is a lovely woman. I know she taught him better. He must've gotten this attitude as part of his rock star ego or something. He definitely didn't learn it at home. He could learn something like that at my home, but not at his."

Gran looks at me, duck-billing her lips and squinting. "What do you mean, he could learn that at your home?"

Shit.

"Nothing, Gran. Just that his house is a lot warmer and kinder than mine, so it's unlikely he would get that attitude from his parents."

"But he could get it from your parents?"

This old broad is more perceptive than she looks. She knows I'm hiding something, and I think she even has a pretty good guess at what it is. I blow out a breath and swivel my head around, making sure we're alone.

"My mother has worked hard my whole life to make sure I never got hurt by trying to have a relationship with someone above my station." I fold my hands in my lap and look down, suddenly unable to look Gran in the eye. "I know that someone like Johnny would never want to spend his life waking up next to someone who looks like me. I just forgot for a moment. When he told me that my mom was right, that we *are* on different levels, it was a wake-up call. I know I needed it, but it still hurt."

A tear falls into my lap. Gran touches my chin, lifting my face so I can see her. "You are perfect the way you are. You deserve love and happiness with someone who loves you wholeheartedly, and who you love the same way." She wipes my cheeks with a papery-skinned hand. "And your mother sounds like a huge bitch."

I choke out a laugh. "Yeah, she is. She is such a bitch."

"And you know what they say about bitches, right?" she asks.

I shake my head.

A huge grin splits Gran's face. "Bitches be trippin'"

We both burst into loud laughs.

"What's going on in here?" Alex says from the entrance to the hallway. "Are you two skipping dinner or will you be joining us in the dining room? We've saved seats for you." She winks at me and turns around.

Fuck. That means I'm sitting by Johnny.

"Now listen here," Gran says, grabbing both of my hands. "You are a talented, smart, funny, and incredibly beautiful woman. Johnny would be lucky to have your attention for even one minute, let alone every day for the rest of his life. This is his loss. Not yours." She pulls me by my hands and squeezes me in her arms. She's another good hugger, just like Johnny's mom. How did I survive so long without good hugs? "Now, let's go get some food. It's like they're trying to let an old lady starve to death around here or something."

I pull back from the hug and stand up. "Well, we can't have that, can we?" I hold my hand out to her. "May I escort you to the dining room?"

Gran pretends to fan herself while she flutters her eyelashes. "Oh my, what a gentleman," she says in a ridiculous falsetto. "I would love that."

We walk into the dining room together and, just as I predicted, I am sitting next to Johnny. Just perfect.

"Can we please talk?" he leans over and whispers in my ear.

"Now's not the time."

"After?"

"Sure. But not for long."

No one knows yet, but I'm leaving town for a while. When I left Johnny's place in the middle of the night on Friday, the first thing I did when I got home, besides bringing in the pile of rocks he left for me, was to book a plane ticket to Las Vegas. It's time I take Uncle Silas up on his offer of a place to stay for a while.

And I'm leaving tonight.

43

Drunk Dickheads

Johnny

"You didn't do anything wrong, Johnny. That's what I'm trying to tell you. You're allowed to feel the way you feel. I just know I can't be with someone who agrees with my mother."

We keep going around in circles and I just don't understand what the issue is.

"You don't want me to agree that we are on different levels?"

She huffs out a breath. "No, Johnny. That's not what I'm saying. Look, I don't have time to keep talking about this. I have to get going. I'm going out to see someone. We can talk another time, okay? We can still be friends." She chokes on the words, and I can see the wetness of tears pooling in her eyes. I want nothing more than to pull her into me, to comfort her, but she's already walking to her car.

"Becca!" I yell. "Come back, please."

She doesn't turn around, just waves as she gets into her car. I watch as she drives away, her tail lights disappearing at the end of Connor's driveway, where she turns onto the main road.

She's really gone.

What did she say? She's going out with someone? She's already dating again? I know our relationship was fake, but I also know I wasn't the only one feeling something more the other night. Did she get scared? Is that what's happening?

Fuck it. Time to get drunk.

I drive my car to the nearest liquor store and buy a couple of bottles of whiskey. I get back in the car and pull out my phone.

Johnny - Hey. You busy? I need to get drunk.

I wait for a few minutes, but when I still get no response, I decide to just drive over to Aiden's and wait for him to get home.

I pull into Aiden's driveway a few minutes later. His old Volvo still isn't here, so I just stay in my car.

Might as well get a head start. I open one of the bottles of whiskey and take a long drink. Not my regular drink of choice. I much prefer the craft beers I usually drink, but those remind me too much of Becca. Plus, whiskey will get me drunk faster and that is the goal tonight.

I sit back and listen to music for a while before Aiden finally pulls into the driveway. I grab both whiskey bottles and get out of my car.

"What are you doing here?" Aiden asks, looking a little irritated. He must not be having a very good night, either.

I hold up the whiskey bottles. "Thought maybe you'd want to have a drink or seven with me? Gotta warn you, though. I got a head start." I take a few swallows, spilling some onto my shirt.

"Fuck, dude. You didn't drive here like that, did you?"

"No. No, no, no." I shake my head and take another drink. "I've been waiting here for a while. Tried to get Becca to talk to me when we were leaving Connor's place and, uh, she was going on another date. So I figured it was just time for me to give up, and I came over here to get drunk with you. Travis has been too busy with whatever secret shit he's been up to lately, so I thought maybe you'd be a good surrogate brother."

Aiden turns and walks to his front door, motioning for me to follow. "Come on in," he says, unlocking the door. "I could use a drink or two."

We've had a few drinks by the time we decide to jam in his garage-turned-rehearsal space. When we first started Sleeping Dogs, we would rehearse here every spare minute we had. That was well before Aiden had the place soundproofed, too. I'm sure the neighbors appreciated it when he finally had the money to do it.

I walk in and grab a vintage Gretsch off the wall. Aiden is a lover of music, and he has a decent collection of instruments. He may be a drummer at heart, as proven by the many percussion instruments he has in here, but he also knows how to play guitar, bass, and piano. I wish I were half as talented as he is.

"So, what are we playing?" I ask. "Start us off."

Aiden gets a little blues shuffle started. Perfect. Some dirty blues feels appropriate for my mood tonight.

We play for a few hours, pouring whiskey down our throats the entire time until I can't even see straight. I know the music still sounds good, though. We are professional musicians, after all. I'm pretty sure I was dead drunk for every show of our first two tours. Aiden's never been much of a drinker, but he's so talented I bet he could still play if he were in a coma. His heartbeat would play the perfect rhythm.

We finish up and lie on the floor, staring up at the ceiling.

"So you're having a shit day too, huh?" I ask him. Shit. My bottle's empty.

"Yeah, you could say that," he says, passing me his nearly empty bottle.

"Is it because of that Rhea chick? You were looking at her with hearts in your eyes this afternoon."

"Shut up," he says. "It's complicated."

"Isn't it always?" I mumble to myself.

After a few quiet minutes, Aiden breaks the silence.

"I have a great idea. Come on." He jumps up from the floor and runs out of the garage. "We need to go somewhere," he yells from the kitchen.

I roll over and force myself to a standing position. Looks like I met my goal of getting drunk. I wonder if I'll remember any of this tomorrow?

"Good morning, my beautiful lads!"

Oh, shit! Who's screaming? And why is it so fucking bright in here?

"Drink this and then get your asses up. We've got work to do."

I try to talk, but all that comes out is a groan

"I don't have all day, sunshine," a gruff-sounding voice says from somewhere above me. "Get off your ass, drink this drink, and get ready to work the rest of the liquor out of you. Ryder, go get a couple of buckets from the janitor's closet. I have a feeling these two shitheads are going to need them."

Ryder's here? And two shitheads? That can only be me and Aiden. The last thing I remember is him having a great idea in his kitchen.

"Can I get some water?" I hear Aiden say from somewhere beside me. "And maybe all the painkillers? Pretty sure I'm dying."

"You and me both, man," I say, still not getting up. The floor is nice and cool and I think I'm just going to lie here for a while. "What did we even do last night? What was your great plan?"

"You drank a LOT of whiskey, and committed some crimes." Devon laughs. "You didn't get arrested, though, so you're good there."

"So why are we at the gym?" Aiden asks.

I sit up and take the disgusting green slime drink that's been left for me.

"Well, by the time I got you guys out of there, it was almost morning. So I figured why not get Ryder to come and let us into the gym? You guys could sleep a bit, I could work out, and then we could put you through the paces to get you sobered up," Devon explains. "So drink up, water and smoothie, and then we'll get started. Alex's Pops says he has a special workout for you, guaranteed to make you sweat out all the alcohol."

"I said puke it out, actually," Pops yells from the back of the gym. "I guarantee you will puke before we're through." He laughs a maniacal old man laugh. "It's been a while since I've made anyone puke. This is going to be fun."

Pops leads us through a workout that I'm pretty sure was designed by the devil himself. I puke up everything I've ever eaten, plus something that smells like the spill mat behind a bar, just a mess of alcohol and rancid mixers.

By the end of the workout, Aiden and I are drenched in sweat, empty of alcohol, and completely exhausted.

I flop down on the floor and enjoy the cool feeling of the black rubber mat against my overheated skin.

"That was a fucking nightmare," I say.

"I'm never drinking again," Aidens promises, like every teenager who's ever had too much to drink.

"Yeah, I'm regretting drinking so much last night, too." I roll onto my stomach. "Oh, that feels nice," I say, spreading my arms and legs on the floor.

"How're the hangovers, boys?" Pops asks, leaning over us where we lie. "I got some whiskey in my desk. Who wants a drink?"

"Fuck off, get that shit away from me," I say at the same time as Aiden says, "No fucking way."

Pops makes us wash out our own puke buckets before we leave with Devon, who drives us back to Aiden's place so I can grab my car.

My head is throbbing the entire drive home and I'm beginning to think drinking a bottle of whiskey was not the right way to go about figuring out what was going on with Becca.

But calling her best friend Alex might be.

As soon as I park my car, I pull out my phone and call Alex. *"Hello?"*

"Alex? It's Johnny. Do you have a minute?"

"Sure. What's up?"

"I fucked up with Becca."

"I was wondering what was going on yesterday. She didn't want to talk about it."

"Fuck. I was hoping you could tell me what I did. But if she didn't tell you, then I'm fucked."

"Did she say anything at all?"

"Nothing helpful. She said that I did nothing wrong."

"That's it?"

"Then she said that she wouldn't settle for someone who agrees with her mother."

"You agree with her mother?" Alex yells so loudly I need to hold the phone away from my ear. *"What the fuck is wrong with you?"*

Okay, now I'm really confused. Why wouldn't Becca's best friend agree that I'm not nearly good enough for her?

"She told me we're not on the same level, and I agree. Becca is way too good for me. I'm lucky she looked at me twice."

Alex laughed into the phone, but there was no humor in it.

"You... you... Are you a fucking idiot?" She continues to laugh.

"Hey now, there's no need for name calling. But yeah, I'm probably an idiot if you're asking me like that. What did I do?"

"Her mother doesn't think you're not good enough for Becca. She thinks Becca isn't good enough for you."

44

Vegas, Baby

Becca

"Becca?"

"Hi, Uncle Silas. You still have room for me?"

I'm standing on the front porch of Uncle Silas and Uncle Patrick's Spring Valley home after an early morning flight and a quick taxi ride. I'm so exhausted that I feel like I walked here from Westborough.

Uncle Silas grabs me and wraps his enormous arms around me, squeezing so tightly I can barely breathe. I missed this.

"Babe," Uncle Silas tilts his head back and yells into the house. "Becca's here. Come grab her and I'll bring her luggage in."

Uncle Patrick comes around the corner wearing a flowing floral romper and runs down the hallway to me. Ugh. Why does he always have to look so much better than me, no matter what he wears?

"Becca, baby," he says, pulling me away from Uncle Silas and wrapping me up in a hug. "Why didn't you tell us you were coming? You know I would have picked you up at the airport."

I heave a huge sigh and sink into his arms just as he's about to let me go. "I know. I sort of decided in a hurry and didn't plan much out. I'm not even sure what I've got packed in my suitcase. I just grabbed stuff and threw it in."

"Oh, honey. Come in. I was just finishing making breakfast." He takes my hand and leads me into the house. "We'll eat, then have a look through your suitcase. We might need to make today a shopping day."

That sounds good to me. I'm thinking I might need one of those rompers Uncle Patrick has on. Or maybe not. I never did like the thought of peeing with my tits hanging out, and besides comfort, that's what rompers are known for.

Over a breakfast of the best pancakes I've ever had outside of a diner, I tell my uncles all about Johnny and what's been going on. Uncle Silas slams his hand down on the table when I tell them he agreed with mom, and what exactly it was he agreed with.

"We'll talk about Johnny in a minute," Uncle Patrick says through gritted teeth, his face a shade of red I've never seen. "I need you to tell me, from the very beginning, exactly what your mother has been saying to you. The very beginning."

I've never told Uncle Patrick or Uncle Silas the full truth, not even way back when Uncle Silas was tattooing over my scars and helping me with Milo. Not any time over the years when I've visited. Not any time over the years when my mother has been extra hard on me. It was my burden to bear. My fault for pulling that soup pot over myself and ruining her life the way I did. I just dealt with it as best I could, alone, because it was what I deserved.

Uncle Patrick has tears in his eyes by the time I'm done with my story. Uncle Silas is another thing altogether. Have you ever seen an almost seven-foot tall, three-hundred-fifty-pound, hairy, bearded, and tattooed giant of a man in a legitimate berserker rage?

It's a terrifying and awesome sight to behold.

He stormed off into the backyard as soon as I stopped talking. A peek out the French doors to the back deck shows that he's out there throwing around lawn furniture and yelling.

"FUCK!" I hear through the doors, seemingly not muffled by the glass in the slightest.

"Is he okay?" I ask Uncle Patrick. "He's going to break all your patio furniture."

Uncle Patrick doesn't even hear me. He's staring off into space while tears silently stream down his cheeks. I reach over and place my hand on his arm. He shakes his head and wipes the tears away, turning to look at me with a sad smile.

"I am so, so sorry, Becca."

"It's not your fault, Uncle Patrick. I never told you. I never told anyone until recently. Hell, I just told my best friend Alex the other day." I chuckle. "It's not like you know my mother, or what kind of person she is."

"I should have," he says sadly. "I should have known."

Uncle Silas is still raging in the backyard. I look out the window and see that he's about halfway through kicking down the storage shed where they store their pool equipment and yard tools. I shake my head. He's madder than I've ever seen him. Madder than I've ever seen anyone. And it's all on my behalf. *Amazing.*

Uncle Patrick is still sitting at the table, looking stunned. It's the least enthusiastic he's ever been. I think maybe we're both a little tired after that story.

"Uncle Patrick? I've been up all night so I'm going to have a quick nap if that's good with you. Then maybe later this afternoon we can go shopping. I have a feeling you're going to need all new patio furniture and a new garden shed."

"Huh? Oh, yes, of course, sweetie. Let me show you to your room." He gets up and takes my hand. But he doesn't go anywhere. Instead, he wraps his arms around me again. "I love you, baby. I will make this right," he whispers before taking my hand again and leading me down the hallway.

He opens the door to the room that's to be mine, and I instantly love it. I haven't been to visit since they moved out to Spring Valley, so I haven't seen this room before. There's a wall shelf full of vintage cameras of all makes and models, and a giant king-size bed that looks like it might actually be made of clouds.

"I've been collecting those for years," Uncle Patrick says when he sees me examining the cameras. "I wanted to make a room just for you, and I thought the cameras would be a fun touch."

"I love them. They're amazing." I say, a true smile creeping up on my face for the first time in days. "I can't wait to inspect them all more closely. I'm going to have to order some film and whatever else these cameras use so I can try them out." My mind races with thoughts of making an art installation, something that hasn't occurred to me in years.

"Okay, darling. I'll let you sleep now."

"Thank you so much. I feel so much better after telling you both about everything."

"I'm glad to hear that. I wish you'd told me sooner, so I could have done more about it. But that was your decision to make. I'm just sorry I wasn't around then to figure it out." He gives me a nod and another sad little smile before leaving the room and closing the door behind him.

I'm planning out the art exhibit in my head when I lay down on the bed. I was right, it's made of clouds. It must be, because it's so soft I'm asleep almost instantly. Even the excitement of finding a passion for art photography again is not enough to keep the exhaustion at bay.

I wake up a little while later to the sounds of yelling. It sounds like I'm hearing one side of an argument. Either the other person is whispering, or this is a phone argument. I have a niggling suspicion that this is something I need to hear, so I roll out of bed and tiptoe to the door, opening it just a crack.

"I don't care what our arrangement was back then. There's nothing you can hold over me now, anyway."

It's Uncle Patrick. He sounds almost as mad as Uncle Silas was earlier. Who's he talking to, though?

I open the door a little further, trying to make out another voice.

"I'm not keeping this secret any longer." Still Uncle Patrick.

"Tell her we're saying something today." That's Uncle Silas. So whoever Uncle Patrick is having an argument with is on the phone. And it's a woman.

"She's worried about her reputation," Uncle Patrick says. "She thinks people will look down on her."

"As they should," Uncle Silas yells, probably so the woman on the phone can hear him. "They should fucking look down on, you bit—"

"Shhh, you'll wake up Becca."

Too late. I'm already awake and I'm so damn curious I'm about to army crawl out there on my belly so I can eavesdrop better. I know I shouldn't be listening in on something that has nothing to do with me, but I can't help it. There's just this... feeling telling me I need to hear this. I don't know what it is, but the only other time my intuition spoke to me this strongly was about Johnny. And maybe that didn't turn out exactly as I finally let myself hope, but it brought about a positive change in me. I consider it a win. A painful, heartbreaking win, but still a win.

"Listen here, you cold-hearted bitch. If I'd known what kind of person you actually were, I'd have taken her long ago. I'm sure the fact that I had to find her purely by accident would have benefited me in family court."

Nope, I can't take it anymore. I need to get closer. I open the door and drop to the floor, slithering on my belly as silently as a snake down to the end of the hallway. I'm still hidden here unless they come around the corner, but I should be okay.

"You think you've had a rough time of it? Imagine you're me. Imagine your bitch of an ex-wife takes your baby and moves to an undisclosed location and you don't find her until she's an adult. Imagine you've already taken a job in a different city when you find her. Now imagine it's fifteen years later and you find out that the mother of your only child has been an abusive cunt all this time."

I... what? I suddenly feel nauseated.

"I don't care. I should have told her when I figured it out. She might hate me when she finds out, but she deserves to know the truth. I'll be begging her for forgiveness, and I suggest you do the same, Rebecca. From Becca, and from whatever gods you believe in because the way you've treated our daughter is despicable. Goodbye, and fuck you."

A sob follows the sound of crunching metal and smashing glass. A sob so loud it nearly breaks my heart. It doesn't because my heart is currently jumping out of my chest, but it comes damn close. I roll onto my back and stare at the ceiling, trying to figure out how I feel about this.

Uncle Patrick is my dad?

What?

"You might as well come out here and join us, Becca. We have some things to talk about. It's time for a long overdue conversation." Uncle Silas is standing at my head, looking down at me. Should I call him Dad? Should I call my father, Uncle Patrick, Dad?

I get to my feet and follow Uncle Silas to the living room, where Uncle Patrick is sitting on the couch, crying his eyes out. And even though I should be mad that he knew and didn't tell me, that they've both hidden this from me for years, I go to him.

I sit next to the man I now know is my father. The man who didn't abandon me because he couldn't deal with my scars. The man who's loved me from a distance all these years. I sit next to him, I rest my head on his shoulder, and I cry with him.

45

This Little Piggy

Johnny

THE LAST TIME I was here, Rebecca helped me track down Becca, and I'm hoping she can do the same for me now. There's one big difference this time, though. Well, two actually.

This time I'm fucking pissed off.

And I have Alex with me. And she's also fucking pissed off.

I spent all day at the shelter with Aiden yesterday. Playing with all the kids there helped to improve my mood, but it certainly didn't remove Becca from my mind. Spending the whole night crafting dicks out of cookies, cakes, and candies with Gran and her best friends, Gladys and Lana, didn't help either. We saved their penis-themed gender reveal party and their new event planning business in the process, though, so at least I accomplished something productive. Plus, I learned how to make circumcised and uncircumcised dicks out of various treats. So if Sleeping Dogs breaks up, and tattooing doesn't pan out for me, I could always open a naughty bakery.

None of that matters if I can't find Becca, though.

"Thanks for coming with me," I say as we approach the house. We had to park further down the street because there was nothing available close by. "You can stop me from throwing her through the window."

I would never actually do it, of course. But I'd be lying if I didn't say I was thinking particularly violent thoughts about this woman.

"Fine," Alex says. "As long as you *don't* stop me from punching her in the face."

"Deal," I say with a chuckle. "But can you wait until after we find out where Becca is? I don't think she'll be very cooperative once you've punched her in the face."

"Ugh, fine," Alex says with a roll of her eyes. "Make it fast."

I shake my head a little. I wonder if Connor knows just how bloodthirsty Alex is. Scratch that. Of course he knows. She rescued him from an attempted rape and beat the perpetrator so badly that she broke her hand while breaking the woman's face. It would be impossible for him not to know.

I lift my hand to knock on the door, but Alex beats me to it, smashing it so hard with the side of her fist that the entire frame shakes. She continues smashing it until it flies open.

"What?" Rebecca snarls. She looks like shit. Her hair is a mess, she's in a ratty bathrobe, and she's holding a bottle of cheap wine. "Oh, it's you. I guess you might as well come in." She stumbles away from the door. "Don't just stand there. Get in here and close the door. It's cold."

Alex and I look at each other. If my eyebrows look like hers, then they're mingling with my hairline. To say I'm shocked would be an understatement. Rebecca's house is a disaster. Broken glass everywhere, torn clothes thrown all over the floor, plus there's the smell of something burning lingering in the air.

"What the hell happened here?" I ask. "Looks like the aftermath of a kegger at a frat house."

"Oh, please. Like you don't know already."

"Uh, no. Did you get robbed or something?" I hate this woman, but I wouldn't wish actual crimes on her. Throwing her through the window is just a therapeutic thought I entertain.

Alex, on the other hand, looks almost gleeful as she takes in the wreckage that is Rebecca's house.

"Looks to me like you got what you deserved," she tells Rebecca. "I might not need to punch you in the face after all."

"Oh sure, come here and inflict more pain on me. Ever since Rebecca was born, my life has been nothing but problem after problem. All anyone ever wanted to do was hold the baby, play with the kid, and talk about her. *What's little Rebecca doing?*" She makes a disgusted face.

"Well, you're not going to like what we're here to ask you, then."

"Then when she had that accident. It got worse. I thought it would get better. People were supposed to think of me, of all the sacrifices I made. But nooo," she says, drawing out the no in a singsong sort of voice. "Of course not. They wanted to know how *little Rebecca* was healing, whether the scarring was bad, and if she was going to be okay in the long run. It wasn't even worth all the trouble I went to in the first place."

"Yeah, we feel terrible for you. Where's Becca?" Alex asks, not bothering to look at Rebecca.

"And after I took her away from her freak of a father. Did she thank me? Of course not. I had to tell her he left because of her scars, even though they came later. Because she was too ugly. And what does she do? She runs right to him. Finds him anyway. *Because* of the damn scars." She scoffs and tries to drink from her bottle but discovers it's empty. "People were supposed to feel bad for me, not for her. And then, when I figure out a way to get my due from her, to keep her tied to me forever by choosing an appropriate husband, she finds you." She points at me, a look of disgust on her face. "All those years I spent telling her no man would want to wake up every day and see her disgusting scars, and then you come along. You should want to be with a model, or an actress, not a scarred photographer who can't even keep a job."

Holy shit, the hate this woman is spewing about her daughter is making me sick. Even Alex looks a little green.

"Listen here. We. Don't. Care. Just tell us where Becca is and we'll leave you to stew in your self-pity."

"I arrange the scars and Silas Mathews finds her because of them. And Silas Mathews is married to my ex-husband. Can you believe that? Not only did my husband turn out to be a gay, but he *married* another man. He'd rather be with a huge, hairy beast of a man than me. It's disgusting if you ask me."

I look at Alex and raise my eyebrows in question. She nods. She heard it, too. Rebecca just said she 'arranged' Becca's scars. Alex tilts her head toward Rebecca and raises her fist a little.

'*Should I hit her now?*' she seems to ask. I shake my head. We still don't know where Becca is. We can't punch her yet. Alex sticks out her lower lip in a pout. It reminds me of when we were kids and my mom used to tell us a rooster would poop on our lip if we did that. A chuckle escapes my lips.

"Oh sure, it sounds funny," Rebecca slurs from her spot on the couch, mistaking my chuckle to be about what she's told us. "Do you know how many times I had to cook soup on the front burner before that stupid kid finally pulled it down? It had to have been hundreds. I finally had to ask her to check on it, to make it happen. It was alright though. She never remembered that I asked her to do it, so the authorities never suspected a thing."

Alex's reflexes are quicker than mine because, by the time I've taken a step, she's on top of Rebecca and holding her by the collar of her robe. "Now listen here, you dumb bitch," she growls in Rebecca's face. "Tell us where Becca is, what her father's name is, and I might let you live. If you don't, I'll get Johnny here to knock you out and drag you to your bathtub so I can dismember you without making a mess. Then I'll throw the pieces of you in the trash where homophobic child-abusing pieces of shit like you belong."

Rebecca's eyes bug out and her mouth moves, but she doesn't seem able to talk.

"Nah," I say. "My great Uncle John owns a farm with pigs. I'm sure they'd love a taste of a homophobic child-abusing piece of shit. Plus, virtually no evidence that way."

Alex drops Rebecca to the couch. "Good thinking. What do you think? Should I count to ten and if she doesn't tell us, you can knock her out? It's getting kind of late. I need to get home to cook dinner."

"Yeah, that sounds fair."

"One…"

"You can't do this," Rebecca stammers.

"Two…"

"But…but…"

"Three…"

"Okay, fine. Her father's name is Patrick Johnson, and he lives in Las Vegas. She said she was planning to go for a visit soon, so she probably went there."

"Do you have his phone number?" I ask.

She glares at me and shakes her head. "You two can leave now."

I look at Alex and give her a nod. She grins, winds up, and spins, throwing a punch with all of her weight behind, knocking Rebecca out.

"Impressive," I say. "You really want me to drag her to the bathtub?"

She shakes out her hand, opening and closing it to work off the pain. "Nah," she says with a chuckle. "I didn't even bring my knives."

I go to Becca's mom and roll her onto her side on the couch. She's a garbage human being, and we may have just been threatening to dismember her and feed her to my uncle's pigs, but I still don't want her to choke to death on her own vomit.

"Ready?"

"You bet," Alex says. "We don't have much time. I have a plan."

We drive back to Alex and Connor's place and get to work. We find a listing for all the people named Patrick Johnson with listed phone numbers in Las Vegas, and another for all the ones named Silas Mathews. Alex gets the listings printed off and I call everyone to come over and help.

Pretty soon we have the two of us, plus Connor, Devon, Xena, and Gran here to help. Everyone else is either busy or not answering. It will be fine though. We only have seventy-five numbers to call, so with six of us, it should go quickly. Plus, maybe we'll get lucky and it will be one of the first calls we make.

46

On Purpose

Becca

THE LAST FEW WEEKS have been intense. I've spent a lot of time getting to know more about my dad. It feels so weird to say that after all these years of thinking my dad had left because of me, but it's nice.

I've settled on calling my biological father, formerly Uncle Patrick, Dad, and calling his husband, formerly Uncle Silas, Poppa Silas.

Dad and I have had several long discussions about why he never told me he knew I was his daughter and even though it hurts that we missed all that time, I understand, and I forgive him. He didn't even figure it out until Poppa Silas was telling him about how he got her permission to tattoo me years after the fact. They opened their home to me before they knew who I was because they cared about me as a person. Because they're good people who saw a kid in pain and knew they could help.

"Well, honey," Dad says, walking into the kitchen where I'm having breakfast. "I'm so excited to have you come see the show tonight. Are you sure it's okay if I introduce you to the audience?"

Dad is going to introduce me as his daughter in the middle of his Dara Mia show tonight and he's more excited than a kid at Christmas. So am I, actually.

"Of course, Dad. I can't wait."

"Can't wait for what?" Poppa Silas walks in behind Dad and gives him a hug before bending to kiss me on the cheek.

"For the show tonight," I say, sipping my coffee. "I still need to find something to wear. Do you have time for some shopping today?"

When I got here, after we sorted through the disaster of a phone call I overheard, Dad and I went shopping for some essentials. It turns out I did a terrible job of packing when I was running away from Johnny. I threw the contents of my underwear and t-shirt drawers in my suitcase, grabbed a toothbrush, and called it a day. Underwear and t-shirts will only get you so far, even in Vegas.

"Oh, me too. I love going to the shows. Your Unc—I mean, Dad is such an amazing performer. I am truly a lucky man." He pulls Dad in and gives him a sweet kiss.

Ugh. True love. I feel a stab of pain in my heart that I *wish* was a heart attack. Instead, it's heartache from missing Johnny.

"I have to get to the club to make sure everything is ready for tonight. I don't want any mistakes. My daughter is going to be on stage with me. This has to go off without a hitch. It's one of the most important days of my life." It's so cute how nervous he is about this.

Being here has been amazing. Spending time with these two men, who both love me more than anything, has me feeling like the Grinch. My heart's grown three sizes. It still hurts from Johnny's confession, but it's getting better with every passing day.

He's been calling and texting me daily, but I haven't read or listened to his messages. I'm not ready to talk yet. I will be soon. I miss him. But I won't settle, not even for him.

"I can take you shopping," Poppa Silas says. "We can drop Patrick off at the club, then hit the shops. Does that sound good?"

"That sounds perfect." I get up and bring my dishes to the sink. "Let me get dressed and I'll be ready to go."

I leave them to eat their own breakfasts and head back to my room. My room full of amazing cameras. Dad helped me track down everything I needed for a couple of the old 35mm cameras and I'm bringing one of them with me to the show tonight.

The art exhibit I thought of creating is underway. I'm taking pictures of things using all the cameras in my collection and comparing them to each other and to current technology. I love it. Dad introduced me around at all the shops he's used to source the cameras and the men and women working there have been amazing resources. One of them is even giving me free rein in his darkroom for the time being, so I'm developing everything myself.

I may have been running away from something, but coming here has changed me in so many good ways that I can't be mad about it. If Johnny hadn't said he agreed with my mother, I never would have come here. I never would have learned Uncle Patrick was really my dad. And now that I know he is, I can't imagine going back to having just my mom.

I've been gone for three weeks, and she hasn't even called me. For a woman who used to leave me upwards of twenty voicemails in a row, it's strange. But she seemed a little weird when I told her I was coming here, so I'm not worried about it. I'm sure she's fine.

I'm pulling on a t-shirt when my phone rings from its place on the nightstand. I look at the screen, see Alex's smiling face, and pick up immediately.

"Alex! I miss you," I say as soon as I press the answer call button.

After a week or so, I finally texted to let Alex know I was in Vegas. She was relieved but didn't seem all that surprised. We haven't had time to talk on the phone though, so this is our first time actually talking since I left. I lay back on my pillows and get comfortable. This could be a long chat.

"Hey, Becca. Oh my god, I have missed you too. When are you coming home?"

"Pretty soon, I think. I've got another couple of series of photographs to take, and then some more developing to do before I'm done with the first part of my art project."

"I can't believe your dad bought you all those cameras. He helped you get your passion back. It makes me want to come there and kiss him silly."

"Yeah, you and me both. After the initial shock wore off, everything started to make sense. I almost can't believe it never occurred to me before."

"Right. Because it would make total sense for you to suspect your surrogate uncle's husband, a gay man, was secretly your biological father who your mother had stolen you from."

I laugh. Of course she's right. It makes no sense, and there is no way in hell I would have ever figured it out on my own.

"Fine. You have a point."

"You know I do. Listen, I don't have too long to chat. It's Aiden and Rhea's housewarming party tonight and we're going gift shopping soon."

"I can't believe how fast they're moving. Last I saw them, they weren't even together. But I guess when you know, you know."

I thought I knew with Johnny, but I was wrong.

"That's true. They bought two houses at the lake, near Denise and Ryder. I'm excited to see both and see which one they're going to live in while they build the house they really want."

"That's crazy to me. This is your life now. You're in with the rich and famous. When are you and Connor going to buy some lakefront property? Will you guys buy three places?" I laugh and shake my head.

I've never had a lot and this all reeks of excess to me. But they're all good people and if that's how they want to spend their money, more power to them. I'll probably end up living in a tiny house somewhere with a dog and three cats.

"Stop distracting me," Alex laughs. *"I have something impor-tant to tell you."*

"Geez, okay. Sorry. Get to it then."

"Sit down."

"I'm laying on my bed." Okay, this sounds serious. "Is everything okay?"

"Yes. Mostly. Just listen. Okay?" Why does she sound so somber all of the sudden?

"Okay. Go ahead."

I hear her take a deep breath. *"Okay. So. After you left, Johnny was going crazy."*

"I don't want to talk about him," I say.

"Don't interrupt. I promise you'll want to hear this. He wasn't doing well. He got drunk with Aiden one night and helped him burn a giant dick into some asshole's lawn." I snicker a little at that, picturing some guy standing in his underwear, ranting and raving at a drawing of a dick. *"After a few days, he got in touch with me. He was confused and couldn't figure out what he did wrong. He told me he said he agreed with your mom that you two were on two different levels."*

"Yeah, thanks for the reminder." As if it didn't hurt enough already.

"Okay, but the thing is, Johnny was an idiot. It's just like I always say: boys are dumb. He misunderstood your mother. He thought she was trying to protect you from him. That she thought you were too good for him, not the other way around."

"Umm, what? Excuse me?" That can't be true. Can it? She's always been pretty clear when she's telling me I don't measure up. "No. I'm sure he knows what she thinks of me. Doesn't he?"

"He does now. That's pretty much what he said when I told him what your mom actually meant. After his initial anger wore off, he realized he needed to find you even more now. So we went over to see your mother."

"Okay," I drawl, suddenly not sure where this is going.

"Long story short, she told us about your father. She told us she stole you because she found out he was gay and she thought it was disgusting or something."

"What a bitch." I knew she never had any gay friends, but I don't think I ever heard her say anything outright homophobic. I'm so ashamed of her right now I feel sick. "I can't believe she would say that."

"It gets worse. She also said that it took her at least a hundred times making soup on the front burner before she finally gave up and just asked you to go grab it."

Something tickles in the back of my brain, a memory. I'm little, my mother is making lunch. I ask her why we're having soup again. We'd had it every day for as long as I could remember. She *told* me to go check on it. She *told* me to pull on the handle to see if it was ready.

Holy shit.

"She burned me on purpose," I whisper.

"She said she thought it would bring attention back to her from you. She was upset that all anyone ever talked to her about was you."

"She burned me and then told me no one could ever love me because of my scars."

"When she told us that, Johnny and I both went a little crazy. We convinced her to tell us where you were or we would knock her out and drag her to the bathtub where I would then dismember her before feeding her to Johnny's uncle's pigs."

A laugh sneaks out of my mouth. I can just see my mother actually believing they would do that. Especially Johnny, because of all his tattoos.

"She finally told us where you were, and that you're okay. And that's when I knocked her out."

I laugh loudly this time, barely able to catch my breath. There's a knock on the door and my dad and Poppa Silas come in.

"Is everything okay, Becca?" Dad asks.

I'm still laughing hysterically. All I can do is nod and pass him the phone. Because as soon as I stop laughing I know I'm going to bawl my eyes out.

"Hello?"

...

"Oh, hello, Alex. So nice to hear from you."

...

"Well, thank you so much. Yes. Okay. Sure. I'll tell her. You have a wonderful day, darling. Bye-bye."

Dad hangs up my phone and puts it on the nightstand.

"Alex says you have something to tell me. But she said that it's not actually funny?"

That sets me off into a fit of giggles, but the giggles quickly turn to sobs. *There they are. I knew I'd cry.*

"She did it on purpose," I choke out. Recognition lights his eyes immediately. "She told me to check the soup. She burned me on purpose."

"Oh, honey," Dad says, wrapping his arms around me.

The bed dips on the other side of me, and then Poppa Silas is hugging me too.

"She did it on purpose, and I can't even hate her."

"Well, I certainly hate her," Dad says, leaning back to look at me. "Why on earth would you not hate her?"

"Because if it weren't for the scars, Becca and I would never have met at my shithead nephew's house. And then she'd never have found you. Isn't that right, darling?"

"Poppa is right, Dad. If it weren't for the scars, and the way she treated me, none of the rest of this would have happened."

Dad pulls me in tighter. "Well, fine. But I still hate her."

"Me too, Dad. Me too."

And then it hits me.

How will I ever apologize to Johnny now?

Finally, I Found You

Johnny

"There you are. It's about time you showed up." A handsome man approaches me, hand out for a shake.

"Patrick?" I ask.

"Yes, sir. And that would make you, Johnny, yes?"

"Yes. It's a pleasure to meet you. Thank you for allowing me to do this."

He turns to lead me past the bar. I'm meeting him at his club to get ready for tonight. He has a big show, and he plans to introduce Becca as his daughter for the first time. He's being kind and allowing me to surprise her here.

He walks into a door tucked away behind the bar which leads to the backstage area. As we walk, he introduces me to the various performers already getting into costume for the show.

"You're familiar with a revue-style show?"

"I think so?" I've been backstage more times than I can count, but I've never been backstage at a drag show. I can't get over how elaborate some of the costumes are.

"Okay, well, here's the general structure. I'm Dara Mia, so I'm kind of the main act slash emcee. We have a bunch of other acts. There's comedy, of course, and musical performances, and some sketches, that sort of thing. I will introduce everyone and also perform several times. Near the end of the show, I will bring Becca up to introduce her, and then I will introduce you."

"Sure, okay. That sounds great."

"So. Now that we have that out of the way," Patrick says, crossing his arms over his barrel chest and looking me up and down. "Tell me your intentions for my daughter."

I chuckle nervously. This is really it.

PATRICK GAVE ME THE dressing room next to his, which is normally reserved for a second headliner who's away on vacation. I'm thankful for the chance to get myself together in private before I go out there. I haven't gotten stage fright in years, but what I'm feeling right now feels suspiciously like it. Becca makes me nervous.

She called me a few times today, and it took everything I had in me to not answer the phone. Alex told me they spoke, and she told Becca everything. About the misunderstanding, about her mother, and about her scars. I couldn't be sure that I wouldn't burst into tears or ruin the surprise, so I forced myself to turn off my phone. After all the work that her dad put in to help me do this, I couldn't not follow through.

There's a knock on the door.

A queen named Regina Rhymes pokes her head in. "Hey, there, hun. Dara told me to tell you that you're up in ten."

"Thanks, Regina." I dab at my sweaty forehead with a paper towel. I'm sitting here in a three-piece suit, dressed up more than I've been since my baptism, and I'm sure my balls are about to melt off. The stage lights are going to kill me at this rate.

"You doing alright, sweetie?" Regina asks. "You nervous? Is this your first time on stage?"

I laugh. I've played in front of sold-out stadiums and here I am, nervous to play for one person. The most important person I've ever met.

"Yeah, something like that."

"Well, take off that jacket for a few minutes and cool yourself off. You don't want to faint on stage in front of your lady."

"Thanks, Regina," I say as she turns and closes the door.

My phone buzzes with an incoming text. It's Alex.

Alex- Good luck. Take a video and send it to us later. Sending our love.

Alex and Connor know what I'm doing here tonight, but no one else does. Except for Patrick, of course. And his husband, Silas.

I take a deep breath and stand up, grabbing my guitar. I've written a little acoustic number that I'm performing for Becca tonight. I just hope she likes it.

Double-checking that I have my phone, I leave my dressing room to see if I can find someone to film for me. Luckily, Regina didn't make it too far.

"Regina," I whisper. "Can you do me a favor?"

"Sure, honey."

"Can you take my phone and film my performance for me?"

"Are you sure? Patrick hired a videographer for the show tonight."

He did? Wow, he's really excited to introduce Becca as his daughter.

"Yeah, please. Our friends back home want to see a video as soon as possible."

"Can do, babe. I'll leave your phone with the bartender if I can't get to you after."

"Thank you so much," I say, giving her my phone.

"Get going, you're running out of time. Break a leg," she smacks my ass as I turn to walk away and gives me a wink and a laugh when I turn back to look at her. I just shake my head and smile.

"And now, ladies and gentlemen, as we come to the end of our evening together, we have a special announcement for you tonight here at the Dara Mia Two Revue." Dara Mia has the audience wrapped around her manicured finger. They're hanging on her every word. "I'm pregnant."

The crowd roars with laughter.

"Alright, alright. I'm not pregnant," she says, walking toward the opposite side of the stage. "I'm much too old for that."

The crowd roars again, Dara Mia laughing right along with them. As I wait, a stagehand comes and mics me up and hooks up my guitar to a small Bluetooth amplifier. He waits with me so he can switch me on just before I head out.

"Okay, enough jokes. I do have a real announcement, a very special one. Come out here, darling." She holds her hand out.

Becca walks out from the shadows on the other side of the stage and she takes my breath away. She's dressed in a short, shimmery, white dress, and she looks like an understated drag queen in all the best ways. She has her signature red lipstick on, and her hair is wavy, hanging just below her chin with her bangs dusting her eyebrows. She's a vision. I swallow hard. She is much too good for me. But I love her. And I need to make her mine.

"This is Becca," Dara Mia says. "And Becca is my daughter." The crowd responds with a mixture of gasps and chuckles. "No, no. It's true. A long time ago, I was married. And then I was gay." A laugh from the crowd. "Well, I was always gay, but then I told my wife about it. And then... then I was divorced." She looks down at the crowd with comically raised eyebrows and pursed lips.

The crowd's laughter swells again. Dara Mia takes the applause, then shushes them with her hands.

"I didn't have my daughter in my life for far too many years. But now she's agreed to give me a second chance and I couldn't be happier." She pulls her in for a hug and it's met with whoops and cheers from the crowd. They love Dara Mia, and they love Becca.

Dara Mia turns to shush the crowd again. "But I'm not the only one who would like forgiveness. I have a young man waiting backstage," she makes a wide-eyed face at the audience and they laugh again. "Not for me, you heathens. There is a young man here who has traveled a long way to ask for my daughter's forgiveness. And guess what? He's a performer, too. And since this is my show, I've decided to give him a shot. Both at asking forgiveness and at performing. Let's see if he's any good, shall we?"

Becca's head is swiveling left and right, looking for me, I hope. She has to know I'm here. Who else could it be?

"Let me introduce to you, a very nice young man, despite the way he looks, Johnny Donovan." Dara Mia turns to face me and does a little golf clap to invite me on stage.

The stagehand who's been waiting with me turns on my mic and amp. I start playing before I even get all the way on stage. Becca looks stunned, but she's smiling, so I take that as a good sign. I stride directly to her, the nervousness fading away, the crowd disappearing, and I sing just for her.

> *Finally, I found you*
> *You showed me the way*
> *I loved you when I met you*
> *I'm finally awake*
> *Finally, I found you*
> *I got lost so many times*
> *But everything I needed*
> *Is here, and now it's mine*
> *True love is real,*
> *I found it in you*
> *True love is real*
> *I found it, it's true*
> *Finally, I found you*
> *I nearly lost you, lost you*
> *Finally, I found you*
> *And you found me too*

Dara Mia steps up next to me while I play the last few chords. She takes my guitar and I get down on one knee.

"Becca, I think we can both agree that I am an idiot." The crowd laughs at my admission. "But I'm an idiot who loves you with everything I am. I still think that you're too good for me, but there's no way I can live without you by my side. Becca, will you marry me?"

Becca is silent. The crowd hushes to a murmur.

Shit. Did I make a critical error? Is this too soon? My breath quickens and I can feel myself panic. She didn't even want to date me. Why the hell did I think she'd want to marry me?

"Yes, Johnny. I will marry you."

The crowd goes crazy. Applause, cheers, whistles. And it's better than any concert I've ever played.

"Oh, thank god." I breathe out and jump to my feet. I take the ring out of the box and slide it onto her finger. It's a vintage emerald in a bezel setting that belonged to my grandmother. "Do you like it?"

"I love it," she says, throwing her arms around me. "And I love you."

"I love you," I say, kissing her. "I love you so fucking much."

"Well, wasn't that nice?" Dara Mia comes up behind us, Silas walking behind her. "Who's ready for another surprise?"

The crowd bursts into cheers and applause.

"Well, then. Let me introduce you to another special guest, here to do a personal favor for us, please put your hands together for... Elvis!"

Silas leans over and whispers into Dar Mia's ear theatrically.

"Oh, thank goodness. Ladies and gentlemen, I was mistaken. Please let me introduce Elvis Herselvis, legendary performer and drag king, here to marry these two crazy kids." Dara claps and nods with a huge grin on her face before Silas leans in and whispers again. "Oh, yes. Marry these two kids to each other, not to Herselvis."

Laughs and cheers and applause meet the announcement.

I lean in and whisper to Becca, "What do you say? Will you marry me right now?"

"Let's do it," she says with a grin. "When in Vegas get married in your dad's drag club by a female Elvis impersonator. That's how that saying goes, right?"

"Sound perfect to me," I say, kissing her softly.

Rules for a Successful Marriage

R̲ULES FOR A SUCCESSFUL ~~FAKE RELATIONSHIP~~ R̲EVISED M̲ARRIAGE

- ~~DON'T~~ FALL IN LOVE!

- ~~DON'T LET OUR FRIENDS KNOW.~~ TELL EVERYONE!

- ~~ONLY SHOW AFFECTION IN FRONT OF BECCA'S MOM.~~ SHOW AFFECTION ALL THE TIME, IN FRONT OF EVERYONE!

- ~~NO SEX.~~ ALL THE SEX!

- NO RELATIONSHIPS WITH OTHER PEOPLE WHILE WE'RE ~~DATING.~~ MARRIED.

- DON'T DO ANYTHING THAT WILL JEOPARDIZE THE FRIENDSHIP.

- SERIOUSLY, ~~DON'T~~ CATCH FEELINGS.

- GET MARRIED IN YOUR DAD'S DRAG CLUB IN LAS VEGAS BY A LADY ELVIS IMPERSONATOR.

- LIVE HAPPILY EVER AFTER

THE END

Keep Reading for a Sneak Peek of Way off Base (Sleeping Dogs Book 5)

Chapter One- Back to Basics

TRAVIS

"Are you heading home already?" Johnny asks when he looks over and notices that I'm packing up my stuff.

We're in the studio today and we should be working on a new album, but Connor, lead singer of Sleeping Dogs and one of my oldest friends, has been too preoccupied to get much done. Ever since reconnecting with his childhood sweetheart and love of his life, Alex, when our last tour ended a couple of weeks ago, he's been spending every spare minute with her, so we've been messing around in the studio. We're not doing anything serious enough to warrant my attendance for a full day, that's for sure. Plus, Ryder didn't even bother to show up, so I refuse to feel bad about leaving early today. At least *I* was here for a bit.

And right now, I need to get the fuck out of here. At the end of the tour, I thought being back in the studio would give me a sense of relief, but these days, being in the studio feels nearly as stifling as being on tour.

Sometimes I think about what it would be like to walk away from it all. To tell everyone I'm done and refuse to record anything or play music at all. And as more time passes, that thought becomes more and more appealing.

I'll never act on it, though, because the guys need me. I couldn't let them down like that. And I do love making and playing music. It's mostly touring that gets to me.

"Not home," I say to my older brother, Johnny. "Heading over to Mom and Dad's. They've got some shit they need done around the house and I said I would work on it this week."

"You're making me look bad." Johnny packs up too, but I know he's not planning to join me at our parents' house. He thinks I don't know, but he's been pining after Alex's best friend Becca since the night he met her. They've been spending a lot of time together, even though they both insist they're just friends. I'd bet anything that's where Johnny goes when he leaves here today. "At least let me know if I can help buy materials or anything. I might be shit at actually doing the work, but I can swipe my credit card like a pro."

I have to laugh. If only he knew that Mom and Dad ask me to fix things around their house because they know I enjoy working with my hands and being in the band doesn't leave me much time to do it. Johnny has always focused on creating art, whereas I've been more interested in building and fixing things. When I would spend time with Dad in his workshop, building stuff out of wood, Johnny would be off somewhere drawing in his sketchbook, or in the kitchen baking with Mom. Not that my woodworking projects aren't artistic, it's that few people can appreciate the art in a well-made piece of furniture the same way they do when looking at the tattoos or paintings Johnny has created.

"Yeah, yeah. You know how Dad feels about that."

"You'd think having two successful musicians with a shitload of money in the family would be a good thing, but not for our folks. I wish he'd let us at least pay for the repairs on the old house since he's never let us buy them a new one."

"You don't need to convince me. But you know how they feel about that place."

"Yeah, I know. That's where they raised the seven of us, and that's where they want their grandkids to visit them. "It's not just our house, it's our home". Mom gives me that same tired line whenever I offer to buy them a new place." Johnny quotes our mother in a high-pitched falsetto that would get him slapped upside the head if she heard it. "At least she let me tattoo her for free after the double mastectomy. That's the only thing she's ever accepted from me, and that's because I refused to take her money after the tattoo was done."

"It's not like she could have returned it and given you the money back like she does with gifts she thinks are too expensive."

"Right? Such a stubborn woman. Let me give you some jewelry, dammit. I can afford it. At least the other women I tattoo give in a little easier than Mom did. Not by much, though. Something about surviving cancer makes women extra fierce."

Besides being a famous guitar player, expert baker, and exceptional tattoo artist, Johnny is also an incredibly kind human being. He doesn't tattoo regular clients. He only works on mastectomy patients, and he only ever does it for free. He says the feeling of giving a woman back her sense of beauty and femininity is worth more than money to him. The only other tattoo he's done in recent years was one for Becca, and that one helped her recover from trauma stemming from a childhood injury.

And he didn't charge her, either.

"I'm sure she'll still try to pay you somehow, even though it's already been years."

Johnny and I walk out of the studio together, tossing a wave to Aiden and Devon on our way out. I try to hide the sigh of relief that escapes me when we walk out those doors. The older

I get, it seems the less I enjoy being in the band and everything that entails. Truthfully, I'm loving that Connor is so distracted right now. It gives me a chance to finally relax. Maybe I'll work my way around to enjoying the music again, or at least to hating it less.

I know, I know. I'm such an asshole for feeling this way, because who doesn't want to be famous? I'm out here living a life most people dream about and I can't even appreciate it.

"I'll see you later," I tell Johnny as I climb into my beat-up truck. Yet another way that I'm not much like a rockstar. I drive a big truck and use it for hauling stuff, not showing off. "Tell Becca I say hello." I pull out past Johnny and give him a two-finger wave before heading down the driveway.

Johnny looks over at me, with his eyebrows raised and mouth open in shock as he watches me drive away. He no doubt thinks I read his mind with the fake twin thing we have from being born ten months apart, but really he's so transparent when he's in love. He's such a romantic he's practically floating on air with hearts circling his head. It would have been impossible for me not to guess that he was going to see Becca. I don't even need to read his mind for that. I think it might be the real thing for him this time, though, so I hope it all works out. He's been looking for *the one* for so long, he deserves to find her after all this time. Not only that, Becca is cool as shit, and we'd be lucky if she joined our family.

Me, on the other hand, I've given up on the idea of finding someone to share my life with. Like the other guys, I spent time at the start of my career messing around with the groupies and assorted models and actresses who wanted to hook up with young musicians, but that got old fast. I want something like my parents have, but I can't see any way to do that while still being a full-time touring musician. I don't want my wife to have to come on tour, and I really don't want my kids to live a life in the spotlight. What would I do if I weren't in the band?

Who am I kidding? I know what I would do if I weren't a musician; it's what I was planning to do before I followed Johnny into this whole music thing in the first place. I wanted to work with my hands like my dad. Building things, creating stuff out of raw materials, fixing stuff. That's the real reason my parents call me instead of Johnny when something needs to repairing or renovating at their house. It's because they know I enjoy doing that kind of stuff. They know it's that kind of work that fulfills me. Playing bass guitar in a famous band is cool and all, but it doesn't light me up like it does the other guys. So yeah, if I ever want to have a family, I won't be doing it while I'm still in Sleeping Dogs. That wouldn't be fair to me, my wife, and any kids we might have.

But that's all a fantasy, anyway. I can't see myself walking away from something that gives me the resources to take care of my parents for life. Even if they won't accept it, it's nice to know that I could help them if they needed it. And it's not like I can let the rest of the guys down. Sure, they could find someone else, but I'm not going to think about that. There's no sense in worrying about it since I'll never leave the band. Problem solved.

Mom and Dad live on the opposite side of Westborough from Connor and Alex, in one of the older neighborhoods. It's not that far, but it takes a little longer to get there because I drive through the middle of the city.

When I finally pull up to my parents' house, I notice a moving truck across the street, and disappointment hits me, a palpable weight on my chest. That house has been vacant for a few years, and I've been playing with the idea of buying it myself so I could fix it up. It was never a solid plan though, more of a daydream I entertained when trying to distract myself from the day-to-day of being in the band. I shouldn't feel a sense of loss now that someone else is moving in. Even so, I can't help but wonder what I could have done with the place if I'd taken that chance.

I hope these new neighbors work out better for my parents than the last ones. The previous tenants weren't exactly what my parents considered good neighbors. Lots of parties, lots of fights, some screaming kids, and an unkempt yard did nothing but make my parents crazy. They still refused to move away, though. There's no scaring them away from this home.

Maybe these new neighbors will do something to fix the state of the house. As it stands now, it looks like it's falling apart, even though I'm pretty sure that's not the case. If Dad were still in the business of taking clients, I'd say he should offer his services as a handyman to help them get things fixed up, but he's pretty much retired and mostly builds for fun now. Kind of how I do it as a hobby.

I park on the street in front of my parents' place and take an appraising look at their house, trying to guess what it is they want me to work on. From what I can see while standing on the sidewalk, the fence needs painting, as does the trim around the windows. I think they need some work done on their roof, as well. Looks like I'm going to have a lot to keep me busy during this break from touring. I can't wait to get started.

"Hey there," Dad calls out as I'm grabbing my tools from the back of my truck. "Ready to do some proper work for a change?" he asks with a chuckle. He thinks that being in the band isn't hard work. He's not entirely wrong. It's not as physical as construction, but it's difficult in its own way. Still, it's easier to let him think what he wants.

"You bet," I say, patting my toolbox. "I even brought some quality tools, so I don't have to use your old, shitty ones."

"Pshh," Dad scoffs and shakes his head. "Didn't anyone ever tell you? It's not the tool that matters, it's how you use it." He waggles his eyebrows and thrusts his hips, really driving home the innuendo. "How do you think your mother and I got all you kids?" he adds with a booming laugh.

I cringe. The thought of my parents having sex is not something I need right now. "Yeah, okay. I don't want to think about that ever again. How about you tell me what needs fixing and let me get to it already?"

He's still snickering when he leads me into the house. "I have it all written down for you here. Come in and sit."

Dad and I go over the list and before I know it, I'm out in the backyard repairing his tool shed. The first task is underway, with at least twenty more to go. I couldn't happier.

KEEP READING IN WAY off Base (Sleeping Dogs Book 5)

Keep Reading Sneak Peek of Santa's Baby (coming late 2023)

Chapter One

PHOEBE

Of all the ways I ever imagined spending the Christmas of my thirty-first year I can say with certainty tracking down the Santa Claus who impregnated me was not one of them.

Yet here we are.

"This place is nice, Phoebe," Gavin says, walking into the living room and setting down a box marked "Lincoln." "Maybe the owners won't ever come back from their trip abroad so you can buy it. The furniture is pretty sweet." My idiot brother then flops face down on my fully furnished rental's overstuffed blue velvet couch and groans obscenely. "Oh, man. I could do dirty things to this couch."

It's not every day I rent a place sight unseen, so you can imagine the relief I felt when we got here and the place looked exactly like it had in the photos. That I could find a fully furnished place on such short notice, right before the holidays, was a miracle in itself. Finding a nice place in a safe neighborhood? Yeah, there had to have been some divine intervention involved for that to happen.

"Ew, don't be gross Gavin. And get your stinky ass off the couch. You're filthy."

"Is that any way to treat the guy who helped you move?" He dragged himself off the couch. "Speaking of which, didn't you promise me pizza and beer as payment for that help?"

"Ha! Nice try, kid. I'll order pizza but you're sticking with soda until you're of legal age. Plus, you still need to drive home so I wouldn't let you drink even if you were old enough."

Gavin is eighteen, my much younger sibling from my mom's second marriage. My bio dad left mom when Lane was born and I was still a few months shy of two years old. Needless to say, after being with such a bastion of paternal fortitude, it took Mom a long time to find another man worth taking a chance on. I was twelve when she started seeing Dennis, and fourteen when they married and Gavin was born.

Like most teenage boys, Gavin's all raging hormones and unrestrained snark. But, despite his many annoying traits, he has the biggest heart and he's one of my favorite people. When I found myself left at the altar almost a year ago no one was angrier than Gavin. He stormed around the hotel, hoping to run into my newly ex-fiance so he could unleash his teenage fury. It's probably a good thing he never found him, though. I doubt it would have been a fair fight.

Seventeen-year-old Gavin was a short, scrawny little shit. Eighteen-year-old Gavin is almost six and a half feet tall and packed with muscle. He's never said so, but I'm pretty sure he started working out after the wedding disaster so he'd be ready if he ever saw my ex again. After a year of protein shakes and lifting weights, not to mention a huge growth spurt, Gavin is formidable. It still wouldn't be a fair fight, but the advantage would go to Gavin, not Webster.

I almost feel guilty for not being as upset as he was about the situation. It was a shock when I got the text telling me he wasn't coming, but not marrying Webster Day was for the best. It was a dick move, but in the end, he made the best decision for both of us.

"No way, Lane said she would drive home." Gavin jumps up off the couch and yells down the back hallway, "Isn't that right, Lane?"

Oh, shit. Despite being one of my favorite people, I may have to murder Gavin if he wakes up Lincoln. That thing they say about never waking a sleeping baby? Yeah, that's totally true.

"Shhh. Will you shut up already?." I slap my hand over his mouth. "Lincoln is sleeping."

He looks so sheepish I might actually believe he felt bad about it if I didn't know better. There's no way Gavin would leave here without saying goodbye to his nephew, even if said nephew is barely old enough to see past his own fist. Gavin is sure Lincoln recognizes him, though, and is so proud of that fact. I believe it, too. Lincoln always seems calmer when his Uncle Gavin is holding him. And Gavin never misses a chance to hold him, even if he has to make his own chances.

"Too late," Lane says, coming out of the back hallway with a tiny baby snuggled in her arms. "Little guy was awake when I tried to sneak into his room to drop off a box. I think he sensed me because as soon as I walked in an unholy rumbling started coming out of his little rear end. You need to do laundry, by the way. I rinsed everything and left it to pre-soak." She looks down at Lincoln with a grin and singsongs, "Isn't that right, Linky? Mommy has to do laundry. Yes, she does. She's lucky Auntie Lane changed you and the sheets instead of running away and letting her deal with it."

My heart swells watching my little sister snuggle my baby and not for the first time since I came up with the plan, I second-guess my decision to move back to Westborough. What am I going to do without my family around to help me for the next three months? This was a terrible idea. But if I want Lincoln to at least have the chance to meet his father, this is where I need to be. And my sense of right and wrong won't let me entertain the thought of not trying to find his father. There's a man out there who doesn't know he has a son, and that doesn't sit right with me. I want him to at least have the choice of whether to be involved in Lincoln's life, even if he ends up being a dickhead like my father and chooses to have nothing to do with him.

"Hey, hey. I can see your brain working from here." Gavin is back on the couch, getting his sweaty teenage boy smell all over it. Whatever, I'll Febreze it when he leaves. He can't stink it up too badly in such a short time, can he? "Everything is going to be fine. Tell her your news, Lane. I can't handle seeing her cry."

I reach up and touch my cheeks, and sure enough, they're wet. "Sorry if my feelings offend you, you little twerp. I'm going to miss you guys, that's all. I'm allowed to be sad about that."

He jumps up off the couch and wraps me in a sweaty hug. "I'm going to miss you too, Feeble," he says, using the nickname he called me when he was little and couldn't quite get his little mouth to say Phoebe. "But you won't have to miss Lane."

I blink a few times and pull myself out of his embrace. "What's he talking about?" I ask Lane. "What are you talking about?"

Gavin takes Lincoln from Lane, snuggling him tightly to his chest, and takes him into the kitchen. I hear the cupboard doors open and close and the water runs in the sink. Sounds like Uncle Gavin is making his nephew a bottle.

"I didn't tell you because I knew you'd try to talk me out of it, but I'm staying with you. You have the third bedroom I can sleep in. I even got myself a part-time job at a coffee shop. I'm staying to help you with Lincoln so you can focus on finding his dad. It will be easier to track him down if you don't have to bring Lincoln with you everywhere you go. Plus, I can't be away from you guys for that long." Lane's eyes are shiny with unshed tears. "I just can't get enough of those midnight feedings," she jokes.

I chuckle. "Are you sure? You don't have to put your life on hold for me, Lane. I love you for wanting to do this, but you don't have to stay."

"I know that," she says, wrapping her arms around me. "I want to stay."

"You're the best sister I could ever ask for," I choke through a sob. "I couldn't have made it this far without you."

And it's true. The seemingly endless months of my pregnancy with Lincoln would have been so much harder if it hadn't been for the help of my brother and sister, and, of course, my mom and stepdad. I won't tell Lane and Gavin, but after living back home with my parents for the last year, and having my family around all the time, I was a little scared to be on my own with Lincoln in the city. I loved living here with Webster, but being on my own with a baby is different. The excitement of Westborough seems almost scary when I think about protecting my son from unseen dangers. I tried to play it cool, but I'm thinking I didn't do such a good job of it if Lane secretly arranged to move here with me. I've never been so happy to be such a shitty liar.

"Are you guys done with all the girly feelings out there? Me and the big guy want to come chill on that sweet-ass couch but we don't want your emotional breakdowns cramping our manly style."

Lane and I both burst into laughter. After one more squeeze, I let her go.

"Yeah, we're done," I call out. "I'll order that pizza now so you can get on the road."

"About that," he says, walking back to the living room with my son in the crook of his arm. "Mom told me to spend the night and drive back in the morning. She doesn't want me driving alone at night in the winter. I don't know what she thinks I do after work at home. It's usually pretty late by the time I get out of the market."

Lane sits next to him on the couch, her eyes on Lincoln. "There's a big difference between driving five minutes in Fallbridge at ten at night and driving on the highway at two in the morning. Especially in the middle of winter."

"Yeah, yeah. Okay, Mom," he teases. "I'm already staying the night. Happy?"

"You bet," she says while ruffling his hair, taking advantage of the fact that he has his hands full feeding Lincoln. "We just wuv you so much, Gavvers," she adds in a baby voice. "We would hate it if anything happened to you."

"Hey, no fair. Hands off my hair. Do you know how long it took to get it like that?"

They sit side by side, alternating between cooing over Lincoln and bickering with each other while I busy myself with ordering the pizzas and unpacking some boxes. The best part about finding a fully furnished rental is how little I had to pack to come here. It would have sucked if I'd had to move my furniture out of storage for such a short stay. Three months isn't long enough to justify renting a moving van. With this rental house, all I needed was some boxes in the back of Gavin's truck and I was ready to move in.

I just hope three months is long enough to find Lincoln's dad.

The doorbell rings, and Gavin hops up to grab the pizzas. "Oh, thank god. I'm starving," he says, spreading the boxes down on the coffee table and flipping one open. "I'm a growing boy, you know." He grabs two slices and stacks them.

I bring plates and napkins out from the kitchen. "We know, Gavin. You tell us every time you get even the tiniest bit hungry."

He wiggles his eyebrows, and grins before shoving the pizza sandwich in his mouth.

"So, Phoebe. Why don't you tell me how you plan on finding this guy? All you said before we came was that you're moving here for three months to look for him. Do you even have any idea where he is?"

I heave a sigh. This is the biggest problem with my plan. It sucks. When you get blind drunk after being left at the altar and hook up with someone you just met, it would be a lot easier to move on with your life if you didn't get yourself pregnant in the process. Failing that, it would be nice if you remember the name of the person or any detail about them other than he'd been dressed as Santa Claus for a Christmas party that was being held at the same hotel as your wedding. The only things I have to go on are the big red velvet coat I stole when I crept out of there in the wee hours of the morning, still drunk from the night before, and a picture I snapped of him with his face mashed so far into the pillow you can't tell with any accuracy what he looks like.

Why did I take his jacket, you ask? I guess I thought my walk of shame would feel less shameful if I covered my wedding dress with Santa's jacket. It didn't. But I made it back to the room without being seen, packed up, and headed home with no one finding out I spent what should have been my wedding night with a stranger.

Until a month and a half later when I got the shock of a lifetime, ensuring that *everyone* would eventually know *exactly* how I spent that night.

That's right.

My fiancé left me at the altar and the first thing I did was run out and get impregnated by Santa Claus.

Talk about Ho Ho Ho.

Want to know when Santa's Baby is available? Get the Roomie Review. Sign up at chantalroome.com/newsletter

Books by Chantal Roome

Sleeping Dogs the complete collection
The men of Sleeping Dogs have had their fair share of women, but now that they're a little older, and a little wiser, they're looking for something more meaningful than the one-night stands typical of their past.

Second Chance (Sleeping Dogs Book 1)
She's an unemployed chef afraid of being burned by love again. He's a world-weary rock star tired of being used. Can a second chance at first love heal them both?

Face the Music (Sleeping Dogs Book 2)
She's a serious control freak of a band manager. He's a jaded joker of a rock star. Will a jealous ex and surprise pregnancy tear them apart before they start?

Skip a Beat (Sleeping Dogs Book 3)
She's a disgraced ex-cop looking for a career change. He's a moody drummer trying to keep his demons at bay. Can vandalism and ill-conceived revenge plans be the glue that mends their lives and binds them to each other?

Only the Best (Sleeping Dogs Book 4)

He's a romantic, guitar-playing tattoo artist looking for true love. She's an emotionally and physically scarred photographer who keeps people at a distance. When one wants true love and the other wants one night, can friendship and a fake relationship ever be enough?

Way off Base (Sleeping Dogs Book 5)

She's a single mom struggling to rebuild her life. He's a reluctant rock star tired of being alone. Can they repair a foundation of lies to build the life they both want?

Chantal Roome writes contemporary romantic comedies and is the author of the Sleeping Dogs series of cinnamon roll rock star rom-coms. She loves writing love stories with just the right mix of sweetness, humour, and sex. When she isn't writing, she's drinking way too much coffee, binge reading romance, and living out her own second chance romance with her husband. She's also a mediocre mom to two frustrating, but hilarious and endlessly loveable kids, and one dog who has eaten every toy he's ever been given.

Keep in touch with Chantal on social media

Visit Chantal's website at: www.chantalroome.com

Get the Roomie Review Newsletter chantalroome.com/roomiereview

Join my readers' group facebook.com/groups/theromcomroome

f   facebook.com/chantalroomeauthor

   instagram.com/chantalroomeauthor

   pinterest.com/chantalroome

   tiktok.com/chantalroomeauthor

   twitter.com/croomeauthor

g   goodreads.com/chantalroome

BB   bookbub.com/authors/chantal-roome

www.ingramcontent.com/pod-product-compliance
Lightning Source LLC
Chambersburg PA
CBHW061602190726

48288CB00007B/2143